California

AUG

1996

GUY
NOVEL

MICHAEL RYAN

THE PERMANENT PRESS
Sag Harbor, NY 11963

For information, address:
    The Permanent Press
    4170 Noyac Road
    Sag Harbor, NY 11963
    www.thepermanentpress.com

Library of Congress Cataloging-in-Publication Data

Ryan, Michael, author.
    Guy novel / Michael Ryan.
    Sag Harbor, NY : The Permanent Press, [2016]
    ISBN 978-1-57962-440-8 (hardcover)
      1. Man-woman relationships—Fiction. 2. Humorous fiction.
    3. Love stories. I. Title.

PS3568.Y39 G89 2016
813'.54—dc23   2016013824

Printed in the United States of America

Men are good in but one way, but bad in many.

—ARISTOTLE, *Nicomachean Ethics*

These miracles wee did, but now alas,
All measure, and all language, I should passe,
Should I tell what a miracle shee was.

—JOHN DONNE, "The Relique"

1.

It was raining in Santa Monica enough to flood the Pacific Coast Highway and knock out some electricity, so the ATMs were down and there were long lines at the bank, inside of which, for some reason, the computers were still working. There must have been a hundred people in there, soaked and steaming among the puddles and yellow plastic warning signs redundantly informing us that the floor was wet. I didn't have any choice but to wait. I was getting married that day and driving to Baja for the honeymoon so I had to have the cash. It's funny how things happen. A freak storm in August. What were the chances of that? If it hadn't been raining so hard, if the ATMs weren't down, if I hadn't had to wait in line so long, I might not have started thinking about the teller. Was she the most beautiful woman I had ever seen? Probably not. She was about thirty, brown hair and black eyes, great bones, great carriage. She'd be gorgeous at eighty. She was standing in front of the counter, not behind it—the water on the floor must have been even deeper behind it. Her cash drawer was perched on the counter, so she had to twist to her right for cash and twist back to count it into the outstretched palms of the customers like kindergartners lined up for their

snacks. She seemed amused by the novelty of it. She wore a
snug green dress and white pumps that drew attention to her
legs, which, as anyone would have to admit, could withstand
the scrutiny. She probably grew up in Southern California—
I had been out here fifteen years and still wasn't used to it,
this dressing for display like flashing a wad of bills, crude
and obvious and almost as laughable, except for the fact that
seeing a woman's body continued to affect me in a way that I
wasn't affected by seeing their money. I guess I had found my
own ways of trying to send the power it had over me back at
them, but I was ready to be done with all that, which was one
reason I was getting married, probably a bad one. Anyway, she
seemed a little on the hard side, despite her delicacy—a little
too savvy, like she had been around the block a couple too
many times. Whatever it was, she had seen it before. Haughty
was the word that came to mind—proud of her beauty, as if
she had earned it herself, or at least was not surprised by it,
which may be the only thing that enables us to forgive someone for being that beautiful, that they know how lucky they
are. Otherwise they might use their beauty against us.

Of course this was all just my head noise. I had no idea
what she thought of herself, physically or any other way, much
less anything she had done in her life, though it passed the
time to imagine it. It couldn't have been too thrilling for her
cashing people's checks and adding up their deposits, much
less dealing with their impatience and grumpiness, but she
seemed to be enjoying herself. She cheered them up. She kept
smiling ironically and making little remarks to her customers
that I couldn't hear, then laughing and showing her sharp little
teeth. Unfortunately I started imagining those teeth sunk into
my shoulder. What a mouth she had, with a lower lip like
the threshold to heaven. She could pout and grin at the same
time. I bet she owned one of those Brazilian bikinis with the

butt-floss bottoms. Bright red, I bet. Merciless. I bet she had a tiny coiled black snake tattooed on her butt. I kept seeing her flouncing toward me on the beach in Baja, a Windex-blue drink with a pastel paper umbrella sticking out of it in each hand and Do-I-Have-A-Surprise-For-You pout-grin on those lips. The woman I was about to marry was not in this picture. She did not own one of those Brazilian bikinis with the butt-floss bottoms. She did not have a tiny coiled black snake tattooed on her butt.

But I am not the sort of person who breaks his commitments, especially what I regard as the ultimate commitment: marriage. I had spent at least twenty minutes in my head with the teller, enough for a few nights together and just about every act one body can perform upon another, but I figured no harm done. I had no intention of saying anything untoward when I walked up to the counter.

Outside the rain was still pounding down in sheets.

"Nice day for the beach," is what I said as I handed her my check.

"I'd like to go back to bed," she said in response.

"That sounds a lot more interesting," came out of my mouth before I could stop it.

She looked at me. She hadn't noticed me at all before. Now she did. I guess that's what I wanted. With women I use my fast mouth. That's what gets me into trouble.

"I meant to sleep," she said.

"Me, too," I answered, with exaggerated innocence.

This got a laugh out of her.

"You men are all alike. One-track minds."

"We're pigs," I said. "You can't trust us."

"Tell me about it," she said.

And this probably would have been the end of it. Except at that moment her supervisor, a young balding guy in a bad brown suit, appeared at her shoulder and told her that the bank was going to close in ten minutes because of the weather. Governor Wilson had declared a state of emergency. The flooding was getting worse. The zillion-dollar cliffside houses overlooking the ocean were sliding down again onto PCH, as they did at least once during the rainy season. The guards were locking the doors right now and letting customers out but not in.

"Looks like you get your wish," I said to her as her supervisor walked away.

"Yeah, how am I going to get home? My roommate dropped me off this morning."

"I'm going to take you," I said, the second remark that was out of my mouth before it had negotiated a route through my cerebral cortex.

"Hmm," she said. (She actually said "Hmm.") She checked me out carefully. "You don't look like an ax murderer."

"I'm afraid of blood," I said.

"Just a ride home," she said. "Don't get any ambitious ideas."

I held up my hand like a Boy Scout. "I'm a very unambitious person," I answered. "A chronic underachiever."

This made her laugh again.

"At least you've got money in the bank. That's better than most guys I know."

This reminded me of why I had come there: to cash a check. I was getting married in six hours. What in the world did I think I was doing? I asked myself this question as I waited in my car outside the bank. Right off I could eliminate the idea that I was being a Good Samaritan. I did not offer a ride to the balding young man in the bad brown suit. I have had many experiences of not knowing what I wanted to do until I did it, but I also have had an equal number of experiences of not knowing until after I did it that I actually didn't want to do what I had done. This was unfortunately shaping up to be one of those. They invariably seemed to involve women. This one looked like it was going to be a doozy, unless I got a handle on it very soon. The rain was running off the windshield in waves as if I were driving head-first into the ocean. I consoled myself by thinking that no one gets married without a little ambiguity beforehand and I was simply acting mine out. I was going to take this person to her house (notice she had suddenly become a "person"), let her out of the car, go home, get dressed, and get married. No one would ever have to know about it. Still, I was not enjoying myself at this moment. The car smelled like my dog, Sparky, after he plays in the ocean. The windows were fogged up. I remembered I forgot to brush my teeth that morning. I could have taken some pleasure in the fact that I was about to have this extraordinary arrangement of female flesh slide into my passenger seat (I was driving a year-old 1995 two-seat cherry pearl 300ZX Turbo with black leather interior and all the aftermarket bells and whistles, which I planned to trade in after I was married for a used white Volvo station wagon), but I knew what I had been enjoying was the fantasy of her not the reality. She was about to become real. I already had a real life. I didn't need another one.

Then the door opened and she was inside my car. What do they call the way a body senses another body? Kinesthetic? She was *there*. Very close. These are the kind of factors that don't show up on the printouts. Her presence, if that's even the word for it, was something else. She didn't have a raincoat or an umbrella, and had run outside holding a huge purse against her chest and the front section of the *Los Angeles Times* over her head, which she dropped into the gutter. The head-line said, "Plane Crash At LAX Kills 223."

"I ran ten feet and I'm soaked," she said. "My shoes are ruined." She pulled her white pumps off by the heels. Her black leather purse was as big as a couch pillow, and there was nowhere to put it except on the floor between her legs, so she did, spreading them a little. Even with the rain smacking the moon roof, I could hear her nylons. I wanted to establish permanent California residence where they met.

"As Gary Gilmore said, 'Let's do it,'" I said, pulling into the gridlocked traffic. "Since I can't see anything, probably nobody else can either."

"Gary Gilmore, *Executioner's Song*. His last words before they executed him. His brother, Mikal, published a memoir last year."

"You read," I said, unable to hide my surprise, and immediately regretted it.

"Was that a pop quiz?" she asked.

I deserved that.

"It really wasn't," I said. "It's just a line I like."

"I like it too. I use it all the time."

I thought about that.

"That's an odd coincidence," I said. "Sort of remarkable."

"If you want," she said. Apparently it wasn't remarkable to her, and certainly not worth further consideration.

"Don't you ever clean this car?" she asked. She held up a piece of inert brown matter that in my best recollection I had never seen before.

"I was going to do it today, honest. That's probably Sparky's. You'd like Sparky. He'll be upset that you moved it from where he buried it."

"Poor Sparky," she said. "This could be a beautiful car. These Zs are so out there. You know who you're dealing with."

"Remnant of a former life," I said. "I'm getting married."

Somehow I had left out the logical transitions that went from the car to the marriage, but she got the point I wanted to make.

"Congratulations," she said after a moment. "When's the big event?"

"In about six hours, actually."

"In about six hours, actually," she repeated. She stuck her tongue into her cheek and twisted that preternatural mouth of hers into a lopsided, ironic grin. "This is becoming an interesting day."

"Where do you live?"

"Malibu. But PCH is closed. Why don't you drop me off at the coffee shop down here at the corner and go get married? I'll sleep in a booth."

"I said I was going to drive you home and I am."

She gave me another one of those appraising looks like she had given me in the bank. This one was something like, *Okay Bucko I'll play this through, it's not going to cost me anything.* Or maybe it didn't mean that at all.

"That's what I like about men," she said. "So flexible. So reasonable."

"You've probably heard the reason only one sperm out of two million ever reaches the egg," I said.

"Why?"

"They won't ask directions."

It was the kind of innocuous stuff that passes for comedy on Leno and Letterman (I should know, since I once told that joke on both shows in the same week—and was never invited back to either of them), but she chuckled politely. "You don't mind me telling you how to get to my place, do you? Or would you rather intuit it?"

To get to Malibu we had to drive all the way up Sunset and around and back through Topanga Canyon. Ordinarily it would have taken about twenty minutes via PCH to get to her place from the bank. Today it took two hours. Her name was Sabine, or so she said. (It is an LA thing to change your name if you don't like the one you were born with. I have met any number of Ashlees, Shannyns, Karmas, and Starrs.) I had fun with Sabine. A lot of fun. Too much fun. She was very sassy and we took that back and forth, mostly on the men-and-women-as-cats-and-dogs-theme. We kept it light all the way. I needed some lightness. My fiancée Doris likes to talk about Her Issues, whereas I am your basic Guy kind of guy. You can talk about feelings until your ears fall off and end up back where you started, only without ears. As far as I'm concerned feelings are just that: feelings. Did you ever see a two-year-old in a restaurant? One second he wants the steak knife more than anything he has ever seen before and it's a tragedy of international proportions that his parents won't let him have it so that he can stick it into his eye. The next second he's happily sucking a paper napkin. The steak knife never existed. I think that's the way we all are when we grow up, too, bouncing from one feeling to the next. So what matters is not what you feel, it's what you do. "Know me by my actions" is my main motto.

So what was I doing with this strange woman in my car on the day of my wedding?

She lived right on the beach in a spectacular house, where the real estate starts at three million and up. One of the Allman brothers was her neighbor. She said he was completely fried by this time of day. He went out on his deck every morning and howled at the moon. As we pulled into the driveway, I couldn't help observing out loud that the Bank of America must be paying its employees very well these days, and she said the house belonged to her roommate's boyfriend, a producer or something who was shooting a movie or something in Africa or somewhere. She and her roommate were house-sitting. In fact, the roommate had flown off last night to rendezvous with the producer (or something) in Paris.

"You told me she dropped you off at work this morning," I said.

"Did I? That was another friend," she said. She opened the passenger-side door and the little light went on over her legs. It had been very dark all day, but it seemed even darker, except for what was illuminated by the little light. "I'd invite you in, but I don't date married men."

"That gives us about four more hours," I said. "Some of my most meaningful relationships have lasted way less than that."

"It's your funeral," she said, getting out. She ran up the stairs to the house in her stocking feet.

"Wedding," I yelled after her as I stepped from the car into the deluge. "Not funeral. Wedding."

2.

When I woke up from the nap afterward, it was six forty-five P.M., which gave me fifteen minutes for the three hours it would take to get dressed, home, changed, and to the church in Palos Verdes, not to mention cleaning out the car. Sabine was still asleep. The rain had stopped and the air had that incredible clarity after a big storm in the LA basin when the smog has been temporarily vaporized. That what you can see then had been there all along is surprising every time, like a great insight that rearranges your understanding of yourself until you forget it and fall back into the usual muddle. The sun was dropping under the ocean's horizon, and the light through the window bathing Sabine's body was a muted bronze, as if we were actually characters shot through a gauze filter in some insufferably wistful French movie.

It was hard to feel sorry for myself at that moment, though later I would manage very nicely. I sat on the side of the bed, naked, facing the ocean, which was still pretty upset, the waves slamming the rocks beneath the house. The only furniture in the room was the mattress and box spring on the floor. All my friends, most of the people I cared about, the woman I supposedly loved, her friends, and most of the people she cared about, were at that moment gathering at the church where I was supposed to appear, flushed and embarrassed, tousled and grinning, running up the walk and tying my tie. I would have an explanation for the delay (gridlock on the freeway would serve fine; in LA, all you have to say is, "It was a parking lot," and everyone instantly forgives—it's part of the liturgy). Doris would kiss me and say something humorously demeaning about my endearing incompetence and everyone would laugh with relief at the disaster averted. I would be chided affectionately. I would be returned to the fold. We would all then compose ourselves and stroll into the church. Afterward we'd have a banquet at Missillac, our favorite restaurant, which Michel Borchard himself was preparing at that very moment. Something with lobster, then rack of lamb, I believe Doris said (she planned the menu, of course; I was not consulted), after Michel's ineffable and sublime *foie gras en croute*. There would be wine from Margaux and oysters from Locmariaquer and live sea snails unobtainable more than five miles inland from the Brittany Coast. The lobster would be flown in from Maine and the lamb from Sonoma, first class, wearing little Dolce & Gabbana suits. Some of Doris's seemingly infinite clients and business associates whom I refused to invite would have extravagant gifts delivered (she once took me to a party of a Disney executive where an electric train driven by a duck took guests to different variously themed parties on the estate, one of which featured a model in a toga walking two white panthers on a leash). Limos would pull up at the restaurant and clowns would pop out carrying balloons and jeroboams of Dom Pérignon sporting bows of red ribbon.

Instead of being at the church amid all that jollity and excess, I was here, in an unfurnished room with bare walls, with an absolute (unconscious) stranger beside me, completely happy with the choice I had made. Nor was I surprised by

my happiness. Temporarily, at least, I had that feeling of
dumb luck, of things turning out right despite my own
bumbling and bewilderment. The sex I just had with Sabine
made me see what a mistake I would have made by marrying
Doris. Marrying Doris made sense. Doris was smart. Doris
was attractive. Doris was generous. Doris was bicoastal. She
helped my career. We shared interests. We had so much in
common. I had every reason in the world to love Doris and
I did love Doris. But I didn't *love* Doris. I had to do what I
had just done with Sabine in order to realize that. Of course
a more responsible person might have chosen a more responsible means of self-realization than screwing an utter stranger
on his wedding day. But I was clearly not a more responsible
person. It didn't really matter how Sabine felt about me when
she woke up or even how I felt about her. It was as if my
body were a separate creature I inhabited, and spoke to me a
language I finally understood: it said, this is what was missing,
you bozo. It's what has been missing in you. Do not marry
Doris. Don't do that to her. Don't do it to yourself.

What I did do to her (and to myself) by standing her up
at the church had not fully descended upon me, as it would
soon, in abundance. Besides the exhilaration of revelation, I
felt the exhilaration of escape, not to mention the afterglow
from the best sex I ever had with the sexiest woman I ever
had it with. There was going to be plenty of downside to that
as well, I suspected, since to the best of my knowledge there's
no free lunch. None of us get out of this world alive. Or
unscathed. But there wasn't much I could do at that moment
about either what I had just done or what might happen in
the future. What the hell. If I felt good, why not just let
myself feel good? Why not just enjoy it?

So I was positively jaunty when I got up and went out to
the living room. There was no furniture in it either, zero. On

the far side of the house was the kitchen. It had zinc counters, and one of those twelve-burner chef's stoves that goes for about twenty grand, and an Italian-hand-painted-tile island in the middle over which you hang your expensive copper pans on hooks and ignore the ho-hum spectacular ocean view as you chop your shallots—but otherwise the room was bare too, except for a single folding metal chair and a card table featuring a pair of prepackaged salt-and-pepper shakers, the kind used by struggling actors and graduate students and day laborers who live by themselves in rented rooms and heat canned chili on a hot plate. In the cupboard was one white plastic bowl and in a drawer was one white plastic spoon. There were four bedrooms and two bathrooms upstairs. I walked through all of them: completely empty. If there was a roommate, she didn't eat or sleep on a bed. If there was no roommate then there was probably no producer or something. But why would Sabine lie about that?

Whatever the reason, I was already feeling less jaunty by the time I returned to the kitchen, where there was another phone on the wall and a twenty-four hour digital clock on the black German microwave: 18:59. One minute until my marriage. It was pointless to call anyone since they were all at the church, so I dialed my own answering machine. I have saved the tape, in case I'm ever asked to contribute to an exhibit of answering machine performance art. It starts with ho-ho ribbings and congratulations from some male friends, segues into quizzical and concerned inquiries from both genders as to my whereabouts, and finally becomes messages of outright distress from Doris. After a few messages, I skipped to six P.M. and this message from my best friend, Don:

Hey buddy. Nobody's seen or heard from you all day, as I guess you know. Doris has been calling here, worried, not wanting to call you in case you were off contemplating the meaning of life or something. So when you get this message, call me. If you got the jitters, hey you should have seen me. I dropped so many Valium I thought I was marrying the minister. Who was not bad looking. And such a spiritual guy. Give a call, pal.

There were a few others, from friends whom Doris also apparently called looking for me. Then there were these three from Doris herself:

6:15: Robert, darling, you were supposed to pick Donald up five minutes ago so he is wondering where you are. We are all wondering, darling. Mother and I are driving to the church right now, so please call me on the car phone when you get this message. I've been so happy all day. I love you, honeypie. Bye-bye.

6:30: Honeypie, it's six thirty P.M. We're just getting off the 405 to Palos Verdes. Donald hasn't heard from you, so he's going to have to drive himself. Robert, are you all right? My God, what if something terrible has happened. If you get this message call me in the car in the next fifteen minutes. We're all worried sick about you.

6:45: Robert, we're about to call the police and the hospitals and there's no trace of you anywhere. Where are you? I am absolutely frantic. We're almost to the church, so you won't be able to reach me in the car anymore. (Mother, how should Robert call me now? Well, doesn't anybody have a freakin' flip phone?) Robert, call my machine, I'll check it every five minutes. This is a hell of a way to get married, you shitweasel. You better be in some hospital unconscious, or I'm going to put you there myself.

This was what I loved about Doris. She was, as we say, up front with her emotions. What you see is what you get. No apologies for it either. Ever. Whereas I tend to be perversely involuted and brooding and self-questioning. This is one reason our friends thought we were so good for each other, on the old opposites attract, two-lovers-make-one-being Platonic principle. They thought I could use her drive and efficiency (which I did) and she could use my introspection and detachment (which she didn't). To Doris's credit, she was usually patient with me, if sometimes a little too obviously so. "What would you do without me?" was one of her favorite lines, delivered with a genuinely affectionate smile. Well, I was about to find out, and so was she.

But I had never wanted to hurt her, and I was hurting her badly. If I knew her at all, she would be vindictive. This thought sent a chill through me, as I stood there in my birthday suit in Sabine's designer kitchen, although the chill might have come from an evening breeze off the ocean. After the sun goes down in Southern California, the temperature drops ten degrees in ten minutes. It was getting dark out now. I could see my reflection just beginning to show up in the window. I must say I was an estimable assemblage of beef. I watched my diet and worked out like a troglodyte. If you were going to do stand-up (which I was, and did—God help me—for the last fifteen years), in front of an audience who has carte blanche to check you out for their pleasure (whatever it may be), you'd better look either good or ridiculous, and I had never wished to look ridiculous (despite the evidence of recent behavior). As Billy Crystal/Fernando said so immortally, "It is better to look good than to feel good." And I sure didn't feel good. Whatever happened with Sabine, I could find another woman. I didn't have to jump into anything. I'd be okay. And so would Doris. But hell hath no fury like a woman scorned, and even Shakespeare could not have imagined Doris, who'd no doubt update his idea to megatonnage for the nuclear age. I just hoped she couldn't get her hands on a Stinger missile. She had never kept an emotion inside herself in her life so it wasn't likely she would do so with this behemoth. She'd take it right out on me. Big time. Some people in this situation might console themselves by asking, "What's the worst she can do?" In my case, this question was not consoling. I have seen her reduce omnipotent studio executives to trembling blobs of ectoplasm. Doris's worst was just this side of Armageddon and she'd be both thorough and relentless in executing it (and me).

This still didn't excuse what I had done to her. I didn't know if it would be more considerate to leave her a message or not. The phone was still in my hand. Maybe as much for that reason as any other, I dialed her number. When her answering machine picked up, I said:

> Doris, this is Robert. I guess you know who it is.
> I didn't plan to do this, but I believe it's for the best that we not be married. At least we didn't make that mistake. I'm sorry I didn't realize it sooner. I know you'll be all right. I hope someday you'll be able to forgive me.

When I hung up, I noticed Sabine was standing across the kitchen on the other side of the island. She had on a white silk robe and thick black-rimmed glasses, so I thought for a moment she was someone else, and I must have jumped.

"Just me," she said. "I live here."

I almost said, "Really? It doesn't look like it," but smiled instead. It wasn't my business, yet, where she lived or how. She certainly *didn't* live here. But maybe she had just moved in? Or out? Or something.

She propped her elbows on the Italian-hand-painted-tile island and cupped her chin in her hands, cutely.

"I think I'll just admire the view," she said looking me up and down. It made me remember I was naked.

"I guess I'll go put on some clothes."

"I brought you a robe." It was also white silk. Large. A man's size. Whose was it? She held it like a coat for me to slide my arms into the sleeves. While my back was to her, she said, "That was a classy message you left your fiancée."

"Classy? If you say so. I did just inconvenience her somewhat."

"Yeah, but you didn't whine. You didn't say anything false. I like that."

"I'm glad you like it. I don't think Doris will," I said, facing Sabine and cinching the robe at the waist.

She looked at me with that ironic grin.

"Are we feeling a little guilt?" she asked. "Are we feeling a little postcoital *tristesse?*"

Postcoital *tristesse?* Who was this woman?

"As a matter of fact, we are not," I answered.

"Good, because I'm not either." She wrapped her arms around my neck and kissed me hard and long. It had authority, no question about it. She said, "I don't know what it is about you, Robert, but you do something to me that goes deep down."

"You, too," I said. I meant it. And it was not just a little scary. It may have been a power like this I had always avoided.

"No, I *really* mean it," she said and kissed me again, expertly, perfectly, instantly transforming my knees into Silly Putty.

She stepped back but kept hold of my hand and looked at me for a long moment, as if she were memorizing me.

"Maybe we were together in another life," she said. Ironically?

"Which life would that be?" I asked.

"The next one."

Okay, she's a nut case, I thought. But what did I have to lose? I had just torched my last life pretty thoroughly. I may as well be with her in the next one—whichever planet she lived on.

"So now what?" she asked, returning us to earth.

"Now what what?" I said. "I believe my calendar has been cleared for this evening."

"It's Friday, I don't have to work tomorrow."

"Yeah?"

"Why don't you take me on a honeymoon?"

"To Baja," I said.

"Why not? It's already paid for, isn't it? The bridal suite with the wet bar and the heart-shaped Jacuzzi."

"I don't think I want to do that," I said.

"At the risk of repeating myself: Why not?"

"It seems disrespectful."

"To whom? Doris is not going to care. She's not going to know."

"To me, I guess. It seems disrespectful to myself." Was I suddenly developing a compunction? I might have to reorganize my entire personality.

"Hmm," she said, the way she had in the bank when she decided to take my ride home. I could hear the wheels clicking inside her brain. She took off her glasses and rubbed the lenses on her robe, pulling it up by the hem and featuring her bare legs. It made me realize that I was leaving a very significant piece of evidence out of this argument.

"Well," she said, "this is the first time I've ever had to try to pester a man into shacking up with me for a weekend. And here I already packed my swimsuit."

She dropped her robe from her shoulders and there it was: the Brazilian bikini with the butt-floss bottom, red as the devil himself. She turned and walked a few steps with her arms held out, in parody of a runway model (or a stripper), the whole time grinning as if she were pulling the trick of the week. The tattoo was there, too, right under the curvature of her butt, at about Rio de Janeiro on the globe, southern latitude thirty degrees, only it wasn't a black snake but a tiny broken heart the size of a dime. I didn't even mention it.

"Baja it is," I said.

"Robert, really?" She threw her arms around me. "We are going to have such a great time!"

3.

I did not have such a great time. More accurately, I had a great time, then a terrible time, and then a weird time, good in its way if you like emotional high colonics. I prefer my emotions more gently purged. The great time was driving down to Baja and having sex again and falling asleep. On the way out of LA we grabbed a bag of Fatburgers and a bottle of champagne, which Sabine insisted on paying for. When I asked why, she said, "I'm trying to get into your pants." I responded, "If you were any more into my pants, you'd be wearing them yourself." In fact, what she was wearing was a workout outfit—halter top and spandex shorts—underneath a bright purple sport coat that just covered her butt. Her traveling suit. Legs up to her ears. When we stopped for the burgers she was shouted and whistled at; a carload of teenagers drummed the side of their car; outside the wine store where she bought the champagne, a beggar who looked like he should be in the ER on life support made kiss-noises at her. When we got back into the car, I stupidly asked her how that kind of attention made her feel. She said, "What attention?" She didn't notice it anymore, or so she claimed. I asked her about when men were more intrusive than that, when they approached her on the street or followed her or tried to touch her. She said she knew how to take care of herself. What I thought of as haughtiness when I first saw her in the bank now seemed more like defiance, a defiance that I myself would find exhausting to maintain. I said something to that effect which I thought sounded feminist and empathetic, but she reacted irritably. "Would you rather I dressed like a nun?" she asked. That was the end of that subject.

I was still feeling lucky though. I had dropped Sparky at the kennel that morning on the way to the bank, and Sabine talked me into not zipping by my house and packing a suitcase, so I'd be beachcombing in Baja in my L.L. Bean rain gear. What did it matter? I was so happy to be with her and not to face my torched life for a couple of days I would have gone to Baja in a hazmat suit. It did seem odd that she was in such a hurry to get on the road: no stopping for dinner, no picking up my stuff. She herself virtually cleaned out her closet in about ten minutes. Four big suitcases, the kind you have to pull on wheels, not including the pillow-sized black leather purse. Okay, it's a girl thing, I thought. Doris wouldn't cross the street without a three-season wardrobe and enough cosmetics to last her a decade into senescence.

But the other oddity was that after Sabine downed her burger and a few hits of champagne she fell asleep and stayed asleep until we got to the hotel in Baja. Six hours. It was as if she had been hit with a hammer. When you don't know someone, you don't know whether their behavior is unusual for them or not. For example, Doris, who always displayed carpet-bomber efficiency, used a whole roll of toilet paper every time she went to the bathroom. All the trees of the world began to scream in unison each time she had to pee. Maybe Sabine always fell asleep as if she were hit with a hammer. But even with our nap earlier it seemed she hadn't slept for a week. At one point after we crossed the border, she mumbled, "Who's there? Who's there?" and, a half hour later, "Don't do it, Softy." Don't do it *softly*? I was sure she said Softy. Who was Softy? The producer? I thought I had plenty of time to find out about that, about why she had lied about the roommate. Anyway, if all we were going to do was hump like puppies, it would be fine with me if she had a boyfriend who spent lots of time in Africa, especially if he were named "Softy." It would mean I wouldn't have to get too involved either, and maybe I needed a break after ten years with Doris of Relationship Building and Communication Skills. God, we had tried hard. The xeroxed handouts from all the weekend couples' seminars Doris and I attended together made a stack that would reach the moon. Doris's personal library on the subject would fill a wing of the Library of Congress if they collect titles like *Women Who Are Just Too Nice*, *Seven Warning Signs He Can't Commit*, and *How To Get More Love From Him (And Everything Else)*. She also bought the tapes, the videos, the CD-ROMs, and an interactive computer game we played with joysticks, the object of which was not to defeat your opponent but to work together in harmony through obstacles presented by the pressures and demands of daily life. We spent so much money on couples' therapy we could have bought the Los Angeles Lakers instead. The Lakers would have probably done more for our relationship. (I understand Shaquille O'Neal is a very empathetic person.) The phrase, "What I'm hearing Doris say to you, Robert . . ." makes me instantly narcoleptic. I fall asleep, boom, just like Sabine did after she finished her hamburger. That phrase has etched by far the deepest groove in my brain, way deeper than more superficial instincts such as food, sex, survival, and breathing.

As you might be able to tell, our Relationship Building was a recurring subject of my stand-up routine, and, to Doris's credit, that was fine with her. She didn't care if I spilled the intimate details of our life to whoever was willing to pay a ten-dollar cover and two-drink minimum. It was art. She respected it. Maybe some of her generosity was compensatory, since she made her money from "novelizations," that miscreant of literary genres. She was the agent who put together the deal. She hired the writers, she wrote the contract, she designed the publicity campaign. Whenever a big movie comes out and the same day you notice at the supermarket checkout stand the unlikely and previously nonexistent novel of that title with the star's picture on the cover, that is the promo work of Doris. Fortunately she did not commission the Jane Austen movies to be novelized. But she did everything else for the paperback of *Sense And Sensibility* with Emma Thompson's picture on the cover that put it on the best-seller list for a couple of weeks until people realized there were so many words inside, and pretty darn big ones at that. The novel of *Pocahontas* totaled about thirty sentences, none of them complex or compound, and did much better. But it didn't really matter. As long as the cover was right and the book was where it was supposed to be when it was supposed to be there, it sold. And Doris made dump trucks full of money. Boxcars full. Toxic waste dumps full. It was more lucrative than murdering drifters for their kidneys.

I think it was the *Pocahontas* guy who sent the fruit basket that was waiting for Sabine and me in the honeymoon suite. It was as big as a gazebo. The card said, "Fruit you can eat! PS Don't drink the water!" There was an enormous sort of flan cake from a writer who hadn't worked for Doris since he novelized *Die Hard II*. There were matching sombreros filled with cookies. What in the world did people think? That newlyweds would spend their honeymoon gorging themselves to death? That they'd sit in the Jacuzzi stuffing their faces? I

was tired enough from the drive that things felt a little surreal anyway (things *were* a little surreal anyway). So far Sabine
and I had spent less time in conversation than having sex. She
barely woke up long enough to check into the hotel (as Doris,
which entertained her) and have sex with me again (not as
Doris, which also entertained her). I had never met anyone
who talked less about herself. But after Doris it was, as I said,
a relief, and, as I also said, I thought we had plenty of time.
I fell asleep like a toddler who just had his first whole day at
the zoo.

But after an hour I woke up with a start, that kind of
waking that must come from our monkey ancestors when
they were about to fall out of a tree. I jumped awake. It was
dawn. I had no idea where I was or how I got there. Then
I remembered. I was hungry. I realized in the past twenty-
four hours I had eaten a total of two hamburgers, not my
usual bill of fare. I got up and went into the sitting room to
look for a banana. I was going to deconstruct the gazebo fruit
basket if the job did not require a backhoe. The bellman had
stacked all of Sabine's luggage next to it. On the coffee table
made out of what seemed to be an actual humongous seashell,
she had placed her purse. I picked one banana from the stalk
of the hundred or so (with leaves) and sat down.

Before I tell what I did next, I want to say that I am not
a snoop. I know this is like Nixon saying I am not a crook,
but snooping has never been one of my problems. I've never
read a diary or a letter addressed to someone else or listened
in on a phone call. I believe I can understand how people feel
about me by the way they act toward me. This may be wrong
but it is simple. If anything, I'm the opposite of paranoid. It
doesn't occur to me that people are hostile to me even when
they *are* hostile to me. It doesn't occur to me that anyone has
a hidden agenda. Anyway, not to put too fine a point on it, I

unzipped Sabine's purse. I was curious about her. I thought I might find out something.

I sure did: it was filled with money. Lots of money. Cash. Hundred-dollar bills in packs of one hundred. Brand-new bills, unused, crisp. I couldn't tell how many of them there were, but there was nothing else in the bag but some tissue paper to round it out. Twenty packs at least. At least $200,000.

My response was perhaps a bit aberrant: I found it erotic. I had never seen that much cash much less touched it. Something about Sabine's purse, the color of the money and the texture of the surprisingly soft black leather, and the way she had run out of the bank in the rain clutching it against her chest. It brought back our sex, the way she felt and kissed and smelled, and the fact that we were soon going to have more sex, a lot more sex, a whole weekend of sex.

Then I thought, *Psycho*. Janet Leigh, the bank teller, the money she had just stolen sticking out of her purse as she drives out of town.

Both of these reactions passed through me in about a nano-second. Then I got scared. Holy shit, I thought. What is going on here? What have I gotten myself into? What should I do?

I started with some deep breathing. I used to have a yoga teacher, an Indian named Miss Gayatri, who would say, "Inn-hale and do nahthing." That's what I did. There were just a whole universe of questions I couldn't get answers to, and there was only one person in the universe who could answer them: Sabine. My options were to call the Mexican police (never an option) or ask her directly what the hell was going on. Or walk out of there right then and drive back to LA. But the room was in my name, and I could be letting myself in for trouble. I might be an accessory to a crime. I might have driven the getaway car. Okay, I'd ask her what the hell was going on. Shall I wake her up and ask her while I am in this state of panic or shall I ask her after we have slept awhile when I may be a bit calmer? What difference would a few hours make?

Pretty fuzzy thinking, I guess, but it had been an over-stimulating twenty-four hours. It's not that I believed she'd provide me with a reasonable explanation for why there was 200 grand in her purse. And I have to admit that, crazy as it was, I wanted to have sex with her again, in fact more than ever. So I left the purse as I found it, trying to make sure it was zipped as it had been zipped, at the exact angle it had been lying on the table. Then I crawled back into bed. Sabine made a sleepy noise as I fit my body against hers from behind. I kissed her neck. She moved against me and reached down and before I could think about it I was inside her again. I put my hand over her mouth as if I were mugging her, and she started sucking my fingers, all of them, like she was trying to get my whole hand into her mouth. Then she started scream-ing in a way that startled me, almost a scream of pain, as if the pain were going out of her as she went into orgasm. Pretty intense. It took me over completely. I just didn't care about anything else, who she was or even who I was. When we were finished, I was the one who fell asleep as if I were hit with a hammer.

When I woke up, it was dark. Sabine wasn't there and, of course, neither was her purse. Or her luggage. The only thing on the coffee table was my banana peel, underneath which was a note on hotel stationery:

> No I am not some avenging angel sent to do you like
> you did Doris. I just had to leave. Some day I hope
> to tell you why in person. Believe it or not, I don't
> go to bed with strangers. I have never done before
> what I did with you. I used you, but I didn't know

you would be *you*, and it has spun me around good.
You may find out some things about me when you
go back to LA that may confuse you or maybe you'll
just not bother and forget me. I will never forget
you. I am sorrier than you will be able to believe
right now that I cannot stay here with you and go
back with you. When we meet again I will make it
up to you. Thank you for your kindness to me. You
are a lovely, gentle, sexy man.

Sexy was underlined three times. At the bottom was a PS:

If you care at all for my safety, please burn this letter.

Burn was also underlined three times.

Well then. What now? I read the letter again. And again.
I read it five times, with a different response each time, rang-
ing from, *My God, what a woman* to *I bumped into a rip-off
artist, that's all. I just got taken for a ride.* The truth is I had
no idea what to think, it was all so bizarre, but I settled on
the last response because it was most obvious and comfortable. Fat chance anyway I'd burn her letter. I might have to
show it to the police. Anyway, it was my only honeymoon
souvenir.

My mouth tasted like I had been sucking dirty pennies.
Here I was in the honeymoon suite, surrounded by food. I
could take a Jacuzzi with the flan cake or perhaps one of the
larger papayas. I could be by myself for a while, which was
what I wanted to do less than anything. But I felt too rotten
to be with anyone else. I could just see the looks: *got what you
deserved.* It was hard enough to feel sorry for myself (at which,
however, I was a life master). No way would anyone else feel
sorry for me.

I called the front desk and found out it was nine P.M. I
had slept twelve or thirteen hours. I put on my rain gear to
go down to the restaurant and have some dinner.

The hotel was huge. The honeymoon suite was about a
half mile from the main lobby. I guess they figured the newlyweds would be screwing so much they wouldn't have time for
the restaurant; they'd eat massive fruit baskets and sombreros-
ful of cookies in their room between gambols in the Jacuzzi.
In contrast to my usual state of antiparanoia, even the hotel
layout seemed conspiratorial. When I asked the desk clerk
where the restaurant was, he said, "My condolences about
your wife's mother, señor."

I said, "Thank you very much."

"What a misfortunate thing to happen on your honeymoon."

"Did my wife get off all right?" I asked.

"Oh yes, no problem," he said cheerily. "The hotel shuttle
took her right to the airport."

"At about what time was that?" I said.

"The plane leaves at nine A.M. so no later than eight."

"And that flight was going to . . ."

"Mexico City, señor. It is only a small plane. From Mexico
City one may fly anywhere in the world."

"Yes, well, thank you," I said. I handed him a tip. He
smiled and bowed elegantly. He was short and had a neat
mustache, nothing like Tony Perkins at the Bates Motel. I
bet he had never dressed up in his dead mother's clothes in
his whole life. I turned to walk toward the restaurant, but he
stopped me.

"A question, señor, if I am not intruding."

"Sure," I said. "What is it?"

"How did your wife find out about her mother?"

"What do you mean?"

"There were no telephone calls to your room."

"Oh, that," I said. "She has a cellular phone. It works any-where. I guess it beams to a satellite or something."

"That was about seven A.M. then."

"It could have been." I looked at his nameplate. "Octavio. Why do you ask?"

"I'm so sorry, señor. I do not mean to invade your privacy in your time of grief. The security guard in that wing heard a terrible screaming coming from the honeymoon suite." Octavio smiled with embarrassment. "We never intrude upon our guests, especially in the honeymoon suite. But such a scream, well, we did not know what to do."

I smiled incongruously. "It was a terrible shock for my wife."

"Yes, I am sure. Again our condolences."

"Right, well, thank you, Octavio."

"My pleasure, señor."

I didn't think about his question until after I was seated in the restaurant, and then it seemed conspiratorial too. How would he know there were no phone calls to the room or why would he pay attention to such a thing? Maybe it was noth-ing. The hotel staff must talk among themselves when a guest has an emergency. Maybe the hotel operator told him there were no calls. Maybe I was completely whacked-out paranoid at this point. I needed to get a purchase on reality here.

Mexico is not the best place to do that for me, which is why I've always liked it. Doris wanted to take the Concorde to Paris for the weekend (she could only take the weekend off), but she indulged me my lower-middle-class preference to drive to Baja. It barely qualified as Mexico anyway. There were more Americans than Mexicans here. Tonight they all seemed to be celebrating birthdays or anniversaries. I was the only one by himself: the dining room was filled with cou-ples drinking margaritas and toasting each other and looking deeply into each other's eyes. There was a buffet at a long table with a number of men in chef's hats slicing hefty beef roasts and hams and women in poofy off-the-shoulder dresses dishing up all varieties of Mexican specialties from silver trays warmed by flaming cans of Sterno. I had to tip the mariachi band ten dollars not to play at my table. They sang "Happy Birthday" as a cha-cha to one of my fellow diners named Earl. I sang along to myself with the words, "How could you be such a chump, Chump? Chump, chump, chump." I had a good time feeling wronged. It kept me from having to think about everything I was going to have to deal with when I got back to LA.

4.

I checked out after dinner.

"No luggage, señor?" asked Octavio.

"Just my anorak," I said, hoisting it onto the counter with one hand while I signed the credit card slip with the other. If I had worn it on the trek from the honeymoon suite to the front desk, I would have been happily dead from heat stroke.

"Anorak," Octavio repeated carefully. "This is a disease that infects cattle. It is a disease of the nerves."

"Yes, nerves. My problem, exactly," I said.

"Oh no, señor. Now you are joking with me. Surely you do not have this disease, because it is fatal."

"Right, just joking, Octavio. You're thinking of anthrax. Thank you very much." I reached over the counter and handed him another tip. I asked him to take home the fruit basket, the flan cake, and the his-'n'-her sombreros filled with cookies. I could tell by his expression that this was not allowed, but he thanked me warmly and assured me that his entire family would think of me as they enjoyed these delicious treats.

There was hardly another car on the road until I crossed the border at three A.M., and then it was the rare pleasure of the I-5 north from San Diego and the 405 into LA at

seventy-five mph without one car ten feet in front and
another car ten feet behind and cars on each side passing and
being passed, with motorcycles splitting the gap and making
my stomach leap to the ceiling. I've seen at least twenty-five
accidents on the freeway in the fifteen years I've lived in LA.
The most recent was a Mercedes a hundred yards in front of
me that shot across three lanes to its left, hit the guardrail,
and flipped onto its roof into the oncoming traffic. The driver
must have either passed out or done it on purpose. I'd never
know which. It became a "fatal injury accident blocking the
405 northbound at La Cienega" on the radio traffic updates
for a couple of hours, then nobody thought about it again.
What does it do to your brain to live like this? It was just
something that happened to somebody else. To most people it
was nothing. To the people who had to drive the 405 at that
time it was an irritating inconvenience. To me it was something I saw that became a story I told for a couple of days to
friends who responded with blank looks that said, "So what?"
If anything, they were concerned about me getting all excited
about the obvious. Because what was there to say about it? It
was just another horrible possibility, like the next big earthquake. The fact that it happened to other people every day
was a fact nobody could do anything about, another unfortu-
nate incident on the news. What are we going to do? Make
bike paths out of the freeways? Stop driving cars? Shut up and
live your life, their patient smiles said.

　　When I pulled into my driveway, it was just dawn. I had
worked myself into the certainty that it would be blocked by
yellow police tape, and a SWAT team would descend on me as
soon as I pulled up. Nothing. Not even two plainclothesmen
napping in an unmarked car. I got out of the Z, stretched my
arms in the air, and breathed. The air is actually breathable
here this close to the ocean. My place is in the Santa Monica

Canyon, at the highest point on a switchback up from PCH, a garage converted into a one-bedroom apartment with a little deck on the back from which I can see the ocean over the trees below and used to be able to see Charles Laughton's old house perched on a cliff in the distance until it slid down onto the highway during a mudslide.

My landlady is named Renate Steiner. She is a big-boned blonde in her late forties with a soft face that shows her suffering. She lives with her daughter Krista in the house on the double lot, an old white wood-frame house built in the late thirties and owned ever since by German immigrants. Krista is a schizophrenic. She has two older sisters: Hannah, who graduated from Harvard Medical School and runs the hospital in a refugee camp in Cambodia; and Greta, who is first cellist with the Chicago Symphony Orchestra. Twenty years ago, after Renate's husband died suddenly, she converted the garage into the apartment and lived in it with all three girls so she could rent the big house and put them through school. Krista is the youngest, twenty-two. She has been home for four years. At eighteen, she went off to Wellesley on a full scholarship and within two months she was back home. If something awful happened to her during that time, she won't tell anybody what it was. Now when one of her sisters has a great accomplishment or good fortune, Krista cuts herself. I've been living in Renate's place for four years; Krista had just moved back home when I moved in. She's a pretty girl, large-boned like her mother, with frizzy hair and a round flat face like a clock. She hates the way she looks. She ducks when she sees a mirror. She smiled brightly when I first met her, then I noticed she had rotated her body a quarter turn and was looking at me sideways out of the corners of her eyes. Her head was oscillating slightly and her smile had become frozen, tense, a rictus. It may have been in response to my putting out my hand to shake hers when Renate introduced us. Renate said, "Krista, shake hands with Mr. Wilder."

"Don't touch me," Krista said.

But in the four years since, she has decided she likes me. More than likes me. Renate says she talks about our future together, that she knows that "we each have to work through our personal issues" but then we will be married. When I travel, I sometimes find her in my apartment when I come home. She waits until Renate is asleep then uses the spare key to let herself in. Sometimes she sleeps in my bed, or eats something from the refrigerator; usually, she just sits in my chair and listens to her Discman, which she does most of her waking hours. Otherwise she doesn't disturb anything. It's still a little creepy, and the first time it happened I of course talked to Renate about it who talked to Krista about it whose response was to slash her breasts with a razor blade. When we hid the key, she broke a window and climbed in. When I asked her myself not to do it, she said, "I don't ever bother you when you're here. Why can't I at least stay with you when you're gone?"

So Krista stays in my place with me when I'm gone. She feeds Sparky (they have a great friendship), although if I'm going to be gone for more than a night I put him in the kennel, since it's impossible to predict what Krista might do. The only alternative to just letting her stay with me when I'm gone seemed to be to move out of my apartment, but I didn't want to move out and after I had given it some thought, it didn't seem like such a big deal, certainly not worth slashed breasts. Plus I slept at Doris's a lot of the time, and I thought I'd be ready to give up my place sometime after we were married, although not immediately. Doris owned a townhouse in Brentwood and a pied-à-terre in Manhattan. It seemed inevitable that my life would gravitate there, that I'd probably start working more in New York. What Krista did drove Doris nuts. She claimed I wouldn't put a stop to it because I was getting an ego stroke. And of course Krista hated Doris, although she never met her and couldn't have seen her more than a couple of times since Doris wouldn't put a foot in what she called my "lair." She claimed she could smell the vaginal secretions on the furniture. Krista called her The Witchbitch. When Renate informed Krista that Doris and I were getting married, Krista said, "No, they're not." The psychiatrist had recommended that Renate tell Krista about my engagement while I was gone for a month on the armpit tour—comedy clubs in the Ohio-Indiana Rust Belt. When I got home, very tired and depressed (from doing comedy for unemployed alcoholics followed every night by the amenities of the local Motel 6), Krista was sitting in my big leather chair with her feet on the ottoman eating Dorritos and watching Montel Williams. When I walked through the door, she said, "You won't marry Witchbitch."

I said, "Time to go back home, Krista." But it turned out she was right.

This time I walked in and Krista was in my bed. She was wearing one of my clean dress shirts, and a pair of my black Calvin Klein briefs on her head. They, happily, were also clean, as it turned out, although I wasn't sure of that when I saw her. I couldn't guess what it was at first. She looked like she was in a hijab, perhaps having converted to one of the more heterodox Islamic sects. She had the briefs pulled all the way down so that her ears stuck through the leg holes. She had never put on my clothes before while I was gone, much less my underwear on her head.

"I'm not asleep," she said.

"Would you mind taking those off your head and giving me back my shirt?"

"I don't have anything on underneath."

"Where are your clothes?"

"I've got them under the covers."

"I'm going into the kitchen and you put them on, okay?"

"You didn't do it, did you?"

She was smiling mischievously with the covers pulled up to her chin. There was no way she could have known what had happened.

"No, I didn't."

"You stood her up at the church."

"How do you know that, Krista?"

"I saw it."

"How did you see it?"

"I saw it in my head. Witchbitch was crying," she said with a huge smile.

"Please get dressed and go home now."

"Make me eggs! Make me eggs!" This was a ritual. Whenever I found Krista sleeping in my bed, I had to make her eggs. I thought she wanted me to show that I wasn't angry at her, but there was probably also some domestic fantasy in it that she wanted played out.

While I was scrambling the eggs, Renate knocked on the door.

"Is Krista here?" she asked.

I told her she was.

"I saw your car," she said when I had let her in. "I thought you were not coming back until Monday."

"I didn't get married," I said. "You want some eggs too?"

"You didn't get married?" Renate repeated.

"I didn't get married." I took two more eggs from the carton and broke them on the edge of the pan and tore into them with a whisk.

"What happened?" Renate asked.

"Let Krista tell you," I said. "She saw it in her head."

Krista came in tucking her T-shirt into her jeans and buckling her belt. Renate did a double take.

"He stood her up at the church!" Krista shouted gleefully.

"Is that true, Robert? Why?" Renate asked, shocked.

"Look how funny he looks, Mama," Krista said. "No one would marry someone who looks so funny."

"That's it," I said to Renate. "No one would marry someone who looks so funny." I dished the eggs up for each of them.

"Witchbitch is dead, Witchbitch is dead," Krista chanted.

"Stop it, Krista," Renate said.

"Eat your eggs, Krista. They're getting cold." I made a pot of coffee and poured myself a cup and sat down with them. Renate kept looking at me, waiting for the explanation which I was not about to give her either then or later, and Krista was shoveling her eggs into her mouth, holding the plate up to her chin like a rice bowl.

"You forgot toast!" she shouted. I had never seen her so happy.

I was actually also happy they were there. This was not a day I was looking forward to. My answering machine pulsed red on overload. No way was I ready to listen to those messages.

The three of us finished our eggs like a normal family having breakfast. Since I clearly did not want to answer Renate's questions, she stopped asking them. Krista, however, wanted to know what I was going to do that day.

"I'm thinking of seeing if I can lock myself in my refrigerator," I answered. "Did you get that when you were a kid in Germany?" I asked Renate. "Never climb into an abandoned refrigerator? Who in the hell would abandon a refrigerator?"

"I want to go to the zoo," Krista said. Renate looked at her and at me. Krista wouldn't leave her house except to sneak into my apartment. She would never go anywhere. When she had her psychiatric appointments (three times a week), she insisted on riding there in the backseat of the car lying on the floor. Renate had to lead her into the building while Krista covered her eyes.

I said, "I can't today, Krista. I'm sorry."

She started to cry. "Why not?" she moaned.

Renate said, "Robert just got home, Krista. He's tired. He has important things to do." But she looked at me as if I had committed a crime.

"We can go this week," I said. "I just can't go today."

"Oh, Robert, you don't have to do that," Renate said.

"Promise?" Krista said.

"Promise," I said. "We'll all go. It's fine, Renate. It'll be fun."

I started clearing the dishes. Renate shooed Krista out of the house in front of her, and whispered to me, "Don't worry if you're too busy. She'll forget about it in twenty minutes." But I knew that wasn't true, and so did Renate.

"It will be fun," I said. "But I can't take her by myself."

"Oh, I'm going. You can count on that."

"Then we're on," I said. As I closed the door behind them, I could see over Renate's shoulder that Krista was throwing me a kiss.

5.

After they left, I surveyed the leavings: four empty cans of Diet Coke on the floor next to my chair, an empty bag of Ripples, the box from a Weight Watchers lemon chicken dinner that Krista must have brought with her to microwave. Since I had been intending to come right home from the bank instead of via the quaint detour to Mexico, I had left papers on my desk (including the unsigned marriage license) and dishes in the sink. Krista didn't disturb the papers nor do the dishes. Her vision of my standing up Doris at the church seemed somewhat less mystical since she no doubt saw the unsigned marriage license on my desk—although her instincts about me were often uncanny, whether they issued from her preternatural attention to me or her schizophrenic brain chemistry. Three of her heavy metal CDs (by Death, Fear Factory, and Weird Looks), which she had probably listened to in my bed, probably at full volume, were on the floor next to the bed, along with her Discman. I pulled the sheets off, which I always did after I found Krista sleeping there, not wanting, frankly, to smell her when I tried to go to sleep. Not her vaginal secretions (despite what Doris thought)—she just had her own smell the way everyone does, and I didn't care to be that intimate with it. I pulled the covers off onto the floor, and underneath them was a vial of pills.

Oh God, I said aloud. Oh no.

It was Demerol, twenty fat tablets shaped like toy footballs, one hundred milligrams each, enough to drop a rhinoceros. Where the hell could she have gotten them? I didn't use drugs except ibuprofen when I had a bad muscle pull, and since Krista had been occupying my apartment I kept even the ibuprofen locked in the glove compartment of my car. I looked at the name on the prescription: Karle Ochte. I didn't know any Karle Ochte. Whoever Karle Ochte was, it was Krista who had been in my bed with these pills, and these pills certainly would have killed her.

It put a new spin on things here. Suddenly there wasn't anything cute about it anymore. I got mad at Renate, mad at the shrink. This wasn't my responsibility. I just wanted to punch something, so I did. I went into the kitchen and punched my refrigerator. It hurt my hand. Surprise. And put a dent in the refrigerator that I'd have to pay to repair (if I didn't abandon it).

I would have to talk to Renate about this. Later. I had enough to take care of right now. Although there weren't any cops waiting for me, I might still be the accessory to a bank robbery. Maybe the bank didn't realize that the money was gone. They may have shut down their computers because of the flooding. It had been Friday (less than forty-eight hours ago!), the bank was closing at the time, and wouldn't open again until tomorrow, Monday. This gave me exactly one day to do something about it. I may not have been arrested when I pulled into my driveway, but I was hardly out of trouble. Now was the time to get some information if I could. Then I had to go to the kennel and pick up Sparky.

I dialed my friend Don's number and he answered on the second ring.

"Don. Robert," I said after his sleepy hello.

"The shitheel," he said. "The infamous cad."

"The very one."

"Where the hell are you? What time is it?"

"Home," I said. "I don't know what time it is. Seven thirty."

"Seven thirty on a Sunday morning. How nice of you to call. I thought I might be getting some sleep after this nightmare weekend you caused, but no. Did you get my message?"

"No, I haven't listened to my messages. The little red number on my machine says 54. I'll need about a day and a half."

"My message said, 'Don't ever call me again.'"

"How nice."

"Francine made me leave it." (Francine was Don's wife and Doris's best friend.) "You are *persona non grata* here, pal. Joseph Goebbels would be more welcome at our house. If Francine ever sees you, you're dead meat."

"Great," I said.

"Lucky for you, she is with Doris on Maui at the moment, spending about $10,000 of our money we had not planned to spend, so you owe me there, too, motherfucker."

"When can I see you?"

"Now if you want to. Kids were asleep until the phone rang. Now they aren't. They're in the next room murdering each other. I've got them the *whole* day the *whole* weekend. For which you also owe me."

"I'll be right there," I said.

"Christ, give me twenty minutes anyway. I've got to brush my teeth."

Don's house was four blocks away, up San Vincente, toward OJ land. Another mile up San Vincente is the Mezzaluna Ristorante where Ron Goldman worked. In this neighborhood it's pretty hard to keep up with the Simpsons. Francine makes 400 grand a year giving lectures on college campuses at five grand a pop on "Images of Women in the Media" and "Anorexia: The Atrocity of Advertising." She bills herself as Dr. Francine Leach, the "doctor" part being an EdD in education, which they give you if you can make the verb agree with the subject for three sentences in a row. I saw her lecture once: she's excellent. Witty, smart—and she's physically attractive. She's also obsessed with being physically attractive, which I happen to know from Don. She's afraid if she gets too old or ugly she's out of business, because her social criticism might seem like personal whining. Francine and I tried very hard to like each other. I respect her work so I could sincerely tell her so, but it seems that she can't even look at me without a palpable twitch of disapproval. She introduced Doris and me, reluctantly (a story in itself). Marrying Doris was my big chance for redemption in Francine's eyes. I can't say I'm sorry about being unredeemed there. I'd positively enjoy never seeing Francine again, although it would be harder on Don if I were the one refusing to see her.

Don is a big bear of a guy, with a beard he'd let go bushy if he lived in Oregon, but which he trims twice a week so he's not a dead ringer for the Unabomber. He manages the Francine corporation, HMR (Hear Me Roar) Enterprises, Inc: the books, the videos, the lecture tours. He's also Mr. Mom. And he writes poems—little Zen things that when he reads them publicly seem incongruously delicate coming out of this flesh-mountain. Plus he does some part-time teaching in both the preppy private schools in Brentwood and the roughest public schools in Compton. But Francine is the breadwinner, and sometimes (in my opinion) she acts like the tyrannical dad in the old sitcoms about the one-earner nuclear family. The irony of this has occasionally worked itself into my routines, to her displeasure when she has heard about it. Whereas Don is so secure in himself and our friendship he has to pretend to be unamused when I do them as a female Archie Bunker and a male Edith. Good for three or four minutes, to an older audience.

Don has a high butcher block table in his kitchen and when I arrived his kids were at it faced off across from each other, scowling. Jeb is nine and Emma is seven. They both look exactly like Francine, which shows who has the dominant genes; they're both petite like she is with sharp pretty features like china dolls. Jeb is going through the stage of hating being so little and pretty and compensates for it with spectacular aggression against his sister whom he whacks every time he can get away with it. Francine goes nuts when she sees him do it, but she's rarely home during the school year. If he whacks Emma in front of Don, he's sent to his room for an hour. Jeb has, in his own opinion, spent a lot of unquality time there recently, so he was currently devising various creative ways to torment Emma without touching her. When I walked in, he was snarling at her, and she was shouting, "Daddy, Jeb is being Monsterdog at me."

"Quit it, Jeb," Don said absently. Don was cleverly making them oatmeal, because it would cause them to unite against him in their refusal to eat it.

"See this oatmeal," he said to me, as he pushed a grotesquely big bowlful in front of each of them. "If you had been here yesterday, Francine would have pummeled your face until it looked like that."

"I've always wanted to look like a healthy breakfast cereal," I said.

"Oat-Meal!" both kids whined in unison. Don then poured them each a bowl of Sugar Stars and whipped cream as he had planned to all along, and put the kids together in the TV room to watch *The Lion King* for the 800th time. Don and Francine owned all the Disney videos compliments of Doris. Plus all the novelizations, the most recent of which Francine displayed on the living room coffee table as if they were actual books.

When Don came back to the kitchen, I was finishing Emma's oatmeal. I had already eaten Jeb's.

"All right, let's hear it," he said.

I told him what happened, from the time I walked into the bank until waking up alone in the hotel to the banana peel atop Sabine's note.

He didn't say anything for a minute. A couple of times, it looked like he was going to interrupt to say something not very nice about me but then stopped himself. Finally he said, "Let's see the note."

I took it out of my anorak and handed it to him. After he read it, he said, "If it weren't for this note, I would have said you must have eaten some funny mushrooms and hallucinated the whole story."

"What the hell am I going to do?" I said.

"About which?"

"About being the getaway driver. What do you think?"

"I didn't hear about any bank robbery. That's big local news. It wasn't in the paper yesterday. We can check the paper this morning, but I bet one of the neighbors would have mentioned it to me if it had been reported."

"So what do I do, walk into the bank tomorrow and say excuse me I was just wondering if you're missing anything?"

"I think you should hire Johnny Cochran."

"Very funny."

"I know of a guy, not personally, I'm happy to say. He got Francine's imbecile brother off the twelfth time he sold crack to an undercover cop. Hot-shot criminal defense lawyer, used to be a prosecutor. LA district attorney until he got the call from Washington. He's still mobbed up with the DA's office. He can make a discreet inquiry. He's expensive though. Six-fifty an hour, and somehow he works thirty billing hours a day even when he plays golf. Amazing how these lawyers can work on your case and play golf at the same time. But you don't have much choice but to hire him. Sometimes these kinds of inside jobs don't get reported in the press. Gives the employees naughty ideas. But if the cops had anything on you, they would have picked you up by now. Maybe because of the rain nobody caught your license."

"Why wouldn't they have come to Sabine's house?" I asked, which I had figured they would have if they knew she had taken the money.

"What house? Sounds to me like she didn't live there. She took all her clothes, right?"

"And then some," I said.

"Who knows where she got the key? There's just too much you don't know. And this note, why would she bother? It only makes her more vulnerable. Why didn't she just split? I don't think you've seen the last of her. Sounds like she's got a major Jones on for you, buddy."

"What I can't figure out," I said, ignoring Don's last bit of literary analysis, "is how it all went click so fast in her brain. I mean, was she planning to pick up some chump at the bank that day? What about the rain and the early closing? Was it all just a spur-of the-moment impulse, or what?"

"*Psycho*," Don said.

"Yeah, that was the second thing I thought of when I found the money in her purse."

Don smiled. "I am not going to ask you what the first thing was. I am not."

"My first thought was: gee, I wish I could give this money to my friend, Don. I could commission him to write a tanka in honor of the Year of the Banana."

"*Your* banana. I'm not even going to visit you in the slammer, you dipshit."

"When are you going to call this lawyer for me?"

"I think I might wait until ten A.M. anyway. It is Sunday, you know. Probably triple rates on Sunday. Hope you have some good gigs coming up."

"I'll never work in this town again."

"Doris is a player, it's true. Of course, she's not at all a vindictive or vengeful person."

"Ho ho hilarious, thanks again," I said.

"Anyway," Don said. "She probably got it all out of her system at the Unwedding Dinner." Don then proceeded to tell me what happened when I didn't show up at the church. I listened, but it wasn't fun:

"Since your lewdness was more important than our friendship and you didn't deign to call to say you wouldn't be picking me up, I left late and had to race to the church in the Friday evening rush-hour traffic nearly widowing my wife and orphaning my children. But worth it so you could pork some megababe, really it's fine, pal. Let me know when you want me to be your best man again."

"Okay, okay, okay," I said. "I get the point."

"I'm not so sure you do," he said. He looked at me with concern and took a deep breath before he continued. "I got there at exactly seven o'clock. Everyone—all twenty-five of your wedding guests—were waiting literally at the church door with poor Doris. Thank God she wasn't wearing a full bridal gown, just a simple white antique lace dress, hand sewn for some Hapsburg princess and worth only about a half a million dollars. By the way, she looked spectacular, you bone-head. Somehow everyone thought I'd know something they didn't. They thought you might have mentioned it to your best man if you were planning to bail. Of course I was sure you were dead. I didn't say that out loud. I couldn't imagine you not showing up otherwise. It was weird standing there believing you were dead and not being able to say it. We didn't know how long to wait or where to go if we didn't. Everyone was trying to make little jokes to relieve the tension and kept giving side-glances at Doris to see how she was han-dling this. Somebody had gotten the yellow pages and people were calling hospitals and police on their flip phones. I had brought mine along too. Doris took charge of it immediately and insisted on calling her home answering machine herself. I was standing there next to her—I think it was 7:10 or 7:15 when she got your message. I watched her for the fifteen sec-onds it took her to listen to it. The blood left her face. She turned so white her face matched her dress. I thought she was going to pass out. Francine knew what happened immediately, I guess everybody did—except me. I thought the message was from the police or somebody. I just couldn't believe that you wouldn't have told me beforehand that you were going to do this, or even that you *would* do it. So like a bumblepuppet, I say to Doris, 'Is he okay?' And Doris says, with great dig-nity, 'Oh yes. I think Robert is just fine.' Then she turns to the group and announces, 'There will be no wedding tonight, friends.' That's when Francine hopped in. She grabbed Doris by the elbow and walked her away. After ten years of mar-riage, I am still amazed by that woman's brain. It goes seventy places at once. I've seen her at book signings writing personal inscriptions one after another while carrying on three other conversations with three different people. Whereas I'm like what Lyndon Johnson said about Gerald Ford: can't walk and chew gum at the same time. My idea of multitasking is to look at the mirror when I comb my hair. Anyway, as Francine was steering Doris away, she called back to us, 'Don't anybody leave. Please just wait for us.' As well as I know her, I had no idea what she was doing.

"Well, what she did was give Doris a talk. These are strong women, pal. They are another species, not like us. They make us look like crème brûlée: a little thin candy crust and mush underneath. These women are made of plain-carbon steel. Five minutes later, they both come back and they're laughing. Doris's makeup is perfect. If she cried, it ain't showing. And it's not a brave front. This is who she is, all the way through. 'Okay, let's go eat,' she says. 'I called Missillac and they're already setting up for us. We're going to have a fabulous dinner. The Unwedding Dinner.' And off they go, the two of them. They walked the six blocks to the restaurant, and we all followed them like Boy Scouts on a hike."

"Wow," I said.

"You ain't heard nothing yet. So we all get seated and Chef Borchard has outdone himself. We start eating our brains out and drinking Cristal Roederer, which Chef Borchard sold at a discount to you, my friend, for only $400 a bottle."

"Me?" I said.

"Oh yes, this dinner was on you. There was something about a blank credit card slip you left with him like you do when you register at a hotel?"

"Oh my God," I said.

"Yes, and we drank *a lot* of champagne. Amazing how much really good champagne you can drink when somebody else is paying for it. Plus Doris insisted on giving every person there a bottle to take home in memory of the evening. She figured you owed us all at least that much."

I did some calculation in my head. Twenty-five people at $400 a bottle plus the dinner at $200 a head plus the champagne during dinner.

"Twenty grand," I said.

"You're not counting tax. Or the tip. Doris felt 20 percent was stingy in these circumstances. She gave the waiters 30 percent. And a bonus for the chef and his kitchen staff. She filled out the slip you signed. Some of your guests were a little drunk at that point and were yelling, 'Fifty percent, Doris. Give everybody fifty.'"

"I don't want to know," I said.

"You're right, you don't," Don said. "You also don't want to know about the Robert Roast."

"The Robert Roast," I repeated.

"Maybe you do want to know about the Robert Roast. I think you do. I think it might be good for you, as you consider your spiritual defects as you enter the monastery. Which may be the only option left to you at this point. It might be a character builder."

"My character's already built," I said.

"It got unbuilt at the Robert Roast. Totally demolished, I'd say, along with whatever miniscule reputation you used to have. I hadn't met some of your guests. Besides Doris's mother, there were twenty-four people, twelve couples, all people you think are your friends. As I said, we were all drinking a lot of champagne. It was Francine who actually had the idea. She got up to make the toast, which I would have made if it had been the Wedding Dinner instead of the Unwedding Dinner. Francine, who has always loved you, said, 'Let's all say something nasty about that miserable shit, Robert.' Everybody got right into the spirit of it. But once again it was your fiancée, Doris, who was most impressive. After everyone had assassinated your character and reduced you to poopy skid-marks on their napkins, Doris said, 'I'm really not happy with this. These are just our subjective opinions of this monster that I almost married. Let's tell his secrets, the ones he's really ashamed of. I'm going to start.'"

"Wow," I said.

"That's the second time you've said that. I admit this is truly impressive. Would you like to hear your worst secrets that your wedding guests have vowed to tell everyone in the entertainment business whom you did not invite to your wedding?"

"Definitely not," I said.

"You fart under the covers," Don said. "You whine doing the dishes. You whine about your career. You bad mouth other comics especially ones more famous than you, which is almost all of them. In your opinion I am pussy-whipped."

"I was just mad that Francine wouldn't let you go to the Lakers game that time."

"That's the cute stuff," Don said. "You also had sex with your college roommate."

"Doris told everyone *that*?" I said. "It was twenty years ago. I was a little lost freshman. We were both stoned."

"You sold cocaine to your middle school debate coach."

"That was twenty-*five* years ago. What can I say? I was fourteen. I was having some problems."

"All right, let's get a little more current. What about this schizophrenic girl? Your landlady's daughter?"

"What about her?" I said.

"You're screwing her, right?"

"Wow," I said, for the third time. "This is evil. I'm only going to say this once, and I'm only going to say it to you. That's a lie. I've never touched her and wouldn't touch her. I've never even thought of touching her."

Don got up from the table and cleared the oatmeal bowls and put them in the dishwasher. He came back and put his arm around my shoulder, and said, "My friend, you've got what they call in Washington, 'a credibility problem.' Your guests took it kind of personally what you did there. I took it personally. I'll get over it, I guess. Francine took it very personally, though she's been looking for years for an excuse to nail your ears back. Doris, now she took it most personally of all. I'd say it *was* personal in her case. I mean, we're all adults. We understand that what goes on between men and women is a mystery. Nobody knows the real truth about the private interaction between two people, probably including the two people themselves. Our social arrangements are built around protecting that privacy. If you don't want to marry Doris, that's fine. Nobody really gives a shit except maybe Doris. But you do not humiliate another person like that. Especially a person like Doris. I mean, public image is her business, for God's sake. That was like springing a trapdoor beneath her. *Public* humiliation. It was a very bad thing to do. And, sorry as I am to say it, I think you're going to pay for it big-time."

That wasn't news, but what Don said to me about how morally repugnant my humiliating Doris was *was* news, and that I had not fully realized it was disturbing. Even if I didn't know I wasn't going to marry her until I woke up at Sabine's fifteen minutes before I was supposed to be at the church. It was in fact my obligation to know, and I felt ashamed.

Emma came in, yelling, "Jeb hit me, Daddy. Jeb hit me!"

Jeb was three inches behind her, yelling, "I did not! I did not!"

"See," Don said to me, "Jeb's got a credibility problem too. Excuse me, I've got to go be a dad." He picked up one of them in each arm, and walked into the TV room. "Time for a peace conference, kids. This crap is going to stop right now."

I looked at the clock. The kennel would be open. I could go pick up Sparky. At least Sparky likes me, I thought. Or maybe he doesn't. How would I like him if he put me in a kennel?

Don stuck his head out of the TV room door. "Leave the megababe's note, okay? If you don't need it to wank off with. I've got to fax it to Johnny Cochran."

6.

Sparky still liked me, unless he's by far the best actor in LA (which is possible). He came bolting through the swinging door that separated the reception area from the kennel at Madge's, and leapt up to lick my face, nearly knocking me over backward. He's a golden lab, seventy pounds of pure muscle with the temperament of Saint Francis of Assisi, but when he wants to investigate a fireplug he can outpull a tractor. Madge followed him, carrying his leash doubled-looped in one hand, a short pigeon-breasted woman with faded blonde hair who favored pink fuzzy sweaters and always wore two pairs of glasses, a rhinestone-studded pair on her face and black half-lenses hanging from her neck. She must have boarded Sparky at least a hundred times in the four years I'd lived at Renate's. At Pico and Lincoln, her kennel was one mile and ten galaxies away from Santa Monica Canyon, in an alley across from Oriental Massage. Madge kept a pot of green tea brewing for "the girls," who came over at slow times during the afternoon to pet the dogs and cry, teenagers who couldn't speak a word of English, illegals in permanent debt to a pimp who smuggled them into the country. They were supposedly at least eighteen, but they looked younger than Madge's twin daughters, who were twelve. They slept on their massage tables and kept their personal effects in a single drawer. Madge met the pimp, who, she said, couldn't have been more than twenty-five himself and arrived chauffeured in a Lincoln Town Car that waited at her door while he thanked her personally for her kindness to his employees. His manners were as elegant as his clothes, fine silks and cashmeres, but the message was made clear by being completely unstated: if Madge interfered with his business in any way, she would regret it. Madge had no such intentions. She just wanted the girls to come over if they wanted to. He was happy to let them do so since it apparently made them act less depressed for the customers.

Sometimes a few of them were there sitting around in kimonos when I picked up Sparky, but at nine Sunday morning they must have all been sleeping in after their biggest night of the week.

"Too early for the girls, Madge?" I asked.

"One of them hung herself Friday night," Madge said casually.

"Jesus Christ," I said.

"Sweet little girl. Mitchie. Mi-hi. It means beauty and joy. Hung herself on an overhead sprinkler using one of the customer's belts. She took it off his pants while he was passed-out drunk. When he woke up, there she was."

"That's awful. God. Were the cops called?"

"No. There's no record of these girls. They don't exist. Took her out in a Hefty bag. Sparky is sure glad to see you," she added in the same tone, as if this sentence proceeded from the previous ones.

"That's awful," I said, again.

Madge gave me a look like, "What planet do you live on?" then said flatly, "Yes, it is."

"Nothing can be done about it," I said. It was a question.

"Not about her. That's for sure."

"The others?"

Madge was behind the counter now, pulling my bill out of her files. The counter was pink and so were the walls. Her complexion was pinkish too. She dropped her rhinestone-studded glasses and put on the half-lenses and spread the bill on the counter.

"You understand, Robert, it doesn't behoove me to become officially involved. But just between us, the cops know all about it. You tell me why they don't do anything."

I stood there looking dumbly at her. She saw that I wasn't willing to become officially involved either.

"Of course we could call Action News," she said. "That's a great humanitarian organization. In for the shoot, out of there, get it in the can for the five o'clock broadcast. They were actually here a few years ago, for about fifteen minutes. I wouldn't talk to them, so they shot me refusing to talk to them. You know, knocking on the door, I open it and there's the camera and an anorexic young woman in a nice suit and good haircut sticking a microphone in my face. Everybody forgot about it five minutes after the broadcast anyway. And guess what? Oriental Massage is still here."

"How about adding a couple of bucks to my bill for the girl's family or something?" I asked lamely.

"Who knows who they are? If they're alive. But sure, I'll buy the girls fortune cookies to go with their tea. Hey," she said, slapping the counter with her hand, "I almost didn't tell you. I rented your video. I watched it last night."

"My video?"

"That one you did—*New Comics: Live at the Improv.*"

"That was eight years ago, with five other guys. I was on six minutes."

"Yeah, well, whatever. You were great. I loved that bit about the midget and the urinal."

"Yeah, thanks," I said, remembering. "That was a good bit."

"It was great. Who thinks of that, how a midget feels when he has to use a men's room, knowing he's going to get smacked in the face by a toilet cake."

"*Stared* in the face," I corrected her.

"That's what I mean," she said. "Where do you guys come up with this stuff? It's the most I can do to talk to dogs."

"You open your mouth and words come out. I work on it beforehand until I could recite it backward. But then you just do it."

"Not me. Not in a million years," Madge said.

"I've actually been wondering if maybe there's something else I could do with my life besides try to make a bunch of drunk twenty-somethings laugh at bathroom jokes. You need any help around here?"

"You're serious, aren't you?" she asked, with genuine concern. I was amazed she could care about my career problems for one second with what she had on her shoulders. "I don't mean working for me, you're serious about quitting comedy."

"About half the time," I said. "It's probably other stuff."

"Well, you've got a gift. You made me laugh. Perked me up on a night I needed it."

"Thanks, Madge."

"I just wanted to tell you that, so I'm glad I didn't forget. I think everybody's got a gift. Mine is animals. I've always loved them. My family didn't have enough money for me to be a vet. I'm probably not smart enough anyway. But I've always been good with animals. Other people come in here and they see the cages and it smells like hell and there's all that barking, and they think, how could anybody stand that?

But to me it's heaven. So this is what I do. My kids don't go hungry, either."

"That's great, Madge," I said. I meant it.

"Yeah, well, I'm bending your ear here, but everybody gets discouraged sometimes. Recession we had here a couple years ago, people didn't board their animals. We ate a lot of Kraft macaroni and cheese. But hey, we got by. You'll be okay. Stick with it. You're really good, you're really funny. I'm not just saying that."

"Thanks, what do I owe you here, two nights at the Ritz? Forty, right? Or did Sparky clean out the minibar as usual and go bonkers on room service?"

"Forty's right, but I ought to pay you. Sparky here, he's my favorite. He is such a sweetie. These golden labs are like holy children. Look at that face. He knows I'm talking about him, don't you, Sparky? I'll tell you something else, these dogs speak volumes about their owners too. Some of these toy poodles these rich bitches bring in here—they ought to have little straitjackets for them. But Sparky, he's just as sweet and good as he can be."

"Hear that, Sparky?" I said. He did hear it. He barked.

I ALWAYS had to take Sparky for a run at the beach after I picked him up at the kennel. It was like making eggs for Krista. He would be hurt if I skipped it and I realized that I didn't in fact have that much to do anyway since I was supposed to still be in Baja honeymooning. I parked in my driveway and hooked Sparky to his leash and walked him wagging and sniffing and dragging me up the block to the highest point in the switchback overlooking PCH where there's a 200-foot stairway leading down to a pedestrian tunnel under the highway to the beach. The tunnel is a nasty place, urinous and graffiti-smeared. It floods when it rains, and the water from the highway sits there in puddles for weeks. It's so bad that the homeless don't sleep there, but on this day a shirtless blond kid wearing a leather necklace and combat fatigues was camped on one of the few dry spots, leaning on a sleeping bag and reading *The Dharma Bums*. Sparky gave his nose a lick. "Hey, doggy," the kid said to Sparky. He had a tray of beaded jewelry on a black cloth next to him.

"Some pretty trinkets for the lady?" he asked me.

"What lady?" I asked.

"Everybody's got a lady, man."

"Not me," I said. "Let's go, Sparky." I bent down and unhooked his leash, and he bolted straight through the puddles out onto the beach.

"Great dog," the kid called at my back. Sparky is much admired—unlike me, I thought as I came out of the tunnel, and got a little laugh from myself out of that. He was already down at the water's edge. He had stopped to sniff something that was black and shiny, which, from where I was, looked like a body bag. All I could think of was the dead Korean girl. Sparky was certainly thrilled by it. He was running around it in a circle, and, as I approached, he began rolling on it, or, I should say, *in* it, since it turned out to be a large mound of black jelly, of marine origin, although it was impossible to say exactly what particular species. Whatever it was, though, Sparky loved it. It smelled worse than any other substance in the known universe. He rolled in it and wiggled ecstatically on his back, his legs flailing like a cockroach's. Then he rubbed his muzzle in it, kneeling on his forelegs and rooting right in there, denting the thing until he pulled his head out and it filled in again with a sucking noise. Doggy heaven. Quintessence of rotted fish matter. I walked ten feet up the beach and yelled at Sparky and threw his stick into the ocean.

He went for it. Getting stinky was big fun but not as much fun as retrieving a stick in the pounding surf. I hoped the ocean would clean some of the suppurating black jelly out of Sparky's fur so I wouldn't have to, but I wasn't greatly optimistic about it.

After fifteen minutes of throwing the stick, I usually sat in the lifeguard stand and watched the water and let Sparky do his own thing investigating the beach and chasing gulls for a while. It was all clearly established and understood and mutually agreed upon: easily my best relationship. I climbed the ladder and lifted myself into the seat. There was still fog over the ocean. The sun sometimes doesn't burn it off until noon. Behind me the bike path that runs from Venice to Malibu was full of Sunday morning traffic: bikers and joggers and Rollerbladers in American Gladiator outfits (helmet, elbow pads, knee pads, and a bikini)—but almost nobody was walking by the water, much less swimming in it. The undertows would be deadly. The waves were still high and strong from Friday's storm. The last time I had looked at the ocean I had been looking through Sabine's kitchen window. It already seemed like another life ago, like a dream, or, as Don said, a hallucination. I remembered the other thing he said too: You don't humiliate people. It was still incomprehensible to me that this was not at all what I was doing while I was doing it. What I was doing was having sex with Sabine. And I was not getting married. Those two things. In that order. I certainly knew that Doris was going to be hurt, but my responsibility to her was such a low third in my consciousness that even this didn't occur to me until I woke up with fifteen minutes to get to the church. I felt like an item in her Life Plan: obtain boyfriend, get married, have baby. I was like one of her deals. A lined-up duck. A sperm donor. Her determination served her so well in her career, maybe I wanted to be the one thing she couldn't have.

That last thought sent a shiver up my spine—as if I had intentionally hurt her, maybe out of jealousy from my own weakness and failure. Her career was spectacular. My career was a mess. I was thirty-nine years old. I had been in LA fifteen years and had pretty much done everything I could do out here and had, as they say, plateaued. I did the circuit of clubs here and around the country, had my shots on Letterman and Leno, showed up on the Comedy Channel now and then, etc. But I hadn't grown. That urinal-midget bit was as good as anything I had done since, and that was eight years ago. I was still trying to fit the six-minute format, still trying to please the twenty-somethings whose frame of reference is limited to TV, sports, dating, and airplane food. It had not been lost on me that spending more time with Doris in New York might have led somewhere. The audience in New York is older and hipper. Maybe I could have pushed myself to another level. Maybe I didn't really need to do bathroom jokes.

Sitting there in the lifeguard stand, I realized I had done it again. I started out thinking about hurting Doris and in half a minute I was thinking about—guess what?—me. My career. Mememe. Was I really so selfish that I could not consider another person for one full minute? Even a person I had supposedly loved? Maybe I deserved everything they said about me at the Robert Roast. (How the hell was I going to pay for that dinner?)

But Sparky didn't think so. He came running up to the lifeguard stand, barking for me to come down. He was followed by a well-shined woman of about forty in a sweat suit and baseball cap. I smiled at her as she approached. I saw that she was about to say something to me and I expected it was going to be something nice about Sparky. She yelled, "You ought to wash that fucking dog. It smells foul."

I said I was just about to go do that.

"It's too late now. He just rubbed that shit on my sweat suit. Blaah. It's horrible," she said, and stomped off up the beach.

It was in fact pretty horrible. People out for their Sunday morning walks crossed the street to get away from us as we walked home. As we squeezed past the kid reading *The Dharma Bums* in the tunnel, he screamed, "Keep that dog away from me!" Sparky's stock had abruptly plummeted. Sharp sell-off in Sparky. Pension funds dump Sparky. I shortened Sparky's leash, so I was holding him almost at the neck. By the time we got home, I smelled like he did.

I always used Renate's old plastic kiddie pool to wash Sparky, which she kept on her back patio next to the hose. The patio was surrounded by a garden, all the flowers in bloom, every variety of extravagant California blossom, which Renate lovingly cultivated every day, the sun just breaking through so you could almost see the flowers stretching toward it. I tied Sparky to the spigot, dumped a whole box of dog shampoo in the pool, and had begun filling it from the hose when Krista came out the back door. She was wearing the same thing she had left my apartment wearing, jeans and an oversized T-shirt and no bra.

"Let me help!" she said.

"He's pretty smelly, Krista. And so am I."

"I don't care," she said, and knelt down in the pool to stir the shampoo in the water with her hand. I could see her breasts down the top of her T-shirt. She splashed water on her shirt and it clung to her. To my horror, I felt a strong sexual charge, like a drug rush, bang. Even worse, Krista seemed to feel my feeling it. At the exact moment it hit me, she looked up and smiled at me, like this spike of lust for her was the loveliest thing in the world. I literally shook my head as if I had been slapped.

"Where's your mom, Krista?" I asked, my voice squeaking.

"She's out," she said.

"Where?" I asked.

"Why? You want to be alone with me?"

I ignored that question. Absolutely ignored it. "I need to talk to her about something," I said.

"Come here, Sparky," she said. "Come here, baby." She hugged him around the neck and kissed his stinky muzzle. "Here he is, here's my good boy," she said. "They don't like you because you stink but Krista loves you no matter what. Let's get you all clean and fluffy."

She began soaping him in great sensual strokes. He hated it when I did it but with Krista he seemed to purr. I could see that I was irrelevant here. And, contrary to what Doris said at the Robert Roast, I was not about to climb into the pool with Krista.

"I'm going to go take a shower, OK? If you really don't mind giving Sparky his bath."

"I like it," Krista said. "I'd like to give you a bath too."

"Ha ha," I said, weakly, and took myself away from there. Fast.

7.

I locked my bathroom door before I stripped and turned on the water, picturing the scene in *Psycho* which in 1960 made everyone in America afraid to take a shower for months. I could hear the screechy violins on the soundtrack as the knife came down over and over again on Janet Leigh's then (weirdly) *my* tender flesh. It spooked me. I had also locked the front and back doors to my apartment and closed all the blinds. And after my shower I dressed in the bathroom. Then I peeked outside: nobody on the patio. Krista had obviously finished washing Sparky and had taken him inside the house. I dreaded going over there to fetch him, dreaded being met by a smiling naked Krista. I knew that my momentary spike of lust was to her as solid as a declaration of love etched in stone. It was as if she lived on another plane of reality, especially in terms of communication. I swear she could read my thoughts. She'd tell her mother that I was sick when she couldn't possibly know I was sick, and she'd be right. It spooked me even more than the shower scene. I had always been simply kind to her, which I'm sure is why she "loved" me. Now I had shown her another feeling, and I was equally sure that sooner or later she would act on it. I was not looking forward to that.

I decided that the best thing for now would be to wait until Renate got home before I fetched Sparky. He'd be okay there, safer than I would be. I went into the living room and sat down in my Swedish recliner and pushed the message button on my answering machine. I was not looking forward to this either. Masochistically, I played the whole tape, all fifty-four messages. There were no more from Doris after her last frantic call from the church which I had already listened to from Sabine's. And there was no Sabine either. I hadn't expected there to be, of course. She had vanished, poof. No doubt to an exotic island in her Brazilian bikini spending her 200 grand on mai tais and pool boys.

There was only one message I listened to twice: from Odom Bucket. One sentence, commanding me to call when I got in. He had certainly wasted no time.

Odom Bucket was my agent. In the eight years he had been my agent, he had called me himself maybe three times. All other communication came through assistants. I had lunch with him once, eight years ago, when he took me on. If it weren't for that, I would have thought he was the Wizard of Oz. He must have been six two and 300 pounds, a dead ringer for Sidney Greenstreet in *The Maltese Falcon* (obviously by design). He always wore a white linen suit and a professionally waxed bald head. I met him at his table in the Polo Lounge at the Beverly Hills Hotel. When I walked in, I certainly didn't have any trouble identifying him, which no doubt was the idea. He seemed to be in his fifties at that time, but nobody knew how old he really was or where he had come from, which no doubt was also the idea. There were plenty of shady rumors about his past—gunrunner, gay porno magnate, Albanian politburo, you name it. He laughed at them, showing a set of teeth that must have had little klieg lights implanted in them, the whitest and shiniest you could buy. He was the Don King of comedy—the power agent, the one you wanted. If he was working for you, you worked. If a club owner didn't book you when Odom Bucket told him to book you, he didn't book anybody else either, since Odom Bucket represented everybody else. So he booked you. It was catch-22. Known comics didn't become known until Odom Bucket represented them and he didn't represent them until they became known. He dealt exclusively in clubs, TV, and videos. When a comic got a bigger offer—a movie, a network series—Bucket immediately sold the contract to ICM or CAA. At a premium, of course. He wouldn't swim with the big fishes. But by limiting what he did, he owned the store. He owned the whole franchise.

When he took me on, my career took off. No more open mics, no more barroom comedy nights, no more "alternative comedy" clubs. That's when I did that video Madge rented. As much as I hated to admit it, he took me on because of Doris. It was never stated, but it was his gift to her. They never did business together. Bucket was much smarter than that. He dealt in influence. It cost him nothing to take me on. What he got from it was Doris's goodwill—highly valuable, since she herself was, as Don put it, a player. This is how Bucket worked. He was crude and obvious only if he needed to be crude and obvious. He knew very well that the power of power is in people's perception, cultivated through favors as well as fear.

He certainly scared me. I knew how he felt about my long off-again on-again engagement to Doris. I worked less when it was off-again. He never dropped me though. Understanding the vagaries of romance, he kept himself covered. We didn't invite him to the wedding, but I had no doubt whatsoever that he had already heard I had stood up Doris at the church. I was about to become gainfully unemployed. In

LA, an unemployed comic lies just south of an unemployed screenwriter and an unemployed actor. But there was no sense putting off calling him, since the only thing worse than his dropping me would be to worry about his dropping me.

He must have had one of those gizmos that displays who's calling because he picked up and said, "Good morning, Robert."

I expected an assistant to answer the phone. "Odom," I said. "How are you?"

"I am excellent, as always. I make a point of it. And if I weren't you'd never guess. How was the honeymoon?"

"No honeymoon, Odom. No marriage. As I think you know."

"That was the rumor. But I like to go to the source. Information, Robert."

Information: Bucket invoked the word as if it were the unspeakable name of God.

"So to business," Bucket continued. "I have bad news and good news. Which do you want first?"

"Yes, Doctor, the bad news is the blood test shows I've got terminal cancer but did I see the great-looking receptionist? Well, the good news is *you're* fucking her," I said. There was dead air on the line. Bucket didn't even sniffle, much less chuckle.

"Which would you like to hear first, the bad news or the good news?" he repeated.

"The patient never does too well hearing the bad news first. Besides I already know what it is. Give me the good news."

"The good news is that I have gotten you an HBO special, my friend. Shoot in a month, airs this fall. Twenty-eight minutes of Wildman Robert Wilder, all new material, no commercials. For years you've been bitching about the six-minute format. This is your chance to show what you can do."

"That is good news," I said, not believing it for a second. "Let me guess the bad news: since you're dropping me, there isn't going to be any HBO special. Or anything else."

"Wrong. The special's on if you want it. But you're right, I am dropping you. After this deal I'm not your agent anymore. After we sign the HBO contract, we're through."

I took a minute to absorb this. I didn't absorb it.

"Still with us, Robert?" Bucket asked.

"Doris, right?" I said.

"Doris said nothing to me. I haven't even talked to her."

"But she will appreciate the gesture."

"Robert," he said impatiently. "This is business. You don't get it. None of you guys get it. I took you on because it was good business. I'm dropping you for the same reason. The end. You'll get another agent."

"Not Odom Bucket."

"True, not Odom Bucket. But there are other good agents out there. Not great agents. Good agents. They'd murder their mothers to represent you."

"I'll be consoled by the deaths of so many elderly women."

"I'll messenger the HBO contract over for you to sign."

"And if I don't?" I don't know why I said this. Of course I was going to sign it.

"If you don't, you're stupid. You're thoughtless and apparently heartless but you're not stupid. Anyway I don't care a whit. Who knows, maybe you and Doris will have a happy reconciliation. If so, I'll give you a call. Until then, good luck."

"Thanks, Odom. You're swell."

"I get the job done," he said, and hung up. I sat there for a moment wondering at my smart mouth. It sometimes worked without me at the controls. My body, too, according to recent evidence with both Sabine and Krista. Where did I

get the chutzpah to talk to Odom Bucket like that? Maybe I
didn't care a whit either anymore.

Then I registered what he had said: I had an HBO special.
Was it really possible? It must have been Odom's wedding gift
to Doris. Pump the hubby. But why was he giving it to me
anyway, after what I had done to her? Like everything else
during the last two days, there wasn't much sense thinking
about it. I might be shooting my HBO special from jail as far
as I knew: Robert Wilder Even Wilder From Prison!

But despite myself, my head started going. I had been
working on a whole different routine. I had guessed Bucket
might do something for me after Doris and I were married,
and I was thinking of trying to do something more ambitious
and cerebral, maybe a small theater piece like Spalding Gray
but not neurotic-psychotherapy-autobiographical. I had been
working on it on my computer. Which was at Doris's. And I
had given her back my key to her townhouse for her mother
to use while she was out here for the wedding.

I heard the back door of Renate's house open and her yell,
"Sparky, get down. Krista, what is Sparky doing here?" It was
obviously time to go over and get him. I got up to open my
door and saw an enormous dark shadow behind the blinds.
Then a hard knock. First thing I thought was: SWAT team. But
I opened the door. It was a black man with his back to me, in
a black T-shirt, with "Comic Relief" written in cursive across
it—a size extra large T-shirt that on him was extra small. When
he turned around he was my friend Charles Coleman.

"Hey, Robert," he said. "Thought I'd come over to the
white folks' neighborhood and scare everybody."

"You scared me," I said.

"I always scare you. You're easy."

I invited him in. His head almost scraped the ceiling.
Charles was my best friend in the business. He had been on

that *New Comics at the Improv* video when I did the midget at the urinal. The man was funny. Much funnier than me that night. He had come out and stood silent at the mic for a full minute doing his bad black glare at the all-white audience as if he were about to beat the bejesus out of every one them for all their racist crimes. When everyone was crawling out of their seats, he said in his best homeboy accent:

"Don't be scared, white people.

"Y'all don't need to be scared of us big black men.

"We just like you.

"We want the same thing you want:

"White women."

That joke made me his fan forever. It's like Eddie Murphy's Mr. Rogers parody, singing to the white audience, "Will you be my neighbor?"—only better, because of all the racist sexual myths. Charles got nailed for it, of course. Anybody who takes real risks in this business gets nailed. That's why I was right on the edge of quitting myself: either I take more risks or I get out. Except they amounted to the same thing. If I took more risks I'd be getting myself out.

Charles checked out my place disapprovingly. "Why is it so dark in here, man? You hiding from somebody?"

"I'll pull up the blinds."

"No, no. Let's go to that Starbucks Nicole Simpson used to hang out at."

That's at Seventh and Montana. Before we got in the car I checked with Renate about leaving Sparky. She answered the door and told me it would be fine. When I slid into Charles's car, he asked, "Who's that staring at us from the upstairs window?"

I didn't have to look. I told him who it was.

"She goofy?" Charles asked.

I told him she was schizophrenic.

He said, "Maybe that's why she's not wearing a shirt. You white folks sure let it all hang out when we're not around to watch you. Maybe you're not all as stiff-assed as you seem."

As we went into the Starbucks, I quoted to Charles my favorite opening sentences in American literature, from a book about OJ and Nicole by her best friend Faye Resnick: "'Nicole and I had a dream. To become financially independent and open a Starbucks together.'"

"So this is *the* Starbucks," Charles said. "Kind of like visiting the Vatican or something. What's the most wastefully expensive thing they got? I'm gonna have that."

"That's the double mocha latte. If you want to be in the spirit of the place, you make it a double decaf mocha latte with nonfat milk."

"No way," Charles said. "I need all the fat and drugs I can get."

We ordered two of them and sat down at a table outside. Late Sunday morning in Santa Monica, more people congregate at the coffee shops than at the churches, mostly singles in workout outfits, but a few couples with kids and dogs. There's a lot of neon-glow spandex uplifting surgically enhanced body parts. Nobody older than twelve is overweight unless they're married. If I gained five pounds in the wrong places a neighborhood intervention committee would show up at my door to confront me about my Food Issues. A line of Porsches (for the boys) and BMWs (for the girls) were double parked at the corner while their owners popped in and got their cappuccinos to go.

"It's nice here," Charles said, smiling. "My, feel that ocean breeze. Maybe I'll buy myself a place over here. All I need to do is start a Mexican drug cartel. I'm going to give OJ a call for some real estate advice."

"Is that why you came over, Charles, to look at real estate?"

"I came over to look at you," he said, seriously.

"Hmm," I said, unintentionally reminding myself of Sabine. I never said "Hmm."

"'Hmm,' the man says," Charles repeated. "I came over to look at you today because I didn't see you on Friday night."

"Yeah, well, I'm sorry you drove to Palos Verdes in all that rain for nothing."

"It wasn't for nothing. We got a free dinner and two primo bottles of champagne to take home." Charles had gone with his wife, Marla, whom he had been married to since college. They had four kids, the oldest of whom was about to start college herself. He was a family man straight through, but didn't let you know that until he trusted you.

"How was the dinner?"

"Dinner was good. You must have heard about it already."

"I have. From Don."

"Yeah, that guy's a brick. He was sitting next to me. I didn't know anybody else and I hardly knew him. When it comes around to his turn when they're roasting you, he gets up and says, 'Robert is my best friend. I love him. I won't say I'm ashamed of him because I don't know why he's not here.' Then he sits down. Blew everybody away. Kind of took the wind out of the Robert Roast. Until I got my turn."

"What did you say?"

"I said one sentence, 'I happen to know for a fact that Robert was the real assassin of Dr. Martin Luther King.' Then I sat down. Nobody makes a sound. They thought I was serious. And nuts. But I can see they're doing the math in their heads."

"I was nine."

"Sure. Marla's laughing her butt off into her napkin. Then everybody gets it. Pretty slow though. Slow and lazy. But I hear y'all got big dicks."

"I step on mine all the time," I said.

"Well, you stepped on it this time, I'll tell you. I wouldn't want to have that Doris woman mad at me. No, I wouldn't."

He took a swig of his latte and left a white mustache on his lip, which he licked off in a swipe. "Amazing they get four bucks for this drink," he said. "It must be like the tulip mania in Holland. When was that? Sixteen hundred something."

"I don't remember," I said abstractly. "I had a lot of book-ings that year."

"So what are you going to do now?" Charles asked. It wasn't curiosity either. It was concern, like Madge. I was pull-ing a lot of sympathy over this career crisis. I should have thought of it earlier.

"I've got some business coming up this week. Bucket just called. He dropped me already. And he got me an HBO special."

"I heard," Charles said.

"How's that possible?" I asked. "I just heard myself ten minutes ago."

"You been in LA long enough to know you can't take a piss in this town without everybody hearing about it before you shake off your wanky. So, you going to do it?"

"What else? Should I not do it?"

"That's a possibility."

"Why's that? You know something I don't?"

He put his cup down on the table. "Could be a set-up."

"How? What do you mean?"

"It may be nothing. I may be paranoid. But I'd want con-trol of choosing the audience. He gets you the wrong audi-ence, you bomb, you're done."

"I'm done anyway," I said. "Without Bucket. Plus I think I've had it. I'm burnt out. I mean, where do I go? You're doing your own thing, you love it, it's working for you. HBO might be my chance to do something good, which is not to say it will be a hit."

"See, that's your problem," Charles said. "You want to do something good. What does that mean? It means you want to do something you think is good. You want to please yourself. But that's not what comedy is. Comedy is for the audience, not for you."

I thought about that. "So I should do more bathroom jokes? Got some real edgy ones for me?"

"No, you're still missing the point. What the audience laughs at is funny. That's what you leave in. What they don't laugh at you take out. Trick is you got to find the right audience."

"What planet do I find it on?"

"Maybe not this one. I didn't say you could make a living from it. You've been jumping over square one is your problem. That's why you're dying, Robert. You're isolated. You're cut off from other people. You're cut off at the root. I've seen that for a long time."

It was an odd moment, sitting there with all the beautiful people and shiny cars, the breeze coming up Montana Street off the ocean. For all the things that had happened in the last two days, including breaking somebody's heart, I hadn't felt like crying. But what Charles said made me see I was lost. I guess he saw the effect it had.

"So I got a proposition for you," he said. "That's what I came over to talk to you about."

"What's that?" I asked quietly.

"An all-black comedy special from the Apollo. Six comics. I'd like you to be one of them."

I looked at him. He wasn't kidding.

"Charles," I said. "There's something I've got to tell you about myself."

"What's that, bro?"

"I'm not black."

"You're shittin' me. You're not black?"

"I'm really not, Charles. I'm kind of surprised you haven't noticed. I thought you were a perceptive guy."

"That's the beauty of it," he said loudly, slapping the table and making everybody around us jump. (They had been hyperaware of him as it was.) "That's the joke. An all-black comedy special, the m.c. is black, the audience is black, there's not a white face in sight anywhere, we open with two or three black comics, then you come out. No warning. You just step out there. There ain't anybody whiter than you, Robert. You dig it?"

"Sounds terrifying," I said.

"Yeah, well, now you know how I felt at just about every gig I used to do. And I was just a baby. But the thing is, it will be *funny*. You start off way up, way higher than normal. You're in a groove before you begin. Everybody's laughing already before you open your mouth. So you stand there for a while, acting confused. Then you open with something like, 'This isn't the Yale Club?' Like you got the wrong driving directions. Then you do a race bit. How often does a white comic do race at all, much less from this angle, in front of this audience? Has it ever happened? I don't think so. You can break some ground here. You can get into some whole new material. We'll get somebody to video it too. What do you say?"

"It doesn't sound like a career path to me, Charles. I don't see how it fits into what you were just saying about audience. I mean, I'm not going to be the black person's white comedian."

"Absolutely right. But you don't know what it's going to do for you, right? Question is, is it a good thing in itself? And the answer to that is yes."

I smiled at him and he gave me a whatthefuckdoesthat-mean look and leaned back in his chair. By this time we had everybody's attention. There was a handsome young couple at the next table with a baby and an Afghan hound. I said to them, "What do you think I ought to do?"

The man said, "Excuse me?"

I said, "Do you think I should accept my friend's offer or not?"

He picked up on it. "How much is he paying you?" he asked.

"That's a good question. How much are you paying me?" I asked Charles.

"Not that much," Charles said.

"Not that much," I said to the man.

"Then the answer is no," the man said.

"Thank you," I said to him. "You ready to go, Charles?"

"Why isn't he paying you better?" the man said.

"Excuse me?" I was the one surprised this time. Didn't the guy see the joke was over?

"Why isn't he paying you better?" the man repeated. "Is he too poor? Or doesn't he like you?"

"He doesn't like me," I answered. "And I don't blame him. You ready to go, Charles?"

Charles didn't answer. As we were crossing the street to his car, Don pulled up in his white Volvo station wagon. Charles tapped on Don's hood and Don waved, then Charles went ahead and unlocked his own car. I stuck my head into Don's window as it glided down. Jeb and Emma were strapped into the backseat, both with four-pound banana splits on their laps. Their T-shirts already looked like action paintings.

"Somebody's getting a bribe from dad," I said into the car.

"No fighting for one hour. Their hourly rate is more than your lawyer's," he said, handing me a sealed envelope. "On second thought, it's not. Nobody's hourly rate is more than your lawyer's. That's his office address. Your appointment's at eight thirty tomorrow morning. Give me a call when he's through with you."

"The one call I'm legally entitled to make?" I asked.

"Not going to happen. If the cops were going to bust you, you'd already be in jail."

I noticed Charles was sitting in his car with his elbow on the steering wheel and his chin on his fist. Jeb had been whispering to Emma in the backseat and now she leaned out of her window and said to Charles, "Are you really Shaquille O'Neal?"

Charles didn't move. He just shifted his eyes when she spoke to him. "No, honey," he said.

Jeb laughed uproariously. "You're such a liar," Emma screamed at him.

"Back to the war zone," Don said. "Stay cool," he added, addressing himself as well as me, then drove off.

I forgot to ask him if Francine had a key to Doris's town-house so I could get my computer. My brain was on overload. I was lucky I didn't walk off a pier, except I wasn't on a pier. I walked over to Charles's car and got in.

"That bit with the guy at the next table wasn't funny," he said through his teeth when I slid in and closed the door.

"I'm sorry, Charles. I'm a little strung out right now."

He didn't say anything but his jaw got even tighter.

"The Apollo gig's a great idea," I said hurriedly. "I appreciate your thinking of me, and I'm probably going to do it just because I could work with you, but I need a few days to think it over."

"That's fine," he said. "But let's get it clear. Number one, I don't care why you do it. Number two, I'm asking you instead of any other white comic in the universe because I think you would do it better than any other white comic in the universe. So it's totally selfish. Number three, that bit with the guy at the next table was disrespectful to me and almost got ugly. Shows an ugly part of you, Robert, that I *don't* like. The part that just doesn't get that other people are people. Not functions. Not joke-functions, career-functions, fiancée-functions, or your one-black-friend-in-the-business functions. So whatever happens please don't do anything like that with me again. Ever."

I apologized again, then apologized probably five more times in the five minutes to my house. I didn't mention Sabine or my potential problem with the LAPD. I said nothing about Krista or the bottle of Demerol or the Korean girl hauled out in a Hefty bag. Plus I hadn't slept since I woke up in Baja to find Sabine gone. There were plenty of reasons I was strung out. I wanted to say, "Charles, if you had a weekend like I just had, you'd be strung out, too." But I didn't. He was much too sane to ever have a weekend like I just had.

8.

The HBO contract in a cardboard envelope was stuck inside my screen door. Krista had signed for it while I was off with Charles, printing her name in wobbly block letters about two inches high. It was about noon. Forty-eight hours ago I had hopped in the car to cash a check for my honeymoon. My future had been clear, or at least only moderately murky. I had never heard of anyone named Sabine. Now all I wanted was sleep. I had left Sparky with Krista, but I thought I'd just take a little nap before I went over to Renate's to get him.

When I woke up from my little (seventeen-hour) nap, it was five A.M. Monday. I jumped awake. I was having a dream in which I needed to do something extremely urgent but nobody would tell me what it was. I went to my car to go buy some Weight Watchers lemon chicken and when I backed out of my driveway I was on the 405 going backward down the steep hill coming from the valley into LA and I realized I was also in the backseat (my Z doesn't have a backseat) and I couldn't reach the wheel and was going faster and faster about to crash. Then I woke up. My heart was slamming as if it were trying to pop through my chest. I lay there a minute, trying to calm down, to become conscious of my breathing and the silence, the physical sensations of the bed and pillow—to enter the moment as it is and turn off the noise in my head. It's your basic meditation technique. This sounds like a joke, but I go to a Vietnamese holy man sometimes for advice. Don's wife, Francine, actually put me onto him. He's got an office in a chic art deco building on Second and Wilshire, where she has her office. His name is Tran Hanh. He has the shaved head, the orange robes, the funny high voice, the whole bit, and is very witty about being a Western entrepreneur of Eastern wisdom. Somehow he can walk that tightrope. Anyway, on one of his videos, when asked what he would do if he had only one minute to live, he said, "I would enjoy my breathing." I guess you can believe that or not, but when I'm panicked, I try to enjoy my breathing.

It worked well enough this time that I emerged from the panic of the dream into the panic of reality. I had to get up, take a shower, get dressed, and make myself some breakfast. I had to go get Sparky from Renate's. I had to feed him and take him on a walk—around the neighborhood, not to the beach. I had to get into my car and go to the lawyer's office. Then I'd see what the day looked like. I might be spending the rest of the day talking to the police, so there was no sense making any other plans.

I did get up, take a shower, and get dressed. That was as far as I got with my scheduled program, because while I was getting dressed, I heard Renate on the patio. She was singing Schubert *Lieder*, softly, as she watered the flowers and clipped the dead buds. I peeked out between the blinds. She had a big green watering can in one hand and her scissors in the other and an enormous straw hat on. It was a picture of joy. She looked like a Bellini Madonna. Her face, which is usually distorted by worry, was in absolute repose. She did not have a great voice, but you could see how the music acted on her as she mouthed the words of those songs. She must have learned them in Germany when she was a little girl, before she went through getting out, getting married and widowed, and raising three girls on no money and finding out one of them was mentally ill.

I hated interrupting her serenity, but I grabbed the bottle of Demerol and went out onto my deck. She looked up when I opened the doors and said good morning and observed that I must have been exhausted to sleep so long. I said I guessed I was and apologized for leaving Sparky with her all night. While we spoke the bottle of Demerol was in my fist.

"Oh, we love Sparky," she said. "Krista loves him so much. No doubt because he is your dog."

"Well, that's what I need to talk to you about."

"I guessed as much," she said, putting down her watering can.

"It's worse than you think, Renate. I found this in my bed yesterday when I was changing the sheets."

She reached up and took the bottle from me.

"In your bed?"

"When I came home yesterday morning Krista was sleeping in my bed as usual, but this time she was wearing one of my shirts." (I spared Renate the detail about my underwear on Krista's head.) "When I was changing the sheets later, I found the bottle of pills."

"I don't understand."

"Renate, what do you mean, you don't understand? She was planning to kill herself in my bed. I'd find her dead when I came home. I don't know if she didn't do it because she saw the unsigned marriage license on my desk, or if she just decided not to do it, or what. But this hasn't happened before, and, to be honest, it's pretty upsetting to me."

She closed her eyes and pinched the bridge of her nose with her thumb and index finger of the hand holding the pills.

"Yes, of course. It's upsetting to me also."

"I'm sure it is, even more than to me. Point is we have to do something about it. We can't just ignore it." I felt impatient with her. It seemed like she was reluctant to deal with the reality here. I guess I couldn't blame her for that.

She absentmindedly cupped an extravagant red hibiscus in one hand and began examining it. Its yellow-tipped black stamen lolled out of the blossom like a tongue. I wanted to shake her by the shoulders. She must have realized that she had gone off somewhere, because she released the blossom abruptly as if there were a wasp inside.

"It's so terrible," she said, "because of her wanting to go to the zoo. That was so hopeful. You should have seen her yesterday, filled with life."

"That is exactly the problem, Renate. I'm being invested with more responsibility than I care to have. I don't want to feel that Krista's life depends upon my playing into some delusion she has about me."

That struck her. It was as if I *had* shaken her physically.

"Yes, well, of course not," she said. "Of course, you're right. I think I will call her doctor."

"Fine, but it may finally be time for me to move."

Renate nodded again. "That would be your decision, perfectly understandable. But I shudder at its effect."

"Shouldn't that tell you something? The situation here is out of hand." I was a bit more emphatic than I had intended to be.

Renate said quietly, "I suppose I have been using you, in a way. Depending on Krista's infatuation with you to keep her wanting to live. It's a strange business, Robert. I don't know if you can imagine being Krista's mother. I am always surprised by what I am willing to do."

This suddenly did make me imagine being her.

"I didn't mean to get angry, Renate. I want to help. Don't worry about my moving or doing anything else that's going to push Krista over the edge. I'll see this through with you if I can. Her life is more important than my convenience."

Renate's eyes reddened, but she did not cry. "Thank you," she said. "You are a gentleman."

I laughed. "I can think of a few people who would not agree with you there."

"They would be wrong," Renate said.

"Do you want me to lock those pills in my car?" I asked.

"No, I have a safe place," she answered.

"By the way, Renate, do you know someone named Karle Ochte?"

She looked at me with puzzlement, almost suspicion.

"She was my grandmother. But how would you know her name?"

"Look at the label on the bottle. It's her prescription."

Renate did look at it and smiled grimly. "Yes, I don't think so. She died in Birkenau."

"Wow," I said, idiotically.

"Krista is obsessed with her, with the death camps. She learned everything about them. In high school, when she was a shining student, it was her special project. I thought then it was morbid, but I couldn't dissuade her. I always let her sisters follow their inclinations, with the happiest results. But I could barely tolerate Krista's. It's too painful, too horrible. But she acted unaffected by it, as if it were truly an academic interest. She did such wonderful work. One of her papers was given an award at a ceremony at the Holocaust museum. It was so hard for me to go, but I did, for her sake. And now you see what has happened. Such nightmares are beyond human tolerance."

"But how did Krista get these pills in Karle Ochte's name? She never goes out alone."

"That I can't tell you. Despite her illness, she is very clever. Sometimes I think the illness makes her more clever. Certainly more willful. And the human will can be very strong, you know. Very powerful. I'm sometimes gone in the mornings. It has been fine of late to leave her home alone. Or so I thought." She picked up her watering can and scissors and looked around distractedly as if there were other things she was forgetting.

"Excuse me, Robert. I'm going to go call her doctor before she wakes up. Perhaps she stole one of his prescription forms. I'm so sorry to have bothered you. I'm sorry to have involved you with my daughter. You're right, it is not your responsibility." She went into the house and brought out Sparky.

I watched him eat a bowl of Gravy Train and took him for a walk. We hadn't walked twenty yards before I saw the woman who had yelled at me the day before about his rubbing marine jelly on her sweat suit. We could have been living on the same block for four years and never noticed each other, such was neighborhood community in Santa Monica Canyon. The gate was ajar—one of those houses built after the riots, a twenty-first century fortress, slits for front windows and a twelve-foot concrete fence surrounding the property and an electronic gate with a video camera built in. She was watering her flowers with Evian, upending one three-dollar bottle, then opening another with an angry twist, as if the flowers were irritating her with their expensive taste. She scowled when she saw me, then I was past her gate. After the walk, I finally got my own breakfast—all that was in the refrigerator was one frozen bagel and two horrific veggie burritos covered with permafrost. I microwaved them and ate them. They tasted like mittens.

Now it was time to go to the lawyer's office. In my opinion, I had done an astounding job of not thinking about getting arrested. I guess it was because I was innocent, and I had that middle-class white-guy assumption that I wouldn't be found guilty if I was innocent. But now I did imagine being in jail. I had actually done some performances in prisons (captive audiences) and I knew how dangerous and brutal they are. I did not want to be in one, even overnight.

I went outside to drive to the lawyer's, still playing *The Shawshank Redemption* in my mind, and opened the driver's side door. The Z is so low that you can't see inside the car until you're in the car, but when I opened the driver's side door I saw the legs of a woman in the passenger seat and her white pumps and green dress. My heart jumped about a foot, not only into my throat, but up my sinuses (it was being very athletic this morning). When I sat down behind the wheel, it was not Sabine but Krista. The white pumps were tennis shoes and the green dress was a skirt. She still had on the T-shirt she had worn to wash Sparky—as if to provoke the same reaction from me—and the car smelled like it. She obviously had not taken it off since except to stand at the bedroom window when Charles and I went for coffee. Now we were being boyfriend and girlfriend, maybe even engaged. She smiled happily at me, the smile of a woman looking at the man she loves.

"Krista, what are you doing sitting in my car?" I asked.

"I'm going with you," she answered. Simple as that.

"We're not going to the zoo today."

"I know."

"Do you know where I'm going?"

"No." She smiled again, as cheery as she could be.

"I've got some business to do, Krista. You can't come with me."

"It doesn't matter," she said.

"I'm glad you feel that way," I said. I thought she meant it didn't matter that she couldn't come with me, and that she would get out. But she didn't move. And she was still smiling, but now it was the nervous rictus smile.

"I'm late, Krista. You're going to have to get out of the car."

"No, Robert. It's all right." She was assuring me that going with me would not be an imposition on her, and indeed what could be sweeter than running a little errand with the love of her life?

"Krista," I said. "Let me say this very plainly. You can't go with me. You must get out of the car now."

"It's all right," she said, but to herself. And she wasn't smiling anymore.

I opened my door, walked around the car, and tried to open her door. She locked it. I unlocked it with the key and opened it. She still didn't move. She was staring straight ahead.

"I want to go with you," she said.

I wasn't going to pull her out by force. But I was shaking with frustration and anger. I turned to walk to Renate's front door. When I got there, Krista yelled at the top of her lungs, "I'm getting out! I'm not going now! I don't want to go with you anymore today!"

I hit Renate's doorbell anyway before I walked back to the car. Krista was standing there next to it, her arms folded across her chest as if to protect her breasts. To protect them from my lecherous gaze, I thought. Her face was twisted into a Medusa expression of fury. I was at least as angry as she was. The passenger door was open, and I threw it shut before getting in on the driver's side, but when I was about to turn the ignition, Krista opened the door again. This time I lost it.

"Close the goddamn door, Krista!" I shouted.

She did, with her right hand, after placing her left thumb just above the latch, slamming the weight of the door on it as hard as she could. She didn't make a sound as it happened, but I knew she had hurt herself badly.

I got out of the car again. Renate was on her front porch, having come out just in time to see Krista slam the door on her thumb. She screamed, "Krista! Krista!" I said, "Krista, Krista," as if I were approaching someone about to jump off a bridge. She was standing there calmly with her thumb smashed in the car door, her gaze riveted on me, watching my reaction. It was one of the spookiest moments of my life. She seemed completely unaware of the pain. She was only interested in me. I was being intently studied. I opened the door gently and held her wrist. The thumbnail was already blue, and blood was seeping out around its borders. She may have broken a bone. She didn't even glance down at it. Her eyes were focused on me.

Renate came running and I handed her Krista's wrist as if it were a dead fish. "Krista hurt herself," I said lamely. All this time Krista's eyes didn't leave my face. And she was smiling again. She had gotten what she wanted.

I got back into my car and drove away.

9.

The lawyer was named Folsom Sheed and his office was in The Ocean Avenue Office Park on the other side of Santa Monica. The Santa Monica Canyon borders Malibu to the north; Ocean Avenue marks the Santa Monica border with Venice to the south. The Ocean Avenue Office Park consists of four matching towers that mirror one another with their black tinted windows, and a chic seafood restaurant called Opus on the ground floor where Doris sometimes bought me lunch when she closed a big deal. There's an underground parking garage but nobody parks their cars themselves. I pulled up at a valet stand shaded by a red-and-white beach umbrella, and one of the five million Chicanos that grind the gears that run LA opened my car door and handed me a stub. I thanked him and he nodded, his black eyes as opaque as the tinted tower lobby windows in which we were reflected. City life. He parks my car, I pay him for it, someone else gets the money. No wonder his eyes were impenetrable.

Sheed's offices were on the top floor of the tallest tower. But of course. I had to leave my driver's license at the security desk and the security guard had to turn a key lock in the elevator to activate the button to the top floor. When I stepped out into Sheed's reception area, the view hit me in the face: a 270-degree panorama, the Santa Monica Mountains to the north, the Pacific Ocean to the west. I stood and looked at the ocean for a minute. At this height, the five-foot waves were peaceful, flat slow-motion ripples, all the wrinkles in LA being Botoxed away. The reception area was soothingly decorated for the nervous client, the furniture mahogany and deep brown leather, the light full-spectrum and indirect, tuned to supplement what came through the windows without revealing its sources. Just like your lawyer. At eight thirty A.M., the receptionist wasn't at her desk, but all the attorneys' offices around the periphery were occupied and probably had been for hours. You didn't work for Folsom Sheed unless you were Productive.

Then from behind her desk the receptionist popped up. She had been fishing in a bottom drawer for her lip gloss and surfaced smearing it on her lower lip, which had a collagen implant in it that must have weighed a pound. She was blonde and blue-eyed and pug-nosed and had a haircut like a little boy. But she did not have a body like a little boy. I knew her. She belonged to my health club. I saw the same people there all the time and never spoke to any of them, but had an impression of each one nonetheless. My impression of her was that she was way out there. I tried to get her phone number once when Doris and I were off-again, but she said she was "dating somebody" and I never asked a second time. I knew it was a bad idea the first time, but I was ready for a bad idea then, and I was ready for an even worse idea now.

"You're Robert Wilder," she said. "You're here to see Mr. Sheed."

I looked at the nameplate on her desk. There was only one name on it. "And you're Tori," I said perceptively. She had on a peach skirt the size of a microchip and a matching top that hovered three inches above her perfect cocoa-buttered navel: California office attire.

"I shouldn't tell you this cause you'll get a big ego, but I saw your video."

"*New Comics: Live at the Improv,*" I said. There must be a sudden run on the thing. Or else Tori was actually Madge in disguise. I couldn't believe two people had ever seen it, much less in the same week, so they had to be the same person.

"You were a riot. I loved the midget and the urinal."

"Thanks," I said.

"So you going to work out today?" she asked, after it became apparent to her that, despite my ability to speak on videotape, in person I was actually a mute.

I said I probably would.

"I'm going after work."

I nodded and smiled.

"It's such a great health club," she said.

"It *is* nice," I said. Was this my initiation into the singles' world? Hours of imbecilic small talk with each other before you earn the right to have sex?

"But here I am chatting away while you're anxious to talk to Mr. Sheed."

"In fact I'd rather talk to you," I said suavely. A terrible line, but technically true since presumably I wouldn't have to pay Tori to talk to her and I was dreading talking to Sheed (and paying him for it). Tori smiled brightly as she pressed a button on her phone console. "You're hiring the hottest legal talent in LA," she said confidentially before Sheed answered. She sounded like an agent. Maybe she could be my agent.

"Mr. Wilder is here, Mr. Sheed," she said. Then she said to me, "I'll show you in."

I followed her undulating peachness to Sheed's office: toned, buffed, and polished. I wondered if she was still "dating somebody." I was single now, wasn't I? Why not try some good old-fashioned sportfucking? It was after all the civic religion and seemed like an excellent way to put my emotional development on hold. And anyway it would be a real stretch for me to spend an entire evening with a person named "Tori." I could develop my tolerance for humanity at large.

She put her hand on my forearm at the door of Sheed's office. "Don't worry, he doesn't bite," she whispered.

I was about to make a witty suggestive comeback about biting when Sheed opened his door. His office was as big as a basketball court, and seemed even bigger because he was so small. He looked like a songbird. His hand, when he shook mine, felt like a child's. Nor was he much bigger than a child. He was in his late forties but his hair was white, and probably had been white since birth. He wore it clipped very close to his egg-shaped skull. His complexion was very fair, and his clothes were clearly chosen to complement it—a custom-tailored suit, of course, and tasseled loafers made of unborn calfskin. Don had mentioned that he wore his ties once then donated them to charity (because after a tie is knotted it bears a trace of the wrinkles), but I never saw any homeless people wearing $100 silk ties, even in Santa Monica.

I followed him to his desk, a French antique writing table—probably Chateaubriand's or some Rothschild's or somebody's. The only things on it were two file folders and a little platinum ellipse two inches high that looked like a trophy ("LA's Most Expensive Lawyer Per Pound"?). He sat down with his back to the window, and the light behind him framed him in a halo that could have been painted by Piero della Francesca. Nothing about this man was without design: the product of the utmost intelligence, will, and financial resources. In other words, exactly what you want in your lawyer.

He clicked a switch at the base of the trophy that made the ellipse begin rotating while it shifted on its axis. It was like a mesmerist's device or something out of those wonderful mad scientist labs in horror films of the fifties.

He noted my amusement and said, "I spent too many years as a prosecutor to ignore the fact that surveillance is the best way to find out what you need to know, even if you never use the information in court. This little device will distort our conversation so that it won't be intelligible to any of the long-range listening devices currently available on the market. I understand they're devising a new apparatus that will unscramble it, but it won't be available through private channels for another six months, at which time there will be another device that the new apparatus can't unscramble. And so it goes, Mr. Wilder. This is what passes for progress these days. But it's for your protection. What you say here will be strictly between us, and will of course be privileged according to law. It is completely in your interest to tell me the unvarnished truth."

I nodded. In contrast to his size, he had a voice like an opera singer: deep timbre that came from his diaphragm. He must have practiced like an opera singer to learn how to speak this way. It gave everything he said absolute authority.

"I'm not taping this, are you?" he asked.

"No," I said, taken aback. It hadn't even occurred to me to tape it.

"Fine. Well, I have good news."

"Yes, I've seen your receptionist."

"Pardon me?"

"It's an old joke, Mr. Sheed. The doctor says to the patient, 'I've got bad news and good news, which do you want to hear first?' "

"Right," he said, unamused. "Don Leach mentioned you were a comedian."

"I'm not so sure anymore."

Sheed removed his hands from his desk and folded them in his lap, a gesture of patience that meant he was losing his. "Would you like to talk about your career plans, Mr. Wilder? Or your legal problem?"

"Please excuse me. My legal problem."

"That's the good news," Sheed said. "You don't have one."

"How's that?"

"There was no money taken illegally from the Bank of America branch at Second and Colorado on Friday."

"There wasn't?" I asked, incredulously.

"There was not. So we have here something more interesting. This is what I was able to find out for you in the twenty-four hours I've had my people working on this: the woman 'Sabine' is in fact named Angela Chase. She has never been employed as a teller at Bank of America. The $200,000 in cash she took with her on Friday belonged to her, part of the profit from the sale of a house in Malibu she owned with her brother."

This was hard for me to believe, despite the basso profundo with which he delivered it.

"Um, wasn't the withdrawal procedure a bit unusual for a real estate transaction?" I asked.

"Yes, it was. The bank agreed to deliver the money to her in cash at the request of Washington, probably the State Department, although I doubt if I'd ever be able to confirm that."

Was this a put-on? A prank Don arranged?

"And why, pray tell, did she take the money to Mexico?"

Sheed sighed almost imperceptibly just to show me that he didn't appreciate the "pray tell," but since I was the client he was nevertheless going to be courteous and tolerant.

"Miss Chase's brother is named Michael. He is a vice president of international marketing for General Mills. He may also be involved in some less wholesome business. From his background, it seems likely. He was kidnapped in Mexico City two weeks ago today. I don't know if he's been released or not. I don't know if Miss Chase raised all the ransom money or not. I don't know if she has delivered the ransom money or not. I don't know if either of them is alive or not. And that is essentially all I know at this point. You do not have a legal problem, because there was no crime. At least no bank robbery."

"I need to rewind a minute," I said. "I don't get something here. Maybe you can explain it to me. Sabine is Angela Chase. Angela Chase has a brother. He's a business executive. General Mills. He was kidnapped, two weeks ago."

"Correct so far."

"I didn't read about it in the papers. He's an American business executive? That usually makes the news."

"Also correct. It didn't make the news, luckily for him."

"And why is that?"

"Two reasons. The current official policy of the United States government is not to negotiate with kidnappers. General Mills has—I believe the figure is—$3 billion in annual contracts with the Defense Department alone. That's a lot of Cheerios. They supply all five branches of the armed services. It's in their interest to be on board. If they refuse to pay ransoms, eventually their executives won't get kidnapped. Eventually. They might lose a few executives at first, but then that's it. The message is, if you want to kidnap a businessman, kidnap a Japanese, because they pay and we don't. Of course it would be bad publicity if this were generally known. You might not buy your child's after-school snack from such a heartless company. But they do want it known to the people in the kidnapping business. They also want to keep it out of the papers."

Sheed could see he was getting through to me. He leaned back in his chair and made a tiny pyramid with his hands by joining them, then held up two tiny forefingers the size of my pinkies.

"Second," he continued, "this Michael Chase may be dirty. He may have been the corporation's point man for bribing Mexican government officials. He may be involved in drugs or arms smuggling or who knows what. In any case, it may be to the corporation's advantage to hang him out to dry. So much so that they may have set it up. But that's completely in the realm of speculation."

"You're still way ahead of me, Mr. Sheed."

"It is a great deal of information to absorb, I'm sure," he said.

"It's not a world I live in."

"You stumbled into it, I'm afraid. And let me tell you something: it's real. It's going on right now as we speak. I am simply trying to describe your situation to you."

"I'm still back asking why Washington would intervene with the Bank of America to allow the money to be withdrawn in cash."

"All we know is that they did. It may have been for humanitarian reasons. However, it's more likely that Angela Chase threatened to inform the press of her brother's kidnapping if the government did not at least help her to obtain her own money for the ransom. And that would have put President Clinton in an awkward position—in an election year. Remember what happened to Jimmy Carter with the Iran hostage crisis? Voters don't like when presidents fail to rescue Americans kidnapped abroad. There are hundreds of such kidnappings a year in Mexico alone. How many do you read about in the papers? Not many. Officially, the ransom's a private transaction. No governments involved. No negotiations. No publicity. Simple quid pro quo among private citizens. As far as the world is concerned, it never happened."

I had an insight at that moment about Sheed. He liked the money but money wasn't the point. Money was only a by-product of the high-powered lawyering, being an insider at the highest level. This was what he liked. He would have taken my case for free.

He opened the top folder on his desk.

"Let's return to your involvement in this situation. I have a few questions for you. You stayed with Angela Chase at the Esperanza Resort Hotel, correct? In the honeymoon suite. She was not registered. She signed nothing nor paid for anything with a credit card."

"I don't believe so."

"But you did." He opened the first folder. "American Express dated Saturday posted yesterday for $873.13."

"How did you get that?"

"That's easy, Mr. Wilder. Any bozo can get it, which means any bozo who wants to can find out where you have been and how you spend your money. You ate chicken enchiladas in the restaurant and drank a bottle of Negra Modelo. Fortunately, we couldn't trace Angela Chase to Mexico at all. Plus, according to the hotel records, you were staying with your new bride."

"I still don't get where I come in. Why would anyone bother to find out any of this about me?"

"Only one reason. To link you to Angela Chase in case you would release the story to the press if she's taken hostage or murdered."

"But I wouldn't know."

"I know that, you know that, Angela Chase knows that, but the government agencies that don't want the story in the news wouldn't know that. Nor would they take a chance. They would assume you will release the story if you do not hear from her by a certain prearranged date."

"Which government agencies? Which *government?*"

"We don't know."

"Am I in some sort of danger?"

"Probably not."

"*Probably* not? Is that supposed to be comforting?"

"As I said, we are completely in the realm of speculation here. But by virtue of the fact that you're sitting here with me instead of lying dead in a ditch, they obviously haven't linked you to Angela Chase. If she flew out of Baja, there's no record of it. She must have had a false passport and paid for her ticket with a dummy credit card or cash, which as you saw she had in abundance. Another question: the note she wrote to you. Where is it now?"

"Don's got it."

"Has anyone else seen the note? Have you told anyone else about it?"

"No."

"Good. Don did fax it to me, but my fax line is secure. It's on hotel stationery but it's not signed. I would destroy it as she advised. She wasn't kidding about it possibly compromising her safety. And yours."

That made me remember her—a tactile memory, the way her body felt against mine, shot through me.

"All right," Sheed continued. "The hotel staff. You must have talked to a desk clerk."

"Yes. His name was Octavio."

Sheed wrote it down in the file. "What did you tell him?"

"Not much. He thought Sabine . . ."

"Miss Chase."

"Whoever she was. He thought she was my wife. He thought her mother had passed away suddenly and that was the reason for her abrupt departure. And the reason for her screaming noises that came from our room an hour or so before she left."

"Screaming noises," Sheed repeated.

I explained her screaming noises, as euphemistically as I could. Sheed thought a minute.

"I don't want you to be alarmed. I'm simply trying to cover all the bases here. This Octavio could still be the one means of linking you to Angela Chase. But first they have to know she was at the hotel and I don't think there's any way to know that, unless Octavio tells them, which means that he would have to be previously connected in some way to the interested parties."

"Gets pretty rococo."

"By which you mean attenuated. Tenuous. I agree," Sheed said. "I don't think you're at risk. Most likely this is a straight-forward American businessman kidnapping not arranged by the US government, the Mexican government, or General Mills. None are likely, but the most likely of the three is General Mills."

"Abducted by Cheerios," I said.

"The world has changed, Mr. Wilder. It's a world of corporations, not nations. There are many surprises coming in the next century."

"Any more surprises for me?"

"At this time, the risk to you is infinitesimal. Statistically insignificant. You are more likely to be run over by a truck crossing the street. As I said, the kidnappers almost certainly work for themselves, so they wouldn't be interested in you at all. It's a thriving business down there. It would be bad business to collect the ransom, then murder the person they kidnapped, much less the person delivering the ransom. So I don't think they'd hurt Angela Chase either. Possibly the kidnappers were hired by a drug cartel or some other illegal organization, but those organizations usually simply kill someone like Michael Chase instead of bothering to kidnap him."

"There's still a few pieces that don't fit," I said. "The woman I took to Mexico was a teller in the bank. She was cashing people's checks. She cashed *my* check."

Sheed pulled a piece a paper from the bottom folder and handed it to me across the desk. It was a xeroxed copy of a California driver's license. The picture on it was Sabine's. The name on it was Angela Chase.

"Is that the woman?" Sheed asked.

I said it was.

"She has never worked in a bank. But she has done some other interesting things." He handed the whole folder across the desk.

"I can look at this?" I asked.

"That's your copy. You're paying for it. Take it home with you."

"I still don't get one thing: why me?"

"Again, speculation: Angela Chase has to transport $200,000 in cash from Santa Monica to someplace in Mexico. By herself. How would you do it if you were she?"

"I have no idea."

"Think about it a minute. There are many people who would be eager to kill someone for considerably less than $200,000. What if she's under surveillance? It's a 100 percent certainty that she was, surely by the government agency that arranged for her to withdraw the cash, and maybe by one or more other black-box agencies. What can she do? General Mills isn't going to pay the ransom, the US government's not going to pay the ransom. She's got to raise the ransom and deliver it, or her brother's dead. You will see in the file that she has a deep attachment to her brother."

I opened the folder on my lap. There were a number of photographs, including one of Angela and her brother at what appeared to be her college graduation. She wore a gown and mortarboard and they had their arms around each other's shoulders and were laughing. The quad where they stood looked familiar to me, but it didn't register why. Michael Chase was as beautiful as Angela was, chiseled and rugged, thick hair, good teeth: what a gene pool.

Sheed continued, "Her first problem is to get the money. That she does. You'll see how she came to own her parents' house. Not a happy story. Her second problem is to get the money out of the bank. She can't just walk in and walk out. She can, but she could be robbed and murdered if she does. There are hundreds of Bank of America branches in Southern California, some of them closer to the Mexican border. Why does she choose the one at Second and Colorado in Santa Monica?"

I said I couldn't guess.

"I can, but it's only a guess: maybe she knew somebody. Her brother had banking connections. Let's say she has arranged to masquerade as a teller. That gives her a little more room to maneuver. At least she doesn't have to walk in and walk out with the money. It gives her time to pick her moment. And there you were: her moment."

"So it wasn't my irresistible manhood?"

"Not by half," said Sheed. "She's an exceptionally attractive woman. That's one power she can use. Let's say this was not the first day she was in the bank. Let's say she was there all week. She could have gotten one hundred rides home but she's going to be observed coming out of the bank with every one. What's different in your case? One thing: the rain. You drove her home in the middle of a deluge. You picked her up at the curb. Even if she was seen coming out, they probably lost you in the traffic. She took the one long shot she had, and it worked."

"But then we went to her house."

"Are you sure it was her house? Remember, she sold her parents' house. Maybe it was a safe house. Maybe it's owned by the US government. Maybe it actually does belong to a producer. Clearly she didn't take you to where she had been living."

I paused a moment to try to absorb this. It meant rearranging my memories like a jigsaw puzzle and trying to make another picture of them, say of the Matterhorn with a goat on top. (I was the goat.)

"All right," I said after the pause. "Let's assume every detail of your version is accurate. How could she possibly know that I would drive her to Mexico?"

"She didn't," Sheed answered, with that unquestionable authority of his. "You wouldn't make a very good lawyer, Mr. Wilder. You have to be able to imagine point of view. She was playing it by ear. Again, look at the situation she's in. She's going to try to rescue her brother. That's boilerplate. You'll see when you read her file. She's going to try to save his life even if it means losing her own. So, under possibly hostile surveillance, she's got to get the money, get out of the bank, and get away safely. How can she do it? You're the ticket. I have no idea how she planned to travel to Mexico before you presented yourself as her chauffeur. I suspect that's why she had a false passport. Once she's out of the bank with the money, having lost the tail, the last step—getting to Mexico—is a stroll through the park. You just made it easier, honeymoon suite and all. You were the perfect dupe."

The perfect dupe. Why did this term not make me particularly merry?

Also quite jolly was Sheed's then informing me that his tab so far was approximately $6,000, not including xeroxing. Add that to the Unwedding Dinner, and being abducted by the Cheerios people was starting to look good. At least I could live on cereal.

Unless the situation changed, Sheed said, he and I would not need to meet again. I should feel free to call him if I had any problems or concerns. He said the private investigators who worked for him would be contacting me when they had further information. They'd certainly tell me who owned the house Angela Chase took me to. I said I'd like to be told if and when Angela Chase got out of Mexico alive and, if she did, where she was. He said he'd try to find that out for me. And with that I said good-bye and shook his little hand.

I felt like I had been picked up by the tornado in Kansas and deposited in the land of Oz. All the reactions I had suppressed to focus on understanding what Sheed was telling me now swirled around me and left me standing outside his office door in Munchkin land dressed in Dorothy's pigtails and powder-blue pinafore. I had completely forgotten about Tori. On the way to the elevator, I glided past her desk like a zombie.

"Robert?" she said to my back.

"Oh, hi," I said, turning around, and recalling her name with difficulty. "Tori."

"How'd it go?"

"Good. I guess."

"I'm not allowed to talk to the clients about their cases. But people don't see lawyers like Mr. Sheed unless they've got a good reason. I just hope everything's okay. You're in good hands with him. He's tough but honest."

I nodded. And smiled (I think).

"He's so busy, though. Call me if you need to get through to him," she went on. "That's one way I *can* help."

I said thanks.

"Oh, don't thank me. It's selfish."

She waited for my response, but I just didn't have it in me. She would have thought I had an electroshock treatment instead of legal counsel, except that she must be used to seeing people come out of Sheed's office looking lobotomized.

"You have the office number here. This is my home number." She wrote it on the back of one of Sheed's business cards and handed it to me.

I looked at it dumbly. She had used red ink. Underneath the number, she had printed "Tori" with two hearts: a big one for the o and a tiny one for the dot over the i.

WHEN I handed my stub to the parking attendant, he looked at me as if I really had just landed from Kansas dressed in pigtails and a powder-blue pinafore. I had forgotten to get my valet parking ticket validated, which for an Angelino is like a Muslim forgetting Ramadan. I don't believe he had ever seen an unvalidated parking stub before.

"Twenty-five dollars, señor," he said. "You want to go back inside for the stamp?"

That didn't appeal to me. I handed him the money. He muttered a sentence to himself in Spanish that had the word *gordo* in it. I assumed he was speaking metaphorically, either about my fat wallet or my fat head or both. When he came back with the car, and held the door for me, I gave him five dollars just so he wouldn't feel undertipped by the big spender. Then I had to go back into the building anyway, because I had forgotten to sign out and pick up my driver's license and I had also forgotten to leave my HBO contract with Sheed for one of his entertainment specialists to review. Bucket's lawyers had surely reviewed it as they always did, but now I didn't trust Bucket either. Maybe I shouldn't trust anybody, I thought. Ever.

10.

I didn't want to go home. I couldn't deal with Krista right now or with Renate dealing with Krista. Lunch with Don was set for noon. My gym stuff was at home, so a therapeutically mind-numbing killer workout was not an option. There was always Starbucks, but sipping a latte with my fellow Californians did not suit my state of mind—if you can call being spun in a cyclotron a state of mind. Sitting calmly in the middle was someone named Angela Chase, smiling at me with that lush lopsided ironic grin of hers.

When I stopped the car, I found myself at Madge's. That's how it happened. I didn't know I was going there. She was leaning on the counter with her half-lens reading glasses on her nose paging through a soap opera magazine. The waiting room smelled like incense instead of the usual Essence of Dog.

"Back already, Robert," she observed. "Where's Sparky?"

"At home," I said. "It's just me that needs boarding."

"What's up?"

"This is going to sound odd, but do you mind if I sit here for a while? I've got something to read and I need a place to do it."

"Make yourself at home. There's a pot of green tea under the cozy. The girls went home already, if you can call a massage parlor home. They had a ceremony for Mitchie here this morning. I guess *we* had a ceremony. I was part of it too. To tell you the truth, it was heartbreaking. The girls got some lotus-flower petals somewhere and some incense. It was all sort of Buddhist, I guess. What would I know? I got dunked in a river in Midgeville, Georgia, washed in the blood of the lamb and all that shit. They had a photo of Mitchie too. They gave it to me as a present."

She handed it across the counter. It was no bigger than a matchbook cover, not the kind of print you get in the US. A ten-year-old in a school uniform smiled happily at me.

"You're good to those girls," I said.

"I've been there myself. There were some mean guys in Midgeville. Pickups with shotgun racks. You've heard the joke about why a Southern town's population always stays the same? Every time a baby's born, a man leaves. Not Midgeville. Motto there was 'Keep the women barefoot and pregnant so they can't outrun you.' But you came here for some privacy. There's your chair," she said, nodding to a legless overstuffed chair in the far corner, fluffy with dog hair.

When I sat down my butt hit the floor. There wasn't any stuffing in the legless overstuffed chair. I opened the folder on my lap and flipped through it: downloaded photographs and newspaper stories; credit reports on Angela and Michael, listing their five most recent addresses; even their college transcripts. Michael got a B in bowling at the University of Miami. Angela went to UCLA. She was a freshman my last year there before I dropped out of the PhD program in English (now I recognized the place her graduation picture was taken—the quad in front of the Humanities Building). There were 40,000 students at UCLA so it wasn't surprising that I never met her. Or had I? That was a bizarre idea. But unless she had a total body transplant, I certainly would remember if I had.

Even more bizarre was to read these things about her. I had made love to this person, I had been inside her most intimate being. Or so I had thought. The person I had spent the most remarkable day of my life with didn't exist. There was no Sabine. She wasn't dead: she had never existed, except as a figment of my imagination, a holographic erotic fantasy she played into. She had been what she knew I wanted her to be, and not even what I personally—Robert Wilder—wanted her to be but what she knew some generic male led around by his dick wanted her to be. Whoever this Angela Chase actually was, I wasn't going to like her—this rip-off queen, this scam artist.

But I did like her, of course: I liked her too much. Just looking at these pieces of paper filled me with longing. This was the summary of her identity provided to Sheed by Advantage Private Investigators:

ANGELA CHASE (aka "Sabine") was born November 14, 1967, in Cedars-Sinai Hospital in Los Angeles to Rev. John Chase and Margaret Chase of Malibu. Rev. Chase was at the time the pastor of Our Lady of Malibu Episcopal Church. Margaret Chase was active in worldwide Episcopal charities especially those concerning children's welfare. She was also a soprano in various choirs, a painter of watercolors exhibited locally, and an organizer of monthly book discussion clubs. Angela was the second of their two children. Her brother, Michael, was born in 1962.

Angela Chase attended elementary school at Miss Waterstone's, a private girls' school in Malibu. Upon graduation at the age of thirteen, she was sent to the Mont Fleur Academy in Lucerne, Switzerland. She returned to Malibu for the summers.

In March 1985, Rev. John Chase committed suicide in gruesome fashion in the backyard of his home. He put a 12-gauge shotgun in his mouth and pushed the trigger with his toe. He apparently slipped as he did so, because the first shot did not kill him. The sound woke his wife, who came out the back door just as he had crawled to the gun and managed to put it into his mouth again. Mrs. Chase witnessed the second shot, which killed him (c.f. *Los Angeles Times*, file item #16).

Angela Chase returned to Malibu to be with her mother. She was two months short of completing her course of study at Mont Fleur, and was never awarded a diploma. Michael Chase did not return to Malibu for his father's funeral. He was then a broker of foreign currency futures for Dean Witter Reynolds in Miami, specializing in the Mexican peso. He had attended the University of Miami from 1979–1985, and during this period was arrested four times for lewd conduct, once for drunk driving, and three times for possession of narcotics (seven acquittals, one misdemeanor conviction). He was incarcerated for short periods of time in city and county jails. He had no contact with his family during this time, and apparently financed the purchase of two nightclubs and a South Beach restaurant by dealing drugs to fraternities and sororities. He was well-known to the Miami police (dossier included: item #5). He was indicted by a grand jury in a bribery scandal involving the South Beach police department during his last year of college, but cooperated with the prosecution and was never brought to trial.

Margaret Chase was periodically hospitalized for depression after her husband's suicide, from March to November

1985. Angela stayed with her mother at their home in Malibu during this time. On November 14, 1985 (Angela's eighteenth birthday), Margaret Chase committed suicide in exactly the same fashion that her husband did, with the same shotgun. Angela was awakened just as her mother had been, and ran to the backyard just as her mother had. Her mother, however, was already dead. Unlike Rev. John Chase, the first self-administered shotgun blast killed Margaret Chase. The story was widely covered by the news media (item #12).

Michael Chase did return to Malibu for his mother's funeral. He continued his brokerage career in Los Angeles. Michael and Angela shared an apartment in Brentwood from November 1985 until September 1990. There is no police record for Michael Chase during these years. Angela Chase enrolled at UCLA in September 1986 and graduated *summa cum laude* in June 1990. In September 1990 she was admitted to the Institut d'Etudes Politiques de Paris, the school for Europe's political and diplomatic elite. Michael Chase was hired as vice president for international marketing by General Mills and moved to Mexico City. The house in Malibu they now owned jointly was maintained as a lease property by Coldwell Realty from November 1985 until it was sold one week ago for $3.2 million. Part of the profit from this sale was delivered to Angela Chase at the Bank of America branch at Second and Colorado in Santa Monica. This unusual procedure was authorized by T. Jefferson St. John, President of B of A (item #33).

Angela Chase completed her graduate studies in Paris in eighteen months. Except for the purchase of plane tickets to various capitals in the Middle East (items #44 through #48), there is no record of her whereabouts from March 1992 until June 1996 (two weeks ago), when she returned to California to arrange the sale of her parents' home to pay her brother's ransom.

Michael Chase resided in Mexico City since leaving Brentwood in September 1990. He was an investment partner in various enterprises with government officials associated with drug and arms smuggling, and has been the subject of investigations both by Mexican panels of inquiry and the CIA (item #17). He has never been indicted. His illegal activities, if any, are unknown. He is a homosexual, and is reputed to frequent the Zona Rosa district. On three occasions, he has undergone inpatient hospitalization in Costa Rica and the United States for cocaine addiction, most recently at the Betty Ford Clinic in Palm Springs. His lifestyle made him an excellent candidate for abduction. His whereabouts are unknown.

The whereabouts of Angela Chase are also unknown.

WHEN I looked up I saw a woman sitting in the pink plastic chair across from me. It was the woman from the beach Sparky had rubbed rotted black marine jelly on, the woman who watered her flowers with Evian.

"Dropping off your dog?" she asked.

"Um, no," I answered.

"Well, you're not picking him up. I saw you with him this morning."

Was that this morning? "He's at home," I said.

"So what are you doing here?" she asked, as if it were her constitutional right to know.

"I'm reading."

"You're reading," she said. "He's reading. At a kennel," she said to the rack of old magazines on the wall. "I love this town."

"Do you mind if I ask you something?" I said, irked at being interrupted. "Why are you so unhappy?"

My mouth ahead of my brain again.

She looked at me angrily. "You doing a survey?"

"Kind of. It's a subject that interests me professionally."

"You a shrink or a priest? Or an undisguised sadist?"

"Comedian," I said.

"An undisguised sadist, in other words. Probably with a high dose of masochism too."

"Guess it depends on how you do comedy," I muttered.

"The answer to your question is none of your business, Mr. Funnybones. But I'm going to tell you anyway. I moved down here from Santa Cruz six months ago, because I got married. I just found out my new husband spent the weekend with another woman. How did I find out? The kennel lady called because Asshole forgot to leave the dog's meds. Asshole told me he was going duck hunting this weekend. Duck hunting! I love that. The outfit, the gun, the decoys, even his stupid duck call. Big masquerade. Loaded his hunting dog into his car then dropped it off here. Where do you men get off screwing around on your wives? Don't you have any integrity? Don't you love anybody but yourselves?"

"I guess all men don't do it," I said, certainly not referring to myself.

"Show me one," she said.

Madge walked through the swinging door from the kennel with a springer spaniel on a leash. It saw me first, since my face was at its eye level, due to my seat in the unstuffed leg-less overstuffed chair. It came right over and tried to lick my mouth. I blocked it with my forearms, so it licked those. I must have smelled like the woman's husband: the infidelity scent.

"Over there, over there," I said to it, pointing to the woman. Madge handed her the leash, and she handed Madge a credit card. She didn't say another word to me. As she was leaving, I said, "See you around the neighborhood."

"Not for long," she answered. "Have a nice life."

"Unusual dog for that kind of woman," Madge said to me after she left. "They don't go together at all."

"It's her husband's," I said from my chair.

Madge raised her eyebrows as if to ask how I knew that. I still was sitting there with Angela's folder on my lap, which had been playing like a tape loop in my mind during my soon-to-be-ex-neighbor's rant. Madge saw I was preoccupied and went back to her soap opera magazine. There was only one more page in the folder: the xerox of the California driver's license that Sheed had already shown me. I looked at the photo more closely. Angela looked startled and scared. Or was this a combination of the DMV flashbulb and my imagination? It wasn't an expression of hers I had seen before. Maybe she had acted the part of Sabine so well I had seen nothing of Angela Chase. Here was this real person somewhere in the world with her own problems and agony—including the agony of losing both parents and now possibly her brother. No wonder she treated me like a function (as Charles put it): the rescue-my-brother function. Didn't I treat her the same way? The escape-from-Doris function? I didn't give her much reason to think I might be interested in anything else.

Yet here she was: Angela Chase. According to the State of California, an official real human being. We had served each other's functions very well. Was that the end of it? What about the note she wrote to me, saying she'd never forget me, the lovely gentle sexy (underlined three times) man? What about that nutty business of being together in the next life? Was that part of the act?

Staci and Laci came flying through the swinging door from the kennel. Madge's twins. Blonde twelve-year-olds with pierced noses and Def Leppard T-shirts, twin hormonal fireworks displays.

"Madonna and Michael Jackson are having a baby!" Staci shouted. Or maybe it was Laci.

"Together?" Madge asked.

"No!" Laci (or Staci) said, punching her sister in the shoulder. "They're having separate babies, but at the same time."

"At the exact same time?" Madge asked.

"Nooo, mom. God," they said. But they knew she was kidding them.

"Maybe they'll share the same hospital room," Madge said.

"Nooo. They're both rich! They'll each have private rooms. They can buy a whole hospital. We decided we're never going to have babies. We're never getting married because guys suck."

"That *is* exciting news. You've met, Robert, girls? What do you say?"

"Hi, Robert," they said in unison. "Mom, can we have some money? Can we go down to the Promenade?" The Third Street Promenade was the downtown Santa Monica mall. Lots of homeless people, street performers, psychotic outpatients, drug pushers, and teenagers sucking it all into their teenage brains.

"I'm going to take off, Madge," I said. "Thanks for the reading chair."

"No trouble, Robert," she said. It was advice, not a statement. She had two good reasons for avoiding trouble, and one was at each elbow as she dug into her purse.

11.

Just a normal morning. It wasn't yet noon and I had watched an insane young woman smash her thumb in my car door so she could study my response; I had spent $6,000 to find out that a) I had not driven the getaway car for b) a bank robbery that wasn't a bank robbery by c) a woman who wasn't who she was; I had been given a phone number by a third young woman for whom I felt nothing but unregenerate lust; and I had been ranted at by a complete stranger (also female) about male infidelity. Not to mention Madge's problems and Mitchie's suicide. That was just about plenty of bad day for one bad day. I had just slept seventeen hours but I needed more sleep—say, a week under the covers, with the door locked, the shades drawn, the phone turned off, and a nice slow morphine drip.

Little Tokyo is in downtown LA, but Little Little Tokyo is in West LA, bordering Santa Monica: two blocks off Sawtelle Boulevard north of Olympic consisting exclusively of Japanese restaurants, karaoke bars, grocery stores, video stores, and shops selling herbal medicine. Don and I met there for our weekly lunch at Asahi Ramen: a big bowl of noodles, vegetables, chicken, and steamed wontons for $6.95: cheap, delicious, filling, and healthy: the best buy in town. It's ten minutes from Madge's. I was early, and claimed a table by the window in advance of the lunchtime crowd. I had brought Angela's file to show to Don, and opened it to look at the photos of her again. She didn't look like Sabine. That is, she did but didn't. They were like pictures of her twin, except she didn't have a twin. Same body, different soul. Then there was the odd coincidence: Angela's freshman year at UCLA was my last year in graduate school at UCLA. I finished course-work for a PhD but like almost everyone else in my class and since, I couldn't get a tenure-track teaching job. I was a teaching assistant for four years. My freshman composition classes became more like stand-up routines as I did more open mics around town at night and less research on my advisor's idea of a dissertation, "Phallocentrism in Restoration Comedy" (which I referred to as "Sheridan's Schlong"). Angela wasn't a student in any of my composition classes, but she could have been in the 800-seat lecture class for which I was one of sixteen TAs. She could have known who I was even if I didn't know her. A disturbing idea.

Even more disturbing was my response to Angela's story. I could see her mother watch her father blow his brains out, could see him crawling to the gun so he could shoot himself again. Her mother had killed herself exactly like her father—what does that do to you? And on Angela's eighteenth birthday? It seemed unimaginably cruel. And if both of your parents kill themselves, how do you keep from killing yourself? Does it terrify you that you will kill yourself someday, that this fate is somehow inside you, part of your DNA? I started asking these questions, and of course they didn't have answers. The problem was that they started to put me into Angela's skin. Sheed was wrong. I could imagine her point of view. Having lost both parents like this, it was easy to understand why she would risk her life for her brother, to sacrifice anything to save him. Including me. She even seemed heroic. Whatever she had done in the years between her parents' suicides and now, she had become a brave person. I recalled what she said to me in Malibu: "You do something to me that goes deep down," and I had responded, "You too," and meant it.

This is how my head was going when Don walked into Asahi Ramen and sat down across from me. A lucky thing, since the ravenous crowd outside waiting for lunch all seemed focused on my occupying a precious table for two to contemplate my situation instead of wolfing my lunch and freeing the table. There were only four tables for two in the whole restaurant. Because I hadn't ordered, a couple outside separated from me by a quarter inch of plate glass had been glaring at me as if I were drowning a baby. Don looked upset. When he's upset, it distracts him and his eyes look everywhere in the room but at you. Asahi Ramen is just not that interesting as interior design: it's a twenty-five-by-fifteen box with a couple of dollar-fifty paper fans nailed to the walls. I asked him what was wrong.

He said, "Francine just called. She wants to stay in Maui with Doris for a few extra days. I think she's really unhappy with her life. With me."

"Did she say something?"

"Just that she's having the best time since before we were married."

"I'm sorry," I said.

"She comes home from her lecture tours exhausted, the kids are starved for her and eat her alive, and she leaves for the next trip more exhausted than when she arrived. It never stops."

"What can you do about it?"

"Nothing. My poems aren't about to pull down 400 grand a year. Somebody's got to be home with the kids occasionally besides the nanny. When Francine *is* home we have nothing left for each other."

I just nodded sympathetically.

"Plus the way Jeb torments Emma drives Francine nuts and he's worse when she's home, probably because he wants all her attention. And of course Francine blames me for 'not parenting him properly.'"

"Maybe you should take a vacation with her."

"Good idea, but first we have to pay for this one."

"Put it on my bill."

"Sure, after your HBO special you can become my patron."

The waitress came over and we ordered our noodles. She was a slight young woman with chopped black hair and a brilliant smile.

"At least you don't have my problem," I said to Don after the waitress left. "Sometimes I think there is a constant fuck movie running in my head. The world can't be as I'm seeing it. Or I should say: them. Women, women, and more women. Even the ugly ones are beautiful."

"Heh," Don snorted. "Well, you live in the right town."

"I even want to get the waitress's phone number. How long do you think it would take me to learn Japanese?"

"What did Sheed have to say?" Don asked, ignoring my question.

I told him. He listened intently without any visible response.

"I knew you weren't going to get arrested," he said when I finished. "At least for this particular adventure. Anyway, Sheed would have gotten you off. If he could get my bone-head brother-in-law off, he could persuade NOW to give you the Future Husband of the Year Award for humping Angela Chase on your wedding day. That's quite a story he told you about her. Quite a woman, this Angela Chase."

"Yeah," I said.

Don read my intonation.

"Uh-oh," he said.

"Yep. She did something to me. If you read this file, you'll probably fall in love with her too. It doesn't make any sense, of course. When did love make sense? Doris made sense."

"You've got a funny idea of love, pal."

"Who doesn't?" I asked. "In the meantime, what am I supposed to do? I feel like screwing every female who isn't incontinent or comatose. I got turned on by Krista yesterday. Krista! And then the babe who works for Sheed gives me her number. I think they can smell it when you're producing testosterone. I think my gonads are on overdrive and the testosterone has flooded my brain pan."

The noodles came. Don ate his while I whined. I said ever since I walked into the bank on Friday I have been living in the Twilight Zone. I told him everything, dumped it all. Don finished his whole bowl of noodles before I started mine. The couple outside the window next to my shoulder were apoplectic. They were called inside for their table and scowled at me as they passed. The guy had a ponytail and wore an expensive leather jacket and ratty Dodgers cap: a uniform that said, *I'm in the Industry*. I thought he was going to make a crack as he walked by, and, if he had, I think I would have punched him. I gave him my best high school tough-guy stare until he broke eye contact. I would have loved to make him pay for the last four days of my life.

Don wiped his mouth with a paper napkin.

"I'd suggest you check into a hospital, but you won't do it," he said.

"You're right," I answered.

"It's just a lot of shit coming to a head at once."

"Like a big zit," I said. "Pop goes my skull."

"Why don't you go see your holy man?"

"I probably will. Make another suggestion."

"Don't have one. You feel suicidal?"

"I already told you: I feel horny."

"Same thing in your case. If you act on it, you could get yourself in trouble, since I think that's what you're looking for. Has it ever occurred to you that the women you want most you like least? Everybody was pulling for you with Doris. Here was somebody your own age with an IQ of more than sixty. I was looking forward to some nice quiet adult evenings together playing Scrabble."

I asked him to talk while I ate, before I was forcibly removed from my chair by the ravenous crowd outside. I asked Don to tell me what he thought of my prospects with the HBO special, Charles's Apollo gig, and Doris's inevitable return. He thought I ought to take both the HBO special and the Apollo gig (work as therapy, plus pay my debts), and he admitted that he couldn't predict what Doris was going to do (my problems would all be solved if she simply murdered me). I asked him if Francine had a key to Doris's townhouse, since my computer and other valuable personal items were locked inside. He said that if Francine did, there was no way in God's universe that he was going to give it to me without her permission. He valued his life slightly more than my possessions. Maybe he too would risk his life to ransom me if I were kidnapped, but giving me the key was not a risk: it was suicide. I asked him if he thought it was impossible that I could fall in love with Angela Chase. He said that since my dick was doing all my thinking, he couldn't imagine why it would be smarter in her case than any other. But when he saw the look on my face, he added:

"I guess I'd have to read the file. Sheed has a gold mine idea here, like a reverse dating service: you get introduced to the person you've already fucked."

"See, I don't need a shrink," I answered. "It's cheaper to have lunch with you and find out how screwed up I am. I'm even going to buy lunch today, you've helped me so much."

I paid and we left. After walking me to my car, Don gave me a hug—in his case, it was always a bear hug. I'm a reasonably big man—six feet, one eighty when I'm in shape—but Don was so much bigger that when he embraced me I felt like a child. He thumped me on the back with both hands, nearly crushing my shoulder blades.

"I'll call you this evening," he said. "You can call anytime until Thursday afternoon: that's when Francine and Doris come home and throw your computer off the pier. After Thursday, let it ring once and hang up and I'll call you back when the coast is clear."

"Francine will think you've got a girlfriend."

"Yeah, hundreds of them. I can barely swat them away they're so thick. I hate to think about how she's going to feel when she gets home and the kids descend on her. I'll call you after I talk to her and pretend I'm glad she's having so much fun without me."

12.

It was the second time in as many hours that I sat in my car not knowing where to drive it. The plush contoured black leather interior of the Z seemed, appropriately, like a padded cell: at the split second between Don's departure and my getting into my car, I was alone in the universe. Plus I had given him Angela's file, so I couldn't go home and read it over and over again and make myself feel even worse. But I decided to go home anyway. I could take Sparky for a walk, check my phone messages, and maybe pick up my gym bag and go work out.

I didn't get to the gym and Sparky didn't get his walk. There were two messages on my machine. The first was from Sheed via Tori:

> Robert, hi. This is Tori. Mr. Sheed asked me to tell you that he has given your HBO contract to Mr. Keene, and that Mr. Keene will contact you after his review. Hey, and that's super awesome you're going to be on HBO! I am totally impressed. Well, I gotta go. You looked so sad when you left this morning I wanted to give you a big teddy-bear hug. Hope I see you at the club or something. Bye. Beep.

Number two:

> Robert Wilder. Gleggi Ungar from Irvine Improv.
> I've booked a room for you at the Laguna Hotel for
> Tuesday and Wednesday nights, assuming you'll be
> driving back to Santa Monica after your last show on
> Thursday. Would you call me if you've made other
> arrangements? Ken Mishima asked me to tell you
> how much he's looking forward to your performances
> here. So am I. I'm a big fan. Please call if there's
> anything I can do for you. Otherwise we'll see you
> here at seven P.M. for the sound check. Have a safe
> drive down to Orange County.

I had completely forgotten about the Irvine Improv gig,
and now I remembered that Doris and I had planned to drive
back from Baja Monday so I could do it Tuesday night. Today
was Monday. A Monday very different than the other Monday
would have been. That life could change so fast like this was
dizzying. But then I had done it myself, hadn't I? I was the
one that started this avalanche sliding down the hill.

Was I in any shape to perform? The show must go on,
right? You just don't cancel in this business or you put yourself
out of business. Ken Mishima, the manager of Irvine Improv,
was a good guy. I didn't want to cancel on him. On the other
hand, it would be worse to have a nervous breakdown on
stage. Stand-up is just at the edge of a public nervous breakdown anyway. I'd rather drop acid and go skydiving. Before
I walk on stage I'm terrified of going blank. I've never gone
blank, but I've had panic attacks during performances which
took me out of my body, so that I was somewhere on the ceiling watching my mouth move. But when I get into a groove
on stage, everything disappears. That's the pleasure, that's why

I do it. I come alive, I'm with the audience, it's a dance: I lead, they follow. I don't need to say how sexual it is. That's obvious. When people laugh, it opens them up—the mouth opens, the breathing changes, body rhythm changes. It heals them. They live longer. It's a cliché, but there's no arguing with it: it's all timing. The pain gets ex-pressed. Tension and release, just like sex.

That's how I got hooked. I never wanted to be a scholar, but I loved teaching and stand-up is just like teaching without books and without decorum. You're supposed to transgress, to reveal surprising, gritty truth, and do it lightly. It goes right to the heart of cherished cultural assumptions. If it doesn't, it's nothing—like Letterman and Leno: polite entertainment. There's such a thin membrane between educating the audience and offending them. You have to make them love you without them thinking you're trying. I have always believed that the only way to do that was in fact not to try. Let the audience make its own decision about me. I disagreed with Charles. Never would I take out a joke because the audience didn't laugh. I'd move it, I'd change the delivery, I'd fiddle with the timing. But if it hit home for me, I wouldn't take it out.

I loved the writing and performing but I didn't like anything else about a comic's life. I didn't like traveling and I didn't like drunks and I'm constitutionally incapable of promoting myself. When I meet somebody "important" I invariably offend them, just to get the issue settled. And what does a comic get when he makes it? A movie or a sitcom. I didn't want a movie or a sitcom. Jerry Seinfeld, Robin Williams, Eddie Murphy: they all quit stand-up. It burns you out, it's too much stress. It can kill you—literally. I started out with those guys. They were all doing the same clubs I was in the early eighties. Now they're them and I'm me. I don't want what they have, I don't want their lives, but when one of them has a big success, I think it should have been me. Envy: pure and nasty. I never told anyone that I really believe stand-up is the modern version of cultural wisdom transmitted around the campfire. I have a reputation for being at best cerebral and at worst arrogant. It hasn't done me any good. After almost fifteen years in the business, I seem to have offended just about everybody with my superior "purist" attitude. But Bucket kept getting me gigs, one after another, treading water, not sinking and drowning. For all I knew, the Irvine Improv could be the last club date I would ever do.

So I'd take it. If I was going to self-destruct it may as well be on stage. Krista and I could share a room in the locked ward. Don was right. The work, and thoughts about the work, were the best way not to think about Angela Chase. Plus I needed the money. But there was no way I could perform in this state. Just the thought of performing made my heart start pounding, which made me remember to breathe, which made me remember Tran Hanh.

Mr. Hanh never made appointments or answered his phone. If you wanted to see him, you had to leave a message. If there were too many people coming on a certain day, he would return your call to gently suggest another day. This was the only concession he made to chronological time. But you could come anyway if you were willing to wait. When you met with him, you stayed as long as you wanted to. Once I showed up at two P.M. and didn't get to talk to him until six. He would simply continue to meet with people until there was no one left. If you didn't want to wait that was fine. The people who felt they really had to see him waited. On this day, I would have waited a month.

As it turned out, I got in pretty quickly. There were only two people sitting on the mats in the anteroom, which was bare except for a discreet incense burner, a woven mandala on each of the walls, and a water cooler that dispensed a fresh fruit juice concoction of Mr. Hanh's invention. The rule was silence. The idea was to be quiet and attend to your breathing. It worked. Usually by the time I saw Mr. Hanh, I already felt better than when I arrived. The two people before me were not a couple. The man was middle-aged, Mediterranean, short and stocky. He wore Michael Jordan's basketball jersey, number 23, which revealed thick black hair that covered his shoulders and arms. His arms looked more like legs: short ugly legs, with forearms like hams. But the ugliest thing about him was a pink inch-wide scar from his collarbone up his neck to the tip of his chin. His throat had obviously once been cut, probably not by accident. I thought he must be proud of it to display it like that. However long he had been quiet and attentive to his breathing, he had an incredibly serene expression on his face, so that, despite his brutal scar and thick arms and hairy shoulders, he appeared happy.

The woman, too: she was in her sixties, sitting cross-legged in a horrible mallard-green pantsuit and heavy jewelry. Her hair had been laminated the color of a brass urn and looked almost as hard, as if it would ring if you tapped it with a quarter. One of my journalist friends used to say that Ronald Reagan had had his face lifted so many times that when he smiled you could see his skull. I thought of that when she smiled as I sat down on the mat across from her. But, like the ugly man, she seemed at peace, at least at this moment, in this place. I wondered what they had gone through in their lives before they landed here.

Whatever it was, it was fine now. Neither of them stayed with Mr. Hanh more than twenty minutes, hardly enough time for a minor tune-up. When I walked in, he was in his usual place in the far corner, cross-legged on his mat next to his plaid thermos of fruit juice. He was a dead ringer for the Dalai Lama, smaller and darker, but the same glasses, the same shaved head and orange robes, and, especially, the same facial muscles that were either smiling or about to, with infinite compassion for all living creatures, twinkly-eyed, welcoming, unshockable.

I sat down facing him where one always did, on the mat in the center of the room.

"How are you today, Mr. Hanh?"

"I am breathing. And you?" This was always his answer.

"Barely breathing." This was always mine.

"I see you are very troubled today. Great turmoil in your soul."

"Yes."

"You speak. I will listen."

I took a deep breath and dumped out everything. He nodded every few seconds, apparently amused at what seemed to me the worst stuff: my untrustworthy impulses, my crashing-and-burning career, my demented adventure with Angela. I speculated that it was reading the report about Angela that had finally unnerved me, or maybe it was realizing what I had done to Doris, or Don reminding me of what Doris might do to me.

When I was finished, Mr. Hanh waited, smiling.

"This is everything?" he asked.

I said it was.

"Not so bad. Now we will breathe together."

We did, for at least a half hour. When I opened my eyes, he was looking at me.

"You are here now?" he asked.

"I guess so," I said.

"Going to lose what you've got, not get what you want. Going to lose what you've got, not get what you want," he repeated a number of times. Then he clapped once. "Here is the moment," he said. "Catch it." He clapped again. This entertained him no end.

"I can't do it," I said.

"Yes," he said. "You are too hungry."

"I'm either fantasizing, or criticizing, or regretting. I'm afraid of everything."

"What do those statements have in common?"

"Tell me," I said.

"I," he said.

"I'm stuck in myself," I admitted.

"What is humility?"

"I have no idea."

"Freedom from self."

"How do I get it?"

"You can't 'get' it."

"Then how does it happen?"

"You must be broken. There must be no choice."

"I think I'm falling apart," I said.

"Very good," Mr. Hanh said. "But you are resisting it. In the resistance is the pain."

"I'm afraid," I repeated.

"Why?"

"I don't want to be insane. Or destitute. Or alone."

"Going to lose what you've got, not get what you want. Are you afraid right now? What is going to hurt you?"

"Doris."

"I don't see anyone here but us."

"I want Angela."

"Have a fruit juice instead," he smiled and poured me a little plastic cupful.

I drank a sip.

"It tastes very good, doesn't it?"

I said it did.

"It's delicious, is it not?"

I admitted it was.

"Physical pleasure. It is lovely. What weather we're having. Sunny but mild. You have enough to eat today. A place to sleep. Your health is excellent, yes? No problems. Mindfulness is all you lack. We are like children. Something shiny dances in front of us and we want it. Perhaps we get it so we are fooled into thinking we can get the next shiny thing and the next and the next. Hunger is infinite. It is eating you. Your hunger is not yours, Robert. You are its."

"I can't stop it," I said.

"Of course you can. But it requires humility. Breathe. Be here now. There is nothing else. Bring reality to mind, bring mind to reality. Mindfulness. Stay in the moment."

"Should I perform tomorrow night?"

"Will you enjoy yourself?"

"I don't know."

"Then I don't know either. Are there others involved?"

"I suppose so."

"Then be kind to them. Don't worry about yourself."

"What if I have a nervous breakdown on stage?"

"Then that is what happens."

"What if I cancel?"

"Then that is what happens. Ask the questions without using I."

"They don't make sense."

"Exactly."

"Who can imagine the world without himself in it?"

"On the contrary, to be fully in it, but only a teeny teeny part of it." He pinched the air in front of his nose to show how small I was. "You are no different from anyone else, Robert. The two people who visited me before you are no different from you. I am no different from you. We only appear different from one another. I have all of your fears and desires. They pass through me. I watch them. They are entertaining."

"How do you decide whether or not to accept an invitation to lecture?"

"Very simple. I accept all invitations. I solicit none."

"Aren't you ever frustrated?"

"I enjoy the tricks the mind plays on us. Our heads are frightfully talkative."

"Mine is driving me crazy."

"Yes," he said. "Stop listening. Or listen and be entertained."

I actually got a glimmer of what he meant. Only a glimmer, but it was like a crack of light inside a cave.

"Thank you," I said.

"Life is joyful," Mr. Hanh said. "If you understand this, you will make others feel joyful also. Then you will feel it more and more yourself."

"I will try," I said, getting up to leave, and shaking his hand.

"Trying is precisely the wrong approach," Mr. Hanh said, laughing. "I'm so glad you have learned nothing from me today."

I wasn't sure how to take this. He wasn't being ironic. He did seem genuinely glad I had learned nothing from him.

There was a basket by the door filled with money. You paid what you wanted to pay for Mr. Hanh's time. The perverse part of me wanted to go every day without dropping any money in the basket until he mentioned it, but this surely would have only entertained him too.

13.

When I got home I called Advantage Private Investigators, Sheed's subcontractor that prepared the report on Angela. The secretary said that number one, they didn't have any more information to give me, and number two, if they did they would be giving it to Mr. Sheed since they were working for him not me.

Then I locked my doors and dropped the blinds and spent the evening with Sparky and a fresh box of veggie burritos (which still tasted like mittens but not frozen mittens). I tried to sketch out a routine for the Irvine Improv that would be neither deranged nor false. I only knew one way to perform: to speak the twisted truth about my life. But I also knew a lot of jokes. And why not give myself a breather (a la Mr. Hanh)? A drop-dead performance wasn't required every time, and I wasn't exactly being carried off the stage on the audience's shoulders anyway. I started writing down all the jokes I knew. They were all about sex, of course. Black comics talk about being black, women comics talk about being women, and white male comics talk about sex. But there was something behind the pattern the jokes made, something I might be able to talk about: it was surely as much about me as about the culture, since these were the jokes *I* loved, but, with luck, it was about the culture, too, and about other people, about something more than myself. I wouldn't find out what it was until the moment it shaped itself on stage. If it turned out to be nothing, I'd end up standing there with my pants down and my dick in my hand. But maybe that was what I needed to quit this business and begin doing something useful: an old-fashioned public humiliation.

Don called at ten. He had read the file. He didn't express much more sympathy for what he called my "infatuation" with Angela than he had at lunch, although he admitted that there must be something substantial in her to endure if in fact she had gone through both parents' suicides and now was risking her life to rescue her troubled brother. I didn't expect more from him than that. I didn't expect him to see what I saw in Angela. I *really* couldn't see what he saw in Francine. I never met a friend's wife I would marry. But then I never met anybody I would marry, including, as it turned out, Doris. According to Don, Angela was just me in the mirror, in love with my own fantasy—if in fact Angela was even her real name.

"What do you mean?" I asked.

"The brother business," he answered.

"What? The kidnapping? What?"

"I'm not sure. The whole story about the ransom seems fabricated. I think Francine knew somebody named Angela Chase from somewhere, maybe from UCLA or some women's group or something. If I can figure out how to ask her about Angela without arousing her suspicion that I was asking for you, I'll do it. If she knew I was asking her about the woman you were screwing when you stood up Doris, she'd grind me into hamburger and use me for pasta sauce."

"But why would Sheed lie? I don't get it."

"I don't either. I haven't figured out that part yet. The whole thing just doesn't add up. How did Sheed get all that information in—what?—twenty hours? On a Sunday night when the rest of the world was asleep?"

"What do you know about Sheed anyway?"

"Not much more than you. You met him, I haven't. I watched him win my bozo brother-in-law's trial, which was some feat, I'll tell you. He's supposed to be the best. All behind the scenes now, never goes into a courtroom himself anymore. Doesn't need to. Hates publicity, hates the press. Used to work at the White House. Likes private dinner parties with heads of state. Still gets lots of calls from political pooh-bahs for advice. He seems to know as much about power as anyone in this town, and that's saying something."

"Would he lie to me?"

"If he had to. Sure. But he'd call it interpreting the facts. I don't think people like Sheed believe there is any truth. Only fallible human impressions, subject to his expert adjustment."

This idea did not fill me with bliss. I sat there holding the phone, trying to run through the implications and possible scenarios. None of them was very clear. If Sheed was lying, I needed to find out why he was lying in order to reckon what might be in store for me—which in any case was probably not a free lunch and a foot rub.

"Did you faint?" Don asked, after a minute of my silence. "Or drop dead?"

"I dropped dead. My last words were 'Thank you, dear Don, for recommending such a trustworthy lawyer to work in my behalf. Remind me to put my fate in your hands the next time my life depends on it.'"

"Only the best for you, pal."

"So did you screw me on purpose as payback for standing you up at the wedding?"

"How was I supposed to know Sheed would do whatever it is he's doing? If he's doing anything. Where can I reach you tomorrow?"

I said I was going to drop off Sparky at Madge's and head down to Orange County and he said he would call me at the Laguna Hotel. I apologized for not being able to help search for information about Angela myself, but reminded him that my computer was temporarily unavailable.

"At least it is not yet polluting Santa Monica Bay with your perverse sense of humor," he said.

"That's it! Tell Doris that if she throws my computer into the ocean she'll be committing an environmental crime. She donates about $40,000 a year to the whales."

"Look at it this way," he said. "You only have to stay out of trouble until Friday and the week is over. And it will be your unwedding's one-week anniversary. When Francine comes home, we'll go shop for your anniversary present."

"There's nothing in Orange County but Republicans and golf courses. How could I get into trouble?"

"How could you get into trouble?" Don said. "That *is* funny. You're going to kill at the Irvine Improv."

"Great. I just don't want to *be* killed."

THE NEXT morning after I dropped Sparky at Madge's, I headed up Lincoln Boulevard toward the entrance ramp to the 10 East that would lead me onto the 405 South to Irvine, but on an impulse turned around and drove directly to Sheed's office. I couldn't wait for Don. I had hardly slept. I had to have some answers.

The same guy was working the valet stand outside of Sheed's office building.

"*Buenas dias, señor!*" he said enthusiastically, when he opened the Big Spender's car door. This was going to cost me another five buck tip, even if I did remember to ask Tori to stamp the ticket, or else I'd be responsible for ruining this man's day. I again had to give my driver's license to the security guard before he'd unlock the elevator to Sheed's penthouse offices. He was a black guy in his fifties with a polite smile and a hip holster with a big gun in it. Since I didn't have an appointment, he called Tori on the house phone, and said, "I got a customer for you."

When I stepped off the elevator, I saw her at her desk. Today's outfit was made of some bright pink material that probably had a useful former life as a neon sign. It was so tight it looked like a sunburn. When she wanted to take it off, it would have to be removed by surgical peel.

"That was fast," she said, as I walked toward her.

"Your elevator is usually slower?"

"Nooo," she laughed, as if I had produced a great witticism. "I just called your house. I left you a message. I hang up and here you are."

"What was the message?" I asked.

"Mr. Keene, our entertainment specialist, has gone over your HBO contract and is ready to meet with you. In fact, you can see him now if you want to. I think he's available."

"I actually came to see Sheed."

"Oh, you can't see Mr. Sheed. He never sees clients without an appointment. He's booked all day. You'd be lucky to see him before next month."

"I've got to see him, Tori. It's urgent."

"Robert," she said, sincerely. "Really, it's impossible. I can't even ring him for you. He left strict instructions. I wish I could do something. I'd be fired if I disobeyed him. Do you want to write a note or something? I promise to give it to him as soon as I can."

"Sure, thanks," I said. She handed me a pen and a memo pad with "Folsom Sheed and Associates" in florid script embossed across the top. I wrote:

> I found out something interesting about Angela's brother: she doesn't have one. What the hell is going on?
>
>   Robert Wilder

I folded the paper and handed it to her.

"Would you mind sealing that in an envelope?" I asked. She took one out of a drawer and licked the edge of its flap very slowly with her tongue tip, meeting my eyes as she licked, but my mind was on the note I just wrote. I had had no idea what I was going to write when the pen touched the paper, but, after I wrote it, I knew it was true. Something really weird was going on. Sheed had lied to me. I wanted him to know that I knew it. The next move was his.

I told Tori that I didn't want to talk about my HBO contract right now, that I was going to be out of town for a few days and I would call when I got back.

"So," she said after a pause, "guess what other message I left on your answering machine."

"Pick up the dry cleaning and a quart of milk on the way home?"

"A comedian," she said. "That's all right. I like a challenge."

"I'd like to find out what else you like," I said. "Let me work out this problem I've got with Sheed. Then I'll have more messages for you than you can handle."

"Oh, I can handle them," she said. "Don't worry about that."

I wanted to jump over the desk into Tori Lalala. But I didn't. I said I'd call her in a few days.

"Better not wait longer than a few days," she said. "I never go a week without a boyfriend. I've got a big appetite."

I laughed out loud at that on the elevator, but who was I to laugh? At least she knew who she was, and was unashamed of it. What was I doing even considering starting something with Tori (of the two red-ink hearts) much less saying what I had just said to her? That question was too easy to answer. But we'd have the shelf life of a leafy vegetable.

By the time the elevator doors opened onto the lobby, I remembered that yet again I hadn't asked her to validate my parking ticket, and yet again I couldn't bring myself to go back up there.

When I handed the parking attendant the twenty-five bucks, he said, "If you are looking for a charity, I can tell you some good ones. The guy who owns the valet concession here, he's doing fine."

I just smiled. He shook his head, got my car, and held the door for me. I pressed the folded fiver into his hand.

"You come back, señor. I'm always glad to see you."

I'm sure he was. At least somebody was telling me the truth.

14.

I had three fortunately quiet days in Laguna Beach and three unfortunately quiet nights at the Irvine Improv. Opening night—Tuesday—I drew eight people. Eight. Not enough for a softball game, even if I pitched for both sides. Ken Mishima apologized before I went on, saying he had beaten the bushes telling everybody he knew not to miss my gig, but he guessed you couldn't be off the circuit as long as I had and expect people to remember you. That was supposed to make me feel better? Oddly I didn't care. I was exhilarated to be in front of a mic again. The last five days since I walked into the Bank of America to cash a check became funny. My life became funny. Nothing seemed like a big deal anymore. My self-concern, self-concern in general, became amusing. Even the fact that I drew an audience of eight people seemed amusing. Two retired couples from Leisure World on a double date and four lonely guys who looked like they had nobody to be with and nowhere else to go. When I picked up the mic, I said, "Hi, I'm Robert. I'm a piece of shit the universe revolves around."

I invited them all to move to tables close to the stage, which many people won't do because they're afraid the comic is going to mock them. I asked for volunteers to tell me their professions. Nobody raised his hand. I told them not to feel self-conscious since they could see by the standing-room-only crowd that I may not have made the best career choice myself. Still nobody raised his hand. I said, "What am I going to say? Oh, you're a trauma surgeon. Well, fuck you." Then they laughed and opened up and we had a good time. I told them about the cartoon of the retired guy with three days' growth of beard reading a book in bed entitled *How To Get Up And Get Dressed*. The lonely guys thought that one was very funny.

The truth is, the audience is a lot funnier than any comedian. The more the audience is packed together the easier for them to laugh. Their laughter becomes infectious. They become a single organism. That's what's fun. The challenge for me was to make White American Middle Class Thirtysomething Guy Behavior at the End of the Twentieth Century sufficiently specific to be both recognizable and ridiculous: moral mastodons limping into extinction, our hypocrisies and habits in tatters and exposed like Nineteenth-Century British colonialists dressing for high tea in the jungles of Africa— or like me on my treadmill running to endless relationship workshops with Doris and driving my Z hoping to score with the babes.

I told them about Angela, sort of. I told them I had spent a night with a woman who left the next morning before I woke up. I tried to call her, but she had given me a false name. Do you think she was trying to communicate something? A certain limit on our relationship? A certain reservation about our future? I said I had been out of the dating scene for so long maybe the protocol had changed. Maybe it had all become speed dating: one minute for talk, one minute for sex, and zero minutes to break up. Actually I thought that was a great idea. If all my relationships were compressed like that, I could date every woman on the planet. Maybe I could even find someone who would give me her real name.

There's only one show a night in midweek gigs, Tuesday–Thursday: on at eight, out by ten. I was back at the Laguna Hotel by eleven. Don's message was waiting for me at the front desk. I picked it up and read it:

No brother. Will call you Friday.

That was it, six words scribbled by the front desk clerk on a Laguna Hotel notepad. I took the elevator to my room, walked in, and sat down in a chair facing the ocean. Spotlights from the hotel roof illuminated the sand and rocks and crashing surf, black shattered into ethereal foamy whiteness. I was right. Sheed had lied. And if there wasn't any brother, then there wasn't any kidnapping and there wasn't any ransom. The 200 grand in Angela's purse must have been for some other purpose, a purpose that, for whatever reason, Sheed didn't want me to know. Why? What was the money for? There was no sense trying to guess. I might never find out what Angela Chase was doing with that money or with me, or even if Angela Chase was her real name. Maybe she had stolen the name of a dead person, or Sheed had, or she would suddenly appear at my hotel room wearing a crotchless Donald Duck outfit and smoking a Cuban cigar.

What do I do now? I asked myself. I did what I always do. I called my answering machine. There was one message:

Mr. Wilder. Folsom Sheed calling. I'd be happy to meet with you at your convenience. Please call Tori and make an appointment.

Click. Beep. Beep beep beep. The end.

All right, I thought. What's behind that? I have never been able to figure out other people's hidden motivations, my own always being embarrassingly obvious. Sheed's willingness to meet with me might be just his slick way to string me along. But I couldn't be sure of that either, could I? Since he knew I knew he had lied, maybe he was afraid of what I might do, although I myself had no idea what that could be. Maybe *I* should be afraid of what *he* might do.

I took a deep breath and remembered Mr. Hanh telling me I was too hungry, that my hunger wasn't mine but I was its. I had gone to see Sheed in the first place not to find out anything about Sabine aka Angela, but to find out if I was an accessory to a bank robbery. I thought I needed a lawyer. I came out of his office enthralled with someone named Angela Chase who had risked her life to save her brother. But Angela was no more real than Sabine. She was nothing but my hunger, a fantasy creation, myself in the mirror. Don was right. Mr. Hanh was right. People put themselves in each other's power when they have sex together. This is what had happened to me.

My poor-me victim story served the good purpose of releasing me from obsessing about Angela for a couple of days. It was in any case pretty hard to obsess about anything in Laguna Beach, with the air at skin temperature and the ocean as background music. The world felt benign and seam- less, as if it actually were made for humans to live in, despite the economic brutalities such lily-white upper-class paradise islands are built upon. Maybe I should move here and have weekly high colonics and eat nothing but organic root veg- etables. I spent Wednesday and Thursday wandering around the town and taking long walks on the beach dissecting my routine, playing it over in my mind, changing it, moving this here and that there. Everybody I walked past seemed at ease, in contrast to LA—nobody acted like they were about to steal your wallet or you were about to steal theirs. It would be eerie to live here, and I'm sure there was plenty else going on underneath this surface, but it was perfect for me now to soak up the quintessential Southern California sun until I calmed down. The only one I missed was Sparky.

The 405 after the Thursday night show was like driving back from Baja: clear and clean, a straight shot, with the great jazz station out of Long Beach on my pumped Bose stereo (standard equipment in the Z). It put me in a good mood, the best I had been in since my Angela adventure. I might have a career again. The audience at the Irvine Improv wasn't much bigger on Wednesday than on Tuesday, but on Thursday the retired double-dating couples brought in a whole minibusful from Leisure World. Since they had all probably seen *Psycho* when it came out in 1960. I did my three-minute rendition of the movie complete with my screeching violin imitation when Norman Bates pulls back the shower curtain dressed in his dead mother's hair bun. Happily I had brought along my gray hair bun, lace collar, and two-foot cardboard knife. They loved it. They yelled out other Hitchcock movies and I did them too. I hadn't performed this routine in years but it was all still there. I couldn't remember the last time I played to an audience who had even heard of Cary Grant, much less Tippi Hedren trying to swat the birds out of her bouffant. Maybe I could specialize in wealthy retirement communities. I might become AARP's Comedian of the Year. I felt renewed and purposeful. Maybe I wouldn't even call Sheed. What was the hook there? Angela? The hell with Angela. The hell with women. I'd burn the pure flame. I'd sign the HBO contract, I'd take Charles's gig at the Apollo, I'd find a new agent. It's all *lieben und arbeiten*, according to Freud: love and work, the best things in life. Screw *lieben*, up with *arbeiten*.

Even at the time, I suspected these ideas were chemically induced by the adrenaline megadose of a good performance. Having hopped into the Z right after the show, I hadn't come down during the fifty-minute trafficless drive from Irvine to Santa Monica. I was sailing when I pulled into my driveway. My life was going to be entirely different. Watch out world, here comes Robert Wilder! It was about midnight. I popped the hatchback, grabbed my suitcase, and rolled it behind me up to my door.

The door was open, about three inches. I thought, Krista. Oh well, here we go again. Back to reality. The lights were out and it was dark. I pushed the door open, stepped inside, and flipped the lights on. There she was all right, sitting at my desk with her back to me, wearing a black robe and head scarf (a real one, not my underwear)—full orthodox Islamic regalia. She had clearly lost it completely.

"My God, Krista," I said. "Now what?"

She swiveled around in my desk chair like Mrs. Bates's skeleton, her black eyes above her veil crinkled in amusement. I'd recognize those eyes blindfolded. They weren't Krista's.

"Hello, Robert," Angela said. She detached the veil, revealing that preternatural mouth of hers arranged in her signature lopsided grin. Why did she have to be so gorgeous? Her beauty made me angry.

"I don't believe it," I said to myself, aloud. What chutzpah. I sat down across the room in my recliner and stared fiercely at her.

"You may be wondering why I'm wearing the hijab," she said.

"I don't care if you're wearing a tutu and antlers," I said. "What are you doing here? What do you want?"

"I need to talk to you."

"Well, here I am. Talk."

"I need you to leave with me. Right now."

"What? Where?"

"If I told you I'd have to kill you."

"Ha. Ha," I said. But I couldn't keep myself from smiling. "If you don't mind, I'll do the jokes."

"I wish it were a joke. I can't tell you where I'm going until you go with me. If you don't go with me you'll be dead before morning."

"Are you fucking crazy? *Go* with you? When I last saw you your name was Sabine and you worked in a bank. I haven't heard from you since your amusing departure from our blissful honeymoon suite. Your pal Folsom Sheed made up some bullshit story about your brother being kidnapped when you don't even have a brother. I have no idea if your name is actually Angela Chase or Daisy Duck. I have no idea why you got me to drive you and your money to Mexico, but it probably wasn't for you to donate it to charity and work in a leper colony. Now you appear in my apartment sitting in my desk chair in the dark dressed like a Muslim. Oh sure, I'd be happy to go with you. I know a nice cliff we can drive over together."

"Of course," Angela said. "I realize you weren't exactly expecting a visit quite like this, much less the news that your life's in danger. And why would you trust me? Don't you think I knew you wouldn't? But I'm telling you the truth."

"You *are* a comedian. I love the straight delivery. Not to mention the Muslim thing. It really works."

She just looked at me sadly.

"I'm sorry I hurt you, okay? But I didn't get you killed. Yet. At the risk of repeating myself, there are elite operatives tracking me right now. They know you drove me to Mexico and they may have been here already looking for you and they will not be nice to you if they find you. They could be five hours away or five minutes. But we don't have time to argue about it."

"But I couldn't tell them anything. I don't know anything about you."

"Unfortunately, they wouldn't buy that."

I stood up from my recliner, and looked out the window as if to espy the "elite operatives" hiding in the bushes. As if I could have done anything but whimper if I actually saw them.

"Jesus fucking Christ," I said, sitting down again. "Is this what you do to all your dates?"

"I don't have 'dates,'" she answered. "Look, what possible motive could I have for coming here but to save your life? I know perfectly well you couldn't tell them anything that would lead them to me. Think about it for one second. Give me one good reason why I'm trying to get you out of here."

She had me there.

"Well?" she said.

"I don't know now, but I'm afraid I'll find out later."

"You don't have to trust me," she said. "You just have to believe me."

Bizarrely, I did. I don't know why but I knew she was telling the truth. Weirdly—like when I wrote the note to Sheed. Why not go with her? What if she *were* actually telling the truth? I certainly had more to lose not going than going. My life, for example. I knew she wouldn't kill me, but the ninjas with their automatic pistols surrounding my apartment appeared in my mind and I started shaking.

"I must be crazy even to consider this."

"You won't regret it. I promise."

I looked hard at her. She didn't flinch. Either she was telling the truth, or she was the best liar who has ever lived.

"One more question," I said. "Did you read Sheed's report about you?"

"I wrote it."

"How much of it was true?"

"UCLA, Paris, my parents. My name *is* Angela Chase. The rest is fiction. With a lot left out."

"Good story," I said. "You ought to write novels."

"Let's go," she said. "You can bring your suitcase."

15.

I rolled my suitcase out to the car, popped the hatchback, and threw it in (ten minutes after I had taken it out), still stuffed with my dirty underwear, the gamy shirts I had performed in, and Norman Bates's gray hair bun, lace collar, and two-foot cardboard knife. Good, I thought, I might need a weapon. And my cardboard knife was surely as effective against "elite operatives" as any high-tech pistol I had no idea how to use, except possibly to blow my dick off—which, had I had the good sense to perform before I met Angela, would have kept me from being in this lunatic situation in the first place.

Angela was quite jolly when I got in to the car. She was clearly one of those people who become calm and focused in dangerous circumstances—SWAT cops, ER nurses, mercenaries who reportedly enjoy battle—very much unlike me. I hadn't stopped shaking since I pictured the ninjas surrounding my apartment. For all I knew, they had their missile launcher aimed at my car or it would blow up when I turned the ignition. But no way was I letting Angela see I was scared.

"Ah, the Z," Angela said, as if relaxing into a warm bath. "I had forgotten the scent of pure testosterone."

"Would you mind telling me where I'm driving? Or would you rather I intuit it?" I asked, backing out of the driveway.

"Santa Monica Airport. 'Would you rather intuit it?': isn't that what I asked you when you drove me to Malibu?"

"I never forget a joke," I said. "Just everything else. Like how to get to Santa Monica Airport."

"Down Ocean up Pico. Twenty-Third Street and across. It's only a couple miles from here. Haven't you ever been there?"

"Why would *I* go there? No commercial flights, only private jets."

"Correct."

"We're flying somewhere, in a private jet."

"Correct."

"My prospects are improving already," I said.

"The jet is probably standard government issue. We'll be lucky if it has a rubber-band propeller."

"So we're on a government mission?" I asked.

"Sort of. Enough questions. We're not flying anywhere unless we get to the airport alive."

I checked the rearview mirrors to see if we were being followed. Nothing. This was fortunate, since I somehow missed the High Speed Evasive Maneuvers unit in high school driver's ed. I also failed to choose the armor-plate and bulletproof windows option when I bought my Z. The streets were empty and we hit all the lights on Ocean Avenue green. The homeless people in the long skinny park fronting the Pacific were bedded down in clumps, orange and olive sleeping bags and trash bags full of clothes and all their worldly belongings clustered together so they wouldn't be robbed or worse during the night. Santa Monica is actually a sleepy town. If anybody goes out after midnight, they go to Hollywood or somewhere else. We'd arrive at the airport in five minutes.

"So that's a lovely outfit you're wearing this evening," I said to Angela, referring to her hijab (black ankle-length robe, black head scarf, black veil revealing only her eyes). "My *Nice Guys Dating Manual* said that's what I'm supposed to say first thing on a date. Oh, I forgot, you don't have 'dates.'"

"You ever try to pee in one of these things in an airplane bathroom?" Angela asked. "Oh, I forgot, you're a guy."

"I often forget I'm a guy too," I said. "I haven't been in a high-speed chase for weeks. I'm also not a Muslim, as far as I know. So what's the deal with the getup?"

"Harder to see in the dark, for one thing. Did you spot that black Mercedes?"

"What black Mercedes?" I yelled. I almost went through the moon roof.

"It was parked. Its lights flicked on as we passed it. Anything behind you?"

"Nothing," I said, frantically checking the mirrors.

"All right, watch out. If there're two cars, one will signal the car ahead to block the road."

"Oh my God," I said.

"Take a left down this alley and a right on Twenty-Fourth. Then right down the next alley and left onto Twenty-Third again."

She was as serene as Saint Theresa instructing a novitiate. I did what she said and, after a few terrifying blocks of racing up and down alleys and scanning intersections for ambushes, we were almost at the airport. I could see it ahead of us. Nobody followed us. Nobody rammed us and machine-gunned our car. Did Angela invent the black Mercedes to go with the ninjas in their black bodysuits? Was she making up the whole story? I had to remind myself that I believed her. She certainly could have seen a black Mercedes I hadn't noticed. Half the cars in Santa Monica are Mercedeses.

"Which gate?" I asked her.

"Any gate," she said. "They know me. They'll want to see your driver's license."

"What do I do with my car?"

"You'll have to burn it," Angela said.

"What? Are you kidding?"

She put her hand on my forearm—the first touch since Mexico. I wished it didn't feel so good.

"Yes, Robert," she said sweetly. "I am kidding. You give your car to the valet and he gives you a little yellow ticket stub. You put the ticket stub in your wallet. You give the ticket stub to the valet when you return and he gives you your car. Just like a normal airport."

"Not funny," I said.

"Oh, you are *such* a Guy guy about this car," she said, affectionately.

We stopped at a guardhouse next to an electronic ten-foot gate with thick steel bars you couldn't drive through with a tank. The guard somehow recognized Angela in her hijab and he wrote down my information on a log-in sheet and asked me to sign it and told us to drive to Sheed's plane, which was waiting for us on the apron with its motors running.

The gate slid open and we drove inside and it closed behind us. *Sheed's* plane? What was Angela's connection to Sheed? I guessed I was about to find out. We drove past a few hangars and rows of parked puddle-jumpers and weekenders, two- and four-seaters with no bathroom and under 500-mile fuel capacity, which didn't rate inside parking. The low-rollers: a mere million or less. How humiliating for them.

"So we're flying in Sheed's plane?" I asked Angela. "Why not Frank Sinatra's?"

"I don't think you'll be disappointed," she answered. "There it is."

A one-hundred-foot-long jet was sitting in front of us with boarding stairs leading to its open door. It had thirteen porthole windows on each side. (I counted them.)

"Are we transporting a battalion?" I asked.

"I think it's just us," Angela answered. "If Folsom's coming along, he'll be on board. Stop the car here."

I did and we got out of the car and the valet appeared out of nowhere and handed me a little yellow ticket stub. I did a double take. It was the same guy who parked cars in front of Sheed's office.

"*Buenos* noches, *señor*," he said, merrily emphasizing the *noches*.

"You're working late," I said.

"My wife likes to have babies," he said. "The babies like to eat."

"Well, I'm not going to lose this baby," I said, holding up the ticket stub.

"I'll believe it when I see it," he answered.

I walked up to the front of my car, embraced the left fender, and kissed it tenderly good-bye—for Angela's benefit, although the valet laughed as well.

"I will take good care of your beloved," he said.

"His beloved. You've got that right," Angela said to the valet.

I popped the hatchback and pulled out my suitcase yet again and rolled it behind me to the plane.

"I wonder if James Bond rolled an overnight bag behind him on dangerous missions," I said to Angela when I caught up to her.

"James Bond is an asshole," Angela said.

"Gee, I always thought he was super cool," I said to irk her, deliberately bouncing my suitcase up the boarding stairs.

The plane inside did not have thirteen rows of seats, or any rows of seats for that matter. It looked like the preferred customer lounge in a Las Vegas casino. Everything was beige—dark beige carpet, light beige suede walls and ceiling, deep beige leather armchairs and sofas arranged around coffee tables and facing big-screen TVs. The only thing missing were hostesses in strapless French maid outfits and fishnet stockings ferrying cocktails on little silver trays. Sheed was sitting at a table for four covered by a white linen tablecloth eating a steak and drinking a glass of red wine.

"Won't you join me, Mr. Wilder?" he asked, without saying hello, apparently expecting me. "Georges would be happy to fry you up a steak." He pronounced "Georges" in flawless French and "fry you up a steak" with a country boy twang.

I shook my head no. Fear takes away my appetite.

"How about you, Angela? There's also sea bass caught this afternoon and a nice Montrachet to go with it."

"That sounds perfect," Angela said. She undid two Velcro strips at her neck and off went the head scarf and robe. Underneath she was wearing jeans and a white dress shirt. Hanging from a waist-length strap under her collar was a big black machine pistol. She bent her neck and looped the strap over her head and dropped the gun into a chair, then sat down next to Sheed as if she had done nothing unusual whatsoever.

The pistol had a separate handle and magazine, so it could be fired with one hand or two, one of those assault weapons used by mass murderers and SWAT teams and SEALs in close combat. I had never seen one before except in movies. The real thing was nasty. It looked like carnage incarnate, bodies piled and blood pooled so thick you'd slip on it. Angela and Sheed both noticed me staring at the gun.

"That's another reason I was wearing the robe," she said to me. "I didn't want to alarm you."

"It certainly would have," I said. "It certainly *does*."

"We might have needed it on the ride here, but there was no sense making you any more nervous than you were," Angela said.

So much for my acting like I wasn't scared. No Academy Award for Best Performance by an Actor While Shitting His Pants.

Still, her remark sounded condescending, implying I'm not the man that she is. As if to answer my thought, she reached up and removed a hair net and fluffed her hair with both hands, raising her arms and pushing her shoulders back and chest forward, a female gesture that always gets my attention. I looked at her breasts and neck and face. I looked at *her*. Her eyes locked on mine.

"It's still me, Robert," she said.

"Please take a seat, Mr. Wilder," Sheed said, motioning to the chair across from him and ignoring this exchange between Angela and me, or in any case not caring in the least about it. "You'll find a seat belt in the chair and we're taking off in a minute. You're sure you're not hungry?"

"Okay, I'll have the steak," I said. "But I don't think I can eat it."

"What are you going to do with it?" Angela asked. "Resole your shoes?"

"Not with this steak," Sheed said. "It melts in your mouth."

He pressed a button on an intercom. "Georges, another *filet de beouf au poivre* for Mr. Wilder, please," he said. I now noticed the wine was a 1974 Chateau Margaux Margaux (about $800 a bottle). I guessed I would have a glass after all.

"Good," Sheed said. The consummate host. He poured me $150 worth or so, and toasted Angela.

"To the most remarkable woman I know," he said. "Don't you think so, Mr. Wilder?"

"Could be," I said. "I don't know her."

"I have never worked with anyone better at what she does," Sheed said.

"And what does she do, Mr. Sheed?" I asked. Angela showed no visible response to our talking about her as if she weren't present.

"I'll let her tell you that herself," he answered. The plane picked up speed and left the ground, the wheels clunking into place under our table. Sheed continued eating without a pause. Angela said nothing. It was as if she were deflating gently after being pumped beyond maximum pressure. Her sea bass and Montrachet appeared and she began eating, too, very slowly. I watched them enjoying their meals in silence, relaxing, savoring every flavor, clearly appreciating Georges's talents. Obviously they felt no urgency to explain anything whatsoever to me. Maybe they planned to sit here and eat gourmet meals for the rest of their lives. When I finally spoke it seemed they had forgotten I was there.

"Not to intrude on your fine dining experience but I think you both owe me a few explanations?"

"Yes, we have a lot to talk about," Sheed answered. "Shall we start with your questions?"

"Sure," I said. "I've got an interesting one: Just what the fuck is going on here? I mean, I'm glad you're enjoying your meal and all but I have no idea what you two are involved in or where we're going or what the hell I'm doing here except for Angela's story that someone was about to kill me."

"*That* is true," Sheed said.

"Would you mind telling me who?"

"It's a little complicated. I'll have to tell you the whole story to explain it."

"Okay," I said. "Let's start at the end and go backward: where are we going?"

"Washington," Sheed answered.

"Washington," I repeated. "Why not? Okay, why are we going to Washington?"

"To meet with the president," Sheed answered.

"The president," I repeated.

"Bill Clinton," Sheed said. "And Richard Clarke, his counter-terrorism expert on the National Security Council."

"So this is a joke, right?" I asked Angela.

"Folsom will explain everything, Robert," she said to me. Then to Sheed, "This sea bass is delicious. And the Montrachet is wonderful."

Sheed smiled and nodded. "Georges is a genius. It's not a joke, Mr. Wilder," he said without a pause or transition between the two sentences. "I work for the president and Angela works for me."

"You work for the president and Angela works for you," I repeated yet again.

"Correct," Sheed said.

I glanced at Angela to see her reaction to what Sheed had told me: none whatsoever. She didn't even look up from her fish.

Georges brought my *filet de beouf au poivre* and Sheed refreshed my wine. I cut the meat and put a bite in my mouth with a sip of the Margaux. It was beyond delicious. No wonder they weren't talking while they ate. "I work for the president and Angela works for me": Sheed had said the sentence with the intonation of "Cloudy today and rain tomorrow." Don said Sheed had Washington connections. I realized there must be other people in the world like these two. People who did secret shit for the rich and powerful and flew on private jets and drank $800 bottles of wine. I had just never met them. Nor had I ever wanted to. And I didn't want to now, despite the best steak and wine I ever had or was likely to have again.

"All right," I said. "Let's try it from the beginning instead of the end. If I have any questions I'll ask them when you're finished telling me the whole story."

Sheed spoke. Angela didn't say a word. She seemed to go into sleep mode without closing her eyes. I wondered if along with her other unusual characteristics she had developed some Yoga-master technique to control her body as she put it through what she needed it to do, which sometimes must have been beyond human limits. Two minutes into Sheed's narrative, she got up and said, "I'm going to bed. Good night, gentlemen." She had eaten only half her fish. She picked up her pistol and hijab like a lunchbox and coveralls after the double shift at the fertilizer plant and staggered back to the bedroom suite at the rear of the plane.

Sheed said, "She's hardly slept for the past week and insisted on rushing to your apartment the minute she touched down from Islamabad."

"What was she doing in Islamabad? Is that where she went from Mexico with the $200,000?"

"Eventually," he said. "But it was a lot more money by the time she got there. We may as well start with Angela, since that's what interests you the most." Sheed offered me the last of the Margaux, which I declined, then he emptied the bottle into his glass, took a long swallow, and began his story.

"I met Angela when she was only eighteen years old and I was Los Angeles district attorney. As the report you read said, her father killed himself. What it didn't say is he killed himself after her mother confessed that she was having an affair with her psychiatrist. Angela came to my office six months later, after her mother also killed herself, cruelly on Angela's eighteenth birthday. Angela had tried to persuade her mother to report the psychiatrist—apparently very vehemently. They had been fighting about it since her father's death. Angela believed the psychiatrist was responsible for both her parents' deaths. Maybe he was, but I had no basis for an investigation. There was no crime committed if the affair was consensual. It's a civil matter, not a criminal case. So entirely on her own—remember this is an eighteen-year-old just out of high school—Angela goes to the psychiatrist's office wearing a wire pretending to be suicidal herself. For whatever reason, he was suspicious and she didn't get anything on tape I could use. Then I received an invitation to work in Washington, and the new DA had no interest in the case."

I pictured Angela as an eighteen-year-old freshman and tried to recall ever seeing her on the UCLA campus or anywhere else. Sheed noticed I had become distracted but didn't try to guess why.

"Are you still with me, Mr. Wilder? As I was saying, Angela impressed me very deeply throughout the whole sordid business. Despite being devastated by what happened, she was strong, focused, and determined, remarkably so for one so young. So much so in fact that when I got to Washington I recruited her, and she's been working for me in various capacities ever since—starting as an undergraduate at UCLA. What could be better cover? No one would suspect someone so young and looked like her—a UCLA coed, a cheerleader or homecoming queen, but not a special agent. Of course I couldn't tell you this to explain her activities on the weekend you met her, so we invented a kidnapped brother. We needed to explain to you why you had not been an accessory to a crime, so we invented a ransom and a brother to be ransomed. The alternative was to tell you the truth, and we obviously couldn't do that."

"Obviously," I said bitterly.

"Must we, Mr. Wilder?" Sheed said. "There's not much sense in resentment at this point. In fact, we were trying not

to put you at risk. Your ignorance was your protection. It
served you as well as us. But now we're in an entirely different situation, with some urgency attached. This time I want
you to accompany Angela to deliver our contribution to the
mujahideen we're supporting in Afghanistan."

I laughed out loud. "You can't be serious, Mr. Sheed. That
is the most ludicrous idea I've ever heard. Why would I ever
do something like that? Do I look like a one-man Special
Forces unit?"

"There's no combat involved. Nor will you be going to
Afghanistan but to a five-star hotel room in a Middle Eastern
capital and then home. With luck, you'll be on the ground
fewer than four hours. As you must know, there are many
places in the Middle East a woman can't go without a male
companion. Have you been following the news lately?"

"Not at all."

"The Taliban are about to enter Kabul, which means they'll
control the country. Osama bin Laden, who I assume you've
heard of, moved his headquarters from the Sudan to Afghanistan on August 18, ten days ago. He issued his 'Declaration of
War Against the Americans Occupying the Land of the Two
Holy Places' and declared terrorism against the US was quote
'a legitimate and moral obligation' unquote. Somebody put a
bomb in that trash can at the Atlanta Olympics last month
killing two and wounding 111. Somebody probably shot a
Stinger missile into American Flight 800 that brought it down
off Long Island ten days before that. Both could have been al-
Qaeda. The Khobar Towers bombing in June in Dhahran *was*
al-Qaeda. It killed nineteen American soldiers and wounded
400 and left a fifty-foot crater where our military hous-
ing complex in Saudi Arabia had been. Things are heating
up very fast. And bin Laden in Afghanistan is one hundred

times as dangerous as when he was based in Sudan. We could observe him and to some extent control him there, but not in Afghanistan. It's too unstable. It's chaos—cities in ruins, tribe fighting tribe, drug lords and armed gangs controlling every road. There's no infrastructure at all, much less for communication. We have zero presence there. We don't even have people who speak the language. The Taliban is the only coherent force in the country. And our only hope is one small faction of the Taliban who still think we are their friends because we supported them for years against the Soviets. Plus they don't want to alienate us because of our money and influence in the world community, and after they take over they will certainly want our recognition as the legitimate government of Afghanistan. This faction of the Taliban considers bin Laden a wealthy nuisance at best and an enemy at worst. They're not in the least interested in worldwide jihad against the United States. Killing innocent people is against their version of Islam and they don't believe bin Laden has the religious authority to declare fatwa. These are obviously the people we want to support. And we have an Afghan mujahideen we think can take out bin Laden. Putting the money in the right hands at the right time is crucial, and that's what I want you to do with Angela."

"Why me? You could get lots of male agents to accompany Angela."

"You're perfect. You have no profile in the intelligence community. We're sure you're not working secretly for anyone else. Plus we don't have time to recruit. We need the money delivered now."

"Who's funding this?" I asked. "The CIA?"

"I already told you, Mr. Wilder. I work for the president."

"Who provides the money? Who pays you? The US government?"

"No. The president. We are not a government agency. We operate entirely outside the law, but we never break the law. What we do is extralegal but not illegal."

"So where does the money come from?"

"Let me just call them 'Friends of Bill,'" Sheed said, smiling. "Donors. What we do is always consonant with US interests, as well as in the president's interest."

"Political interest?" I asked.

"Certainly that," Sheed answered. "But more generally that he thrive and do well."

"Do well in the polls," I said.

"Of course. But it also may not surprise you to learn that there are powerful people in Washington who prefer that Bill Clinton not thrive and do well. We're only two months from the election, are we not?"

"Against Dole and Perot, two geriatric crankbuckets," I said. "Dole has one expression: irritated. He's like your grumpy grandpa with a bad case of hemorrhoids. And Perot is a certified nutcase. Clinton is creaming them in the polls. It'll be a landslide."

"Right. If nothing happens."

"What could happen?" I asked.

"What if the American people felt the president wasn't protecting them against terrorism? What if there was a huge terrorist incident right before the election? What if there was a series of them?"

"Is there going to be?"

"We're trying to make sure there isn't. Now let me ask you a question. Politically, whose interest would it serve if there were?"

"The Republicans', I guess," I answered.

"That's who is trying to kill you," Sheed said.

"The *Republicans?* Please, Mr. Sheed. You can't be serious. All I see are fat fiftyish pasty white guys in straw boaters with red-white-and-blue streamers on them."

"Yes, well, there are other Republicans. You'll remember the CIA was run by George Bush. Many agents are glad to do a little moonlighting. Especially the frustrated ones, which almost all of them are. What begins as patriotism shades easily into fanaticism. They are very well-trained and they are neither fat nor fiftyish."

A different picture appeared in my mind, which wasn't so funny.

"They're funded by Republican donors," Sheed continued. "Fanatical billionaire right-wing donors. They *hate* Bill Clinton. They'd kill him if they could get away with it. But they couldn't get away with it. You on the other hand—it would be nothing for them to kill you. After they extracted from you every detail about Democrats' covert operations that would bring down Clinton."

"But I don't know anything! I have no idea what Angela was doing in Mexico!"

"But they don't know that, do they? You drove her there. As far as they're concerned, you work for Clinton. You're a valuable undercover operative just like her."

Sheed seemed to enjoy telling me this quite a bit too much.

"Of course, you're under no obligation to accompany Angela," Sheed continued. "You can leave anytime. But we have no way to protect you if you do. Since we're not a government agency, we have no access to government protection. I would hate to see you exposed to harm and on your own."

I tried to detect irony in Sheed's last remark, but there wasn't a trace of it. He probably would hate to see me hurt. But I also knew he'd accept it as collateral damage, another civilian killed in the war, and go on with his business.

"It doesn't seem I have much choice," I said.

"Not much choice, no," Sheed replied. "Your stipend by the way is $20,000, payable after the delivery is complete."

"Well, that's more than I made last year. I didn't imagine embarking on a new career, but the old one was sort of tanking anyway."

"This is one and done, Mr. Wilder. I'm afraid you're stuck with making jokes. The people looking for you want to cause the president problems before the election, not after. After will do them no good. They'll simply turn their attention elsewhere. There's a world of people who can cause problems for Bill Clinton."

"Such as every woman he's ever met?"

Sheed sighed. "Oh yes, the dick problem. Every woman he's ever met has already been paraded before the microphones. That's old news."

I certainly had a dick problem myself—hence my current circumstances—but Sheed was diplomatic enough not to remind me, although he probably knew about it and everything else about me.

He continued, "You can sleep on this and give me your decision before we get off the plane in Washington. If you're not coming along, I'll buy you a cab ride to Dulles and a ticket to LAX. We'd have to pick up a male agent provided by Richard Clarke, but this could put Angela in peril."

"Because?"

"Because we can't trust anybody else. It's that simple. There's too much money involved. Can you guess how much the presidency is worth? Federal subsidies, regulations, penalties— every industry, every enterprise. That's a fraction of the money in play. I'm talking about the men who have that money and mean to keep it and make more."

I had no doubt that Sheed was accurately describing this secret world of money, politics, and intrigue. I suddenly felt very tired. Maybe I was asleep already, because it seemed that I had entered a nightmare universe populated by aliens. Including Angela, Murderous Princess of Planet Lovetron. A very depressing thought.

"Georges will make you a bed up front," Sheed said. "Why don't you catch a nap before we land? You look like you could use it."

I got up and walked meekly to the front of the plane where one of the seats had already been made into a single bed complete with percale sheets, a down comforter, and a foil-wrapped chocolate on the pillow spotlighted by a reading light above the porthole window. A pair of 100 percent Egyptian cotton baby blue pajamas was folded neatly at the foot of the bed. I changed into them in the airplane bathroom behind the pilot's cabin, picturing Angela in there trying to pee in her hijab. Before I clicked off the reading light above the bed, I glanced back at Sheed at the dining table. He had taken out a briefcase and was reviewing a stack of file folders as if it were eight A.M. in the office and he had just finished his second cup of coffee. Of course he can bill thirty hours a day. He never sleeps.

16.

Sheed and Angela were up and dressed before I even awoke (of course): the power couple. They were halfway through their conquer-the-universe power breakfast when I trundled past the dining table in my 100 percent Egyptian cotton baby blue pajamas carrying my shoes, socks, pants, and anxiety-soaked shirt of the night before, which—because I had no clean one—I would have the privilege of wearing to Meet The President (hoping he has lost his sense of smell).

"*Baby blue* pajamas!" Angela said. "Be still my beating heart."

She was arrayed in a tailored black suit with no blouse underneath, a single strand of pearls around her neck, and black pumps on her feet, which unfortunately were connected to those remarkable legs of hers. Be still *my* beating heart.

I asked, "Any place a girl can go to freshen up?"

"You can use the girls-only bedroom suite if you don't mind it being decorated with yesterday's underthings," Angela said.

"Only kind I wear," I said.

As before, Sheed didn't blink at her remarks, or mine. He had perfected the absolute deadpan. Very useful in his profession(s).

The bedroom suite was as beige as the rest of the plane, with dark wood paneling on the closets and dark brown granite counters. Angela's black machine pistol hung from a strap on an open closet door and her wispy black underwear was clumped like a ball of Kleenex on the rumpled bed. The combination kind of said it all about her: you go for the underwear and get the pistol. The last time I had seen her underwear she was wearing it. I had no intention of becoming enthralled, enamored, enchanted, or en-anything else. My dick was not leading me into perdition this time (I vowed). I would go with her to the unnamed "Middle-Eastern capital," but I was not going cheerfully. I planned to sulk, pout, and complain like a fourteen-year-old with PMS—which is exactly (?) how I felt.

Her black machine pistol was definitely not wispy, and happily it didn't have the effect on me that her big black soft leather purse did after I discovered it in the Baja honeymoon suite stuffed with money. The gun was repugnant. It angered me—the thought that Angela had probably shot people with it. How could she choose a life like this? How could she or any of these people believe what they were doing was good? On the other hand, what did I know about anything? Much less covert international power politics. None of these thoughts were in the least consoling. They just made me crankier and I had awakened plenty cranky already.

After I washed my face and dressed and gobbled one of Georges's sublime fresh-baked croissants, we landed at what appeared to be a military base and were met at the bottom of the stairs by a helicopter with its rotors whirring. When I pulled my little suitcase behind me on board, Angela yelled above the rotor noise, "You could have left that on the plane."

"Thanks for telling me now," I yelled back. Maybe we would become like an old married couple sniping at each other in public. Both she and Sheed were dressed as if they had just stepped out of a Park Avenue boutique and there I was pulling my suitcase on rollers and smelling like a walking armpit.

The helicopter lifted off and within minutes we were over Washington and approaching the Capitol Dome on the Congressional Building. All the famous federal buildings and monuments came into view, the ones that every American has seen pictures of since they were babies. I guess that's when this became real—we actually were going to meet with the president. I still couldn't believe it. Didn't I have to accomplish something first? I hadn't done anything except learn to imitate the screechy violins in *Psycho*. Maybe that qualified me for high-level security missions. I'd be about as useful to Angela as a pair of concrete waders. Not only would I not be protecting her, she'd have to protect me. It was like giving a soldier a toddler to take into battle.

We landed on a helicopter pad atop a tall building and ducked under the rotors into an elevator that took us to the lowest level: minus eight—eight floors underground. To access that floor, Sheed punched a code into a keypad next to the button—from memory, instantly and automatically, as if he used it every day. The minus-eighth "floor" was nothing but a long corridor no higher or wider than the elevator itself, which led to one room at its end. Sheed opened the door and switched on the lights. The room was huge, a couple hundred feet from wall to wall, its walls covered with computer screens and electronic maps. Banks of keyboards on desks surrounded an elevated command center in the middle. It looked like the situation room in a bad disaster movie. Only no one was there. It was silent and all the screens were blank. No crusty generals barking orders, no passionate disputes between the egomaniac colonel and the handsome lieutenant. The contrast between the room's emptiness and the noisy frenetic activity for which it was designed was eerie. Neither Sheed nor Angela appeared startled. They obviously had been here before and knew where they were going—which was to a conference room behind a door off to the side. This room was also dark and Sheed flipped on the lights to reveal a seminar table surrounded by leather chairs. The three of us sat down, Angela between Sheed and me, across the table from where the president obviously sat, which you could tell because his chair was higher than the other chairs and had a headrest on it. This seemed funny to me. Angela asked what the joke was.

"Why does the president get the best chair?" I said.

"Is that how the joke opens?" Angela asked. "Okay, why does the president get the best chair?"

"No," I said, pointing to the big chair across the table from her. "He gets the best chair. Doesn't that seem ridiculous to you?"

"Washington runs on symbols," Sheed said.

"But the best *chair?*" I said.

They both looked at me like I was from Mars.

I still had my suitcase, of course. I had rolled it behind me the whole way—off the helicopter, into the elevator, down the corridor, through the situation room, and now it was here for my meeting with the president stuffed with my dirty underwear and *Psycho* props. Maybe the president would like to see my imitation of Norman Bates complete with the screechy violins. I tried to shove the suitcase under my chair so nobody would notice. But it didn't fit.

I also could smell myself. In this windowless conference room, it was only a matter of time before everyone else smelled me too.

The door opened and Clinton and Clarke walked in, dressed in elegant blue suits and crisp white shirts, a breath of fresh laundry. Clarke was small and trim, but muscled and not as slight as Sheed. He looked like a rat terrier, and had the same affect: scrappy. If there were only one bone in the room, he'd end up with it. I bet he chased the mailman up the block. At the same time, he was so pale he was translucent, a former redhead whose hair had turned white, so he also seemed incongruously vulnerable and, because of it, hyperalert, like a ground squirrel.

Clinton, by contrast, was *big*. I knew he was six three and 240 pounds when he was gorging, but he seemed as big as the rest of us put together. Plus he exuded bonhomie, which probably took up additional space. The consummate pol. "Jolly" was the word that might come to mind, but it would be the wrong one. He made all the gracious gestures to make you like him, but he was ready to deal with you effectively if you didn't.

"*Good* morning, everyone," he said, taking his presidential chair. "Folsom, looking sharp as usual. And Angela, what can I say? Will you marry me?"

"I'm unfortunately all booked up today, Mr. President," Angela replied.

Clinton smiled. "And I have yet to have the pleasure of meeting this gentleman," he said to Sheed about me.

"Robert Wilder, Mr. President," Sheed said.

"Bill Clinton," Clinton said, extending his hand across the table for me to shake.

"I recognize you from your picture on the dollar bill," I said.

Clinton laughed heartily. "Yes, Richard told me you were a comedian. We could use a comedian at all our meetings, couldn't we, Richard? Mr. Wilder, Richard Clarke."

Clarke was already seated and reading a file folder in front of him and glanced up at me as if he noticed a fly landing on the table. I realized the file he was reading was about me.

"Yes, let's start right here, please," Clarke said. "Mr. Wilder should not even be in this building, much less in this room. Why is he at this meeting?"

"To provide the jokes," Clinton answered. "What about it, Folsom?"

"He's escorting Miss Chase," Sheed said.

"An *escort*?" Clarke asked. "From an escort service?"

"Richard, you know very well that Angela needs male accompaniment where she's going. Mr. Wilder is unknown. If you provide her an escort from one of the agencies, he might be identified. Mr. Wilder won't be. Plus I have vetted him completely and he's completely trustworthy."

("I *am*?" I thought.)

"I don't like it, Folsom. I didn't get his file until a half hour ago. We haven't had a chance to run it though our databases. There's been no clearance, no waiver, no thorough background check, nothing. And it's illegal to involve citizens."

Clinton laughed. "I never thought I'd hear *that* objection from you, Richard."

Clarke glowered. He was so pale his skull lit up red as a Christmas bulb. "What if he writes a book and goes on Oprah?"

Angela laughed at that, and Sheed smiled. Clinton put his hand affectionately on Clarke's shoulder.

"I'm sure Mr. Wilder will sign a nondisclosure agreement. Right, Mr. Wilder? I'm in enough stand-up routines as it is."

"Sure," I said. "No one would believe this happened anyway."

"Let's go with it," Clinton said. "If you're killed in the line of duty, we'll have your funeral on Comedy Central."

"Doesn't sound like a speaking part," I said.

Clinton laughed again. "See, Richard, that was a joke."

Clarke smiled so tightly it looked like his face would split.

"All right," Clinton said. "Folsom, what's the plan?"

Sheed produced his briefcase out of nowhere, laid it in front of him on the table, and popped open the solid fourteen-carat gold locks. He took out four copies of a sheet of notes and passed them to Angela and she gave three to me. I kept one and handed the last two across the table to the president, who gave one to Richard Clarke. Suddenly we were all graduate students in Sheed's seminar, and we looked at his handout.

"This is the situation in Afghanistan," Sheed said. "These forces define the only order underneath the chaos." He repeated what he had told me about bin Laden and the Taliban and how this was a climactic historical moment that could go either way: either the Taliban would support bin Laden and provide a base for al-Qaeda's international terrorism or they would not. If they did, bin Laden's long-planned operations could start occurring very quickly, in rapid sequence, possibly before the election. To discourage that, the differences—both political and religious—between bin Laden and the Taliban must be amplified. "The best way we can accomplish this," Sheed concluded, "is to support the mujahideen whose interests align with ours. I now defer to Miss Chase, who has taught me all I know about Islam and was a classmate of Ahmad Jalalzada, the mujahideen we want to support."

"Thank you, Folsom," Angela said. "I should mention that all I know about Islam Ahmad Jalalzada taught me when we were students in Paris. Few Westerners knew much about Islam then, and they still don't. Worse, what they do know now is derived from bin Laden's videotaped threats and murderous bombings. They think Islam is a fanatical religion that encourages violence and hatred. This is totally false. Islam is a religion founded on love and brotherhood. It's based on four principles that must be practiced: Dharma (duty), Karma (virtue), Ardha (success), and Kama (pleasure). It encourages acts of kindness as the most powerful expression of devotion to God. This is Jalalzada's version of Islam, which sees bin Laden's version as heretical, and vice versa. The opposition between them could not be more absolute. The Taliban's version of Islam is actually closer to Jalalzada's than to bin Laden's. The opposition between the Taliban and Jalalzada is political—that is to say, they don't agree on the nature of the government in Afghanistan under which Islam is to be practiced. For the Taliban, the state must be a totalitarian theocracy enforcing fundamentalist religious practices, including purdah for women and the wearing of beards for men 'longer than the length of your hand.' Jalalzada graduated from Harvard and the Institut d'Etudes Politiques de Paris, where I met him. He is the scion of an old royal family and grandson of King Zahir Shah, the last king of Afghanistan. He believes Islam would best thrive in a parliamentary democracy modeled on Western Europe and Turkey. Obviously our interests coincide with Jalalzada's. The more power he has, the less bin Laden has. In any case, the more support we give Jalalzada the more time we buy from both the inevitable takeover by the Taliban and their possible sponsorship of bin Laden. In fact, Jalalzada may attack bin Laden's compound if he becomes strong enough. This would be the ideal of what our money could achieve and we could achieve it relatively cheaply."

"How cheaply?" Clinton asked.

Sheed took over again. "Ten million for this installment. With $10 million Jalalzada could field an army of 10,000 men for three months. Bin Laden has a couple hundred fighters guarding his compound. The rest are Taliban. If the Taliban can be persuaded to look the other way, bin Laden is toast."

During Sheed's and Angela's presentation, Clarke had looked increasingly like his head was about to pop off his neck like a cork.

"This is a complete distraction," he said vehemently. "Our problems are with Iran and Hezbollah, not bin Laden. He's a freelancer, a spoiled brat terrorist financier. All he's got is money. He's probably going to fade away by himself. He's not a general, he has no army, he has no nation behind him, much less one the size and strength of Iran. Get serious, Folsom. There's no comparison between bin Laden and Iran. We need to concentrate our resources on Iran."

"I think we *are*, Richard," Clinton said. "Didn't Congress just approve a billion dollars of emergency supplementals to upgrade security for airlines and military bases? The CIA and FBI got a bonus too. And, as I recall, a gentleman who walked into our embassy in Eritrea mentioned that al-Qaeda currently has at least fifty sleeper cells in various cities around the world. That's what we got for the million dollars we paid him compliments of the American taxpayer. What Folsom is proposing is off the books. What if he's right?"

"If he's right, every intelligence agency we've got is wrong."

"They've been wrong before," Clinton responded. "Folsom has not."

Clarke knew he had lost and so did the rest of us. No one spoke for a moment, as if to acknowledge it. Of course, I hadn't spoken at all since I made my last joke—a good thing, since I would have made a complete dick of myself. I felt like a junior college transfer at the Nobel physicists' convention.

Now that he had won, Sheed saw it was time for the caveat.

"Mr. President, before you sign off on this, I must add that we don't intend to ask Jalalzada to attack bin Laden's compound. In fact, we won't ask him to do anything. We just give him the money to spend as he sees fit. Of course he understands that if he doesn't produce results in accordance with our interests he'll never see another penny."

Clinton nodded, then came Sheed's olive branch for Clarke. "Richard, I completely agree with you about Iran. The measures you've put in place to contain Hezbollah have been brilliant. A war with Iran would be an expensive disaster and you've devised an effective strategy to avoid it. But a war in Afghanistan would be worse. We wouldn't be able to get out of there for ten years and a trillion dollars, minimum. Ten million for Jalalzada is .001 percent of a trillion. And as the president said, it's not even taxpayer money."

"I don't think we have any more to talk about," Clinton said. "The money will be on your plane, Folsom. It will be unloaded for Angela at her destination. Angela, when you return I'd appreciate a *personal* debriefing," he added, consciously parodying his lecherous reputation.

This was obviously a routine Clinton and Angela had done before.

"I never go anywhere without Folsom," Angela said.

"Or Mr. Wilder," Clinton said, reaching across to shake my hand. "You're a lucky man, sir. Have a lovely trip with this lovely lady. And don't cut yourself on your cardboard knife."

Clinton and Clarke walked out of the room. I stood there dumbfounded. Sheed was fussing with his briefcase and Angela was laughing at me.

"Could have been worse," she said. "He could have asked for the name of your cologne. I was thinking 'Men's Locker Room,' but we could brainstorm it before we market it worldwide."

"How . . ." I began.

"The elevator has a scanner," she said. "It's automatic, as soon as you get on. I hate to think of how many low-level functionaries have seen me naked. If it detects anything, the elevator doors don't open. I think it can release a range of noxious gases in there as well to brighten up your day. I just hope it never malfunctions."

"What a world you live in," I said to her, without thinking.

She looked at me intently, as if to consider exactly what I meant, then said nothing. We were a million miles away from each other. And probably always would be.

"So you two take my plane," Sheed said. "Clinton has a fund-raiser tonight at Barbra Streisand's and offered me a ride. I'm taking Georges back with me, though."

"It's true," I said. "You don't ever sleep."

"Not much," Sheed replied. "Great job, Angela. As usual. And Mr. Wilder, you set the perfect tone with your jokes. As the president said, we could use you at all our meetings."

"Probably the best booking I'll be offered this year," I said.

"I don't think that could have gone more smoothly, do you?" Sheed asked Angela.

"Clinton had made up his mind before the meeting started," Angela replied. "I worry about alienating Clarke, but it was unavoidable. He doesn't like to lose. He also will be listening to every word we're saying right now, as you know. But I don't think any of it will surprise him."

"I'm sure it won't," Sheed said, and with that he picked up his briefcase and headed for the door.

17.

Sheed rode up to the roof with Angela and me to say good-bye, then stepped back into the elevator and disappeared. His good-bye to Angela was characteristic: a hearty handshake. A hug would have been worse, I guess, since he barely reached her shoulders and, with her high heels on, she might have poked his eyes out with her breasts. He'd have looked like a ten-year-old hugging his mom. No way would Sheed ever subject himself to that. I had never met anyone so self-possessed. He had designed himself for maximum efficacy, part of which was his resolute placid dignity. If he suffered conflict and anxiety like every other human being who has ever lived, he masked it masterfully, and he made you want to act as calm and rational as he was by agreeing to whatever perfectly reasonable plan he proposed. Like me flying to an undisclosed "Middle Eastern capital" and secretly delivering $10 million to an Afghan mujahideen. What could be more reasonable than that? Especially since there were probably a good many people with very large guns who would prefer I didn't. If Sheed ever got angry or frustrated or just let off a little steam, no one ever witnessed it. Maybe after work he chopped up pizza deliverymen in his basement and played

Twister with the pieces or donned a monkey suit and partied with a tribe of horny bonobos, but what he seemed to like to do most *was* work because his work was the one manifestation of cosmic order left in the modern world as the millennium spluttered to its conclusion.

His relationship to Angela was a mystery to me. He clearly admired and appreciated her, but affection? Desire? Paternal tenderness? Not in the deepest recesses of his brain. He did his job and she did hers—and together they prospered. If Sheed were her surrogate father or some other psychobabble replacement figure, it was not apparent. She seemed to have found the perfect arrangement—one that asked nothing personal of her—and the perfect profession, which asked her only to do and not to feel. Emotion in fact would be a hindrance in their line of work. It might make them nice instead of effective. I felt more than ever like an alien on their planet. Clinton and Clarke, Sheed and Angela—for all their personality differences, they belonged together. They were all relentless brilliant psychopaths, who felt no emotional bonds to anyone, including one another.

But who was I to talk about "emotional bonds," the notorious shitweasel who left his bride-to-be literally standing at the altar?

The helicopter took us back to the plane and the plane took off immediately. We were hardly off the ground before Angela was on the radio in the copilot's seat talking to whomever—Sheed no doubt, among others. Besides the pilot, who I had still not met, there was no one else on the plane. I realized Angela *was* the copilot, for this flight. Among her many talents, she apparently also knew how to fly jet planes. For some reason, this thought depressed me most of all. I supposed she'd be the Cordon Bleu chef, too, since Georges had gone with Sheed back to LA. But what was I supposed to eat now?

I checked the refrigerator. Georges had made croissant sandwiches from the leftover *filet de beouf au poivre* and I wolfed down three of them while wandering about the plane. He had tidied up everywhere but the bedroom suite. It looked exactly like I left it before the meeting with Clinton. Angela's gun was still hanging by its strap from the closet door and her wispy bra-and-panties were still crumpled into a ball on the bed. They each presented problems for me. I couldn't sleep with the gun hanging over my head—what if we hit turbulence and it bounced off and shot me?—nor could I sleep with Angela's underwear, much less on it. I picked up the underwear no less gingerly than the gun and put them in an empty drawer together—the two faces of Angela. If she had luggage it wasn't here, nor was the $10 million. Of course, I checked all the drawers and closets but they were empty. Then I stripped and crawled under the covers. They smelled of Angela. The whole bed smelled of her—her hair and flesh, her scent—which I hadn't smelled since being in bed with her in Baja. It was like sleeping with her ghost, and made me feel all the desire for her that I never wanted to feel again, and I resolved to get through this delivery and away from her forever or die trying, which seemed all too possible.

Blessedly I passed out and when I woke up Angela was standing next to the bed, still arrayed in her tailored black suit.

"Robert, wake up, we're landing in an hour," I heard through the fog that filled my skull.

"How can that be?" I asked. "I only just went to sleep."

"Yes, twelve hours ago. You didn't even wake while we refueled. I brought you a coffee."

I sat up in bed and propped the pillow behind me, the bed sheet covering my lap. I was suddenly aware that I was completely naked, and that Angela was aware that I was completely naked. I took the coffee from her and thanked her.

"Where's my gun?" she asked.

"It's in the top drawer with your underwear. They're becoming friends."

"How about us, Robert? Are we becoming friends?"

"I don't know," I said.

"You don't make a very good liar," Angela said.

"It's kind of a silly question, isn't it? We haven't exchanged a personal word since you appeared at my place in your Muslim fashion statement."

"Would you like to talk about something?"

"I'd like to talk about everything," I said.

"Maybe we'll have the chance," she said. "I've just been doing my job."

"Was it your job to fuck me all the way to Mexico?"

Angela paused a moment before answering. She was still standing next to the bed, about a tenth of an inch away from me. She gave me a look like I had reminded her of something: sex. She said, "What do you think?"

"I don't know," I said.

She reached for my coffee cup and gently lifted it out of my hand, brushing my fingertips with hers. It sent a charge right to my brain stem. She set the coffee cup on the counter and looked that look of hers at me, waiting for my answer.

"I think you wanted to," I said quietly.

"And I want to even more right now." She slid out of her tailored black suit and there she was in her Brazilian bikini with the butt-floss bottom, red as the devil himself. Happy memories of Malibu. Its effect on me was instantaneous.

"Remember this?" she asked.

"Unfortunately I do," I answered.

"Let me see," she said, and slowly pulled the sheet off of me. "Oh, you have an excellent memory." Private Wanky was standing at full attention, a fine soldier. If he stood up any straighter, he'd be saluting.

Angela moved to the foot of the bed and reached down and pushed my legs apart and knelt between them.

"You have the most beautiful cock in the universe," she said.

"That's what my grandma tells me," I said.

That one surprised her (surprised me too). She laughed, nothing held back, the laugh I love. "Isn't there anything you can't make a joke of?"

"Like what?" I asked.

She smiled and sat upright on her knees and undid the two teeny shoestring bows that impossibly held her bikini on.

"How about this?" she asked. She took me in one hand and straddled me and slipped me all the way inside her. I couldn't make a joke of it, all right—nor of anything else, for quite some time.

ANGELA MADE *omelettes aux fines herbes* in the galley kitchen and served them with fresh coffee and warm brioches that Georges had parbaked and frozen. She had put on the same white silk robe she had worn in Malibu and I watched it move like thick cream over the contours of her body as she cooked. I must have died and gone to heaven—weird heaven, but heaven nonetheless. Here we were setting up house in the airborne Vegas casino preferred-customer lounge. I wore my skivvies, the same pair I had been wearing for the last three days. They were starting to become a life form independent of me. Angela's luggage—the same four big bags she took to Mexico—perched on chairs around a coffee table as if they were having a business conference, and a big cardboard box sat at their feet like a mastiff. A box packed with money, probably. Since neither the box nor the luggage were here before,

I assumed they had been brought up from the baggage compartment during the refueling I slept through.

Angela folded the omelette, flipped it, halved it, then slid the two halves onto plates and set one in front of me and sat down across from me with the other.

"So did you learn to make this omelette at Le Cordon Bleu?" I asked.

"Where did you get that idea?"

"I thought maybe you picked up your chef certificate on the side while you studied in Paris. Probably you also learned to juggle on the high wire and occasionally perform with Cirque du Soleil."

"I can barely balance on one foot and make toast," she said. "This omelette is the one thing I can manage without setting the kitchen on fire. What other fantasies do you have about me?"

"Lots," I said, pointing to my skull. "Not a nice neighborhood. Never go there alone."

"Well, you behave fairly respectably. Most of the time."

"I'm almost grown up now," I said. "By the way, it's been more than an hour since you woke me and we haven't landed."

"I exaggerated a little."

"So we weren't landing in an hour. And that coffee you brought me—you were just trying to get into my pants?"

"You weren't wearing pants."

"Well, thank you. It was the best cup of coffee I've ever had."

Angela smiled. "You're pretty tasty yourself. Would you like to know where we're going?"

"'A five-star hotel in a Middle-Eastern capital.'"

"Is that what Folsom told you?"

"Yes, did he exaggerate a little?"

"Not at all. We're going to a yurt in a Central Asian Republic."

"You're kidding," I said.

"We're landing—actually in about an hour—in Turkmenistan."

"Turkmenistan? I don't even know where it is."

"Borders Afghanistan to the north. It's the only place we can meet Ahmad. Believe me, I tried everywhere. That's what I was doing on the radio for twelve hours. I'm sorry I couldn't book us at the Four Seasons in Amman, but they're having a little 'unrest' in Jordan at the moment, as is just about every other country in the region. We're lucky this worked out. It's not at all the way I like to do these things, but we should get in and get out safely and so should Ahmad, so that's all that matters."

"What's the problem?"

"None, really. I'm just more comfortable going under the radar, but Ahmad can't be away right now so we have to go to him, or as close to him as we can. Which meant Clinton had to call President Niyazov and arrange a military escort for us and for Ahmad when he reaches the border. Niyazov agreed on one condition: we pretend we're Saudis. So I'm wearing my hijab and you're wearing this."

She reached into the chair next to her and held up this fall's latest fashion line in Saudi menswear: a white ankle-length robe. The same as last fall's fashion line and the previous fall's fashion line for the last 3,000 years or so. I thought it was an extra tablecloth Georges had left for us.

"A robe?" I said.

"A 'thobe,'" Angela said.

"*Thobe*?" I asked. "Or did you suddenly develop a lisp?"

"Your first word in Arabic. We also have the *tagiyah*, the *ghutra*, and the *agal*." She held up each one for display—a skull cap, a scarf, and a black cord, the three parts of the head covering. "As we girls know, the outfit is all in the accessories."

"I'm supposed to wear that," I said flatly. "May I ask why?"

"Turkmenistan foreign relations. Would you like to hear an interminable lecture on Turkmenistan foreign relations?"

"Turkmenistan foreign relations make me hot. I'm not sure I could control myself."

"Then here's the short version: oil. Turkmenistan has massive undeveloped oil and gas reserves. Everyone knows Americans invade for oil. Americans with a military escort make Turkmen nervous. Saudis don't. Saudis need oil like you need a penis splint."

Then she picked up a pair of boxy underpants, too tight to be boxers and too long to be briefs, with an Arabic letter under the right butt cheek. I had never seen underpants like it.

"Do Arabs have square butts?" I asked.

"I'm happy to say I have no idea. You can't see their butts through their *thobes*."

"What does the Arabic letter under the right butt cheek mean?"

" 'If you can read this, you're driving too close.' "

"All that with one letter?"

"It's the company logo, I think."

"How about my beard? Don't Saudis wear beards?"

"Oh yes, the best part." She arranged on the table a little black mustache, goatee, and mouche in the shape of a face.

"All right. Now I know you're pulling my chain."

"Honestly, I am not." She held up her hand like a Girl Scout. "You can't imagine how hard it was to have your Arab facial hair delivered to the Abu Dhabi naval base where we refueled."

"Well, you might get away with wearing your hijab, but who's going to believe I'm a Saudi? I sweat in deserts. What if this little muffin thing under my lip falls off?"

"There so much glue on it you'll be lucky if it doesn't rip off your face when you try to remove it. But maybe you'll like it so much, you'll wear it from now on. It's the Prince Abdullah autograph model. If I have my way, no Turkmen soldiers will get close enough to see it's fake. That's the thing about former Soviet Republics. The people are still in the habit of seeing what they're told they see. So we'll be Saudis to them even if your mouche falls off. Plus I want you to wear it the next time we have sex."

"You mean there will be a next time?"

"If you're a good boy and wear your nice costume."

I fingered the mustache, goatee, and mouche. They felt like Brillo. There was clear tape on the backs of each of them, under which I could see a thick adhesive gel.

"Scratchy," I said, holding up the mouche. "This is really crazy."

"Welcome to my world," Angela said.

"I mean *really* crazy."

"Yes, well, Niyazov *is* clinically insane." She offered me a brioche. "Would you like a nice warm piece of Gurban-soltanenedzhe?"

"Say what?"

"Gurbansoltanenedzhe. In Turkmenistan it's illegal to use the Turkmen word for bread. The word for bread is now the name of Niyazov's mother: Gurbansoltanenedzhe."

I took a bite of the brioche. "Mom is delicious," I said.

"Want to hear some more of my favorites? No makeup on TV, no lip-synching to recorded music, no gold teeth—because Niyazov believes if the people chew bones like he does they'll have healthy teeth like he does. He closed all the libraries and declared that the people should read only two books: the *Koran* and *Ruhnama*. You never heard of *Ruhnama*? Guess who wrote it? Guess whose autobiography it is? And all Turkmen must pass a test on it to get a driver's license. Niyazov proclaimed that any youth who reads it three times will go to heaven. Criticism of it is high treason punishable by imprisonment. He's erected hundreds of gold statues of himself, in every city. There's one that's 250 feet high that automatically rotates to face the sun and plays recordings from the *Ruhnama* at dawn and dusk. Niyazov's official title is not president but His Excellency Saparmurat Niyazov Turkmenbashi, 'Leader of all ethnic Turkmen.' He makes Stalin look like Mr. Rogers. He won the election last year with a majority of 99.9 percent. Of course he was the only candidate and anybody who doesn't vote gets a phone call from the secret police. But my most favorite decree is his renaming the days of the week and months of the year after himself and his family. September is called Ruhnama, after his book. What's today, Wednesday? When we land in Turkmenistan it won't be Wednesday, it will be Hosgun, 'The Good Day.' Aren't you glad? It could have been tomorrow, 'Justice Day,' which is also the first day of Ruhnama. Then we might have been arrested."

"How did you learn all this in twelve hours?"

"That's nothing. You should try learning to speak Turkmen with a Saudi accent. Fortunately I know a little Arabic."

"Is there anything you can't do?" I asked.

"Yeah, I can't be happy," she said.

She was dead serious. I was so surprised I was speechless.

"You want to do something about it?" she asked, as if challenging me to a bar fight.

"I might," I said.

"Well, you can't," she said. I had obviously said the wrong thing.

"Why are you pissed? I'd like to make you happy. I think."

"You think," she said. "It was a stupid thing for me to say. Just forget it. Let's see how you look in your *thobe*." She literally threw the robe over my head. I stood up and she slapped the mouche onto my face, hard. I grabbed her and kissed her, also hard, rubbing her face with the bristles.

"You're such an ath-hole," she said, wiping her mouth.

"Good one," I said.

"Put on the rest of your outfit. No more talk."

"Okay," I said. "I'm sorry I said the wrong thing. About wanting to make you happy."

"You didn't. That was the right thing." She kissed me again, voluntarily this time. "I'll tell you, I could get to like that little muffin."

"It already likes you," I said.

The pilot came on the intercom. "Angela, we'll be on the ground in fifteen minutes."

"We'll be ready," she said, not to the pilot but to me.

18.

I never had more fun with a woman, in bed or out of bed, than with Angela. Not even close. I tried not to think about what it "meant," although as soon as the plane touched down I wished it would lift off again to Paris or somewhere we could spend the $20,000 I would not earn being Bill Clinton's bagman or shot full of remanufactured Soviet bullets or blown into a bazillion Islamic pieces. But Angela was definitely running this show, and clearly she intended to "do her job," as she put it. It mattered to her, which was fine with me (or sort of fine), yet wasn't there anything that mattered more? Me, for instance? Maybe even "us"? Of course I didn't say this to her. I couldn't think of "us" without quotation marks, since we actually hardly had an "us," and even the term "us" made me feel girly. It did seem to me a gender-neutral preference to prefer not to die in Turkmenistan disguised as an Arab, but for Angela it was all just another day at the office.

She strapped on her machine pistol over the Kevlar vest she dug out of the big brown box, which turned out to be not filled with money but martial equipment of various alarming sorts. I was sitting at the dining table in my *thobe* and Prince Abdullah, the latter slanted at the jaunty angle Angela had stuck it onto my face. She looked like a one-woman SWAT team and I looked ridiculous. I had no idea what was in her mind but she knew what was in mine as I watched her adjust her vest.

"Just a precaution, Robert. There won't be any trouble. We're going to be fine." She dug into the box again and tossed another Kevlar vest to me. "His 'n' her outfits," she said. This one had a crotch protector that pulled under from the back and snapped in the front, which she merrily snapped for me before slipping into her hijab. Between the crotch protector and the Arab underpants, Private Wanky felt a bit put upon.

"What am I supposed to do with my dick?" I asked after she snapped me up.

"Keep him snug for later," she said, giving it a gentle pat.

I thought this was a thought I should hold onto until we were safely in the air out of Toonloonistan. It was all beginning to seem like an incredibly elaborate hazing ritual, after which I might aspire to be inducted into Angela's fraternity-of-one.

"Are you sure we need to go through with this?" I asked her. "I can be a lot more fun if I'm alive."

She kissed me on the cheek. "My Proud Lion," she said and walked up to the opening exit door, through which blasted brutally bright sunlight and summer desert heat. The Turkmenistan military escort was waiting for us: four open trucks packed with soldiers in sand-colored combat gear and an olive green 4x4 with opaque windows and a cannon mounted on its roof. An officer stood at its rear door, which he opened chivalrously as we descended the boarding stairs, me in a pair of stiff pinching sandals no doubt designed for self-mortification on the pilgrimage to Mecca, plus the *thobe* whose hem I kept stepping on and the headgear that kept blowing into my eyes. At the foot of the stairs we had to pass under the crossed swords of an honor guard in full-dress uniform and two-foot black Turkmen hats that looked like enormous Afros. I held up the hem of my *thobe* like a matron stepping over a puddle, lest I stumble into the swords and lose a valued appendage. The officer looked more Russian than Asian. He was short, stocky, and strong, a noseguard, one of those little guys who could pick up a Volkswagen. His chest was plastered with medals, and he wore epaulettes signifying his lofty rank.

I bowed to him and said, "*Asalaam Alaykum*," in my best Muslim Brotherhood Arabic (as Angela had taught me), expecting him to return my greeting with "*Alaykum Asalaam*" (as she also taught me). But instead he just laughed, apparently truly amused, and gestured for me to get into the 4x4 with a large friendly grin. It scared the bejesus out of me, but what other choice was there but to start running the 7,000 miles or so to Los Angeles? Angela was already sitting next to a console and cup-holders with little bottles of chilled sparkling water in them, and I thought, well if they were going to shoot us why bother to chill the sparkling water? The officer took a seat facing us and pulled the door shut.

"My husband wishes to thank you for your generous hospitality, Allah be praised," Angela said to him in her best Arabic-accented Turkmen.

"No need for the masquerade, Miss Chase. I know who you are. And as you see we can speak English," the officer responded. "I am Major General Tirkish Trymyev, Commander of the Turkmenistan Border Guard, at your service. Turkmenbashi personally commissioned me to accommodate your every comfort during your all too brief visit to our happy country."

"Yes, thank you, General," Angela responded politely, as if unfazed by the general's unmasking us (in English no less).

"You may remove your head scarf if you wish," Trymyev said, rapping the tinted window with his knuckles. "No one can see us, including the driver."

"Thank you, I'd rather wear it," she said.

"How about you, Mr. Wilder?" Trymyev asked me. "Not that you're not the spitting image of Prince Abdullah himself, on a day he awoke to find his mustache and beard somewhat askew."

"I'm fine," I answered, following Angela's lead, although I would have liked to rip off the whole costume and burn it.

The rap on the window may have been the command for the convoy to start. In any case, it did—two trucks ahead of us and two behind us. Before long we were barreling along at one hundred kilometers an hour down a highway bordered by oil rigs, pumpjacks, concrete block houses, and lots of dirt— which I realized was actually a kind of dingy oil-tinged sand. It looked like West Texas only worse. But unlike West Texas this highway was only two narrow lanes and we took up both of them, causing the profuse Russian minicars to swerve onto the shoulders on both sides until we passed. No one shook their fists at us, nor yelled curses about our mothers sleeping with pigs, nor did they appear in the least surprised by the sudden military convoy. In this place the state was supreme.

"We'll be at your destination in about forty minutes," Trymyev said. "So let us use the time pleasantly in conversation."

"Where did you learn to speak English?" I asked him amiably, as if we had just met at an exchange student cocktail party. I could see Angela roll her eyes as the words came out of my mouth, all the more emphatically because everything but her eyes was covered by her hijab.

"Yootee," Trymyev said.

"Yootee?" I asked pensively. "Is that in Australia?"

"Yootee, yootee," he repeated.

"UT," Angela said dryly. "The University of Texas."

"Hook 'em Horns," Trymyev said, forming the Long-horn hand signal with his pinky and index finger. "Happy

Hour half-price Lonestar Longnecks killer nachos Waylon and Willie. Petroleum and Geosystems Engineering Class of '84."

I smiled and nodded. Obviously my job was to keep my mouth shut.

"Has the money for Ahmad Jalalzada been transferred from our plane to this car?" Angela asked Trymyev, without so much as a word of transition from chitchat to business.

"It has all been arranged, Miss Chase," he answered.

"We have it with us, in this car?"

"It's all taken care of," Trymyev said again, with exaggerated patience.

"It's in *this car*," Angela said again, this time gesturing "this car" with her finger pointing to the floor.

Trymyev paused a moment, to consider what and who he was dealing with.

"It is," he said.

"All right," Angela said. "When we arrive at our destination, I want the trucks halted one hundred meters from the yurt. Our car will then drive to the yurt's doorway. None of us will get out of the car including you until your driver has transferred the money into the yurt. When he returns to his position in the driver's seat and has fastened his seat belt, Mr. Wilder and I will get out of the car and go into the yurt. The car will then join the trucks one hundred meters away and your soldiers will establish a perimeter of a one-hundred-meter radius on all sides surrounding the yurt as the center of the circle. No soldier or vehicle will venture within the circumference of that circle for the duration of our meeting with Ahmad Jalalzada, and he will be delivered before the meeting and picked up after the meeting in the same fashion, and so will we. We will then be transported directly to our plane, which will be cleared for takeoff five minutes before we arrive at the airport."

Trymyev bristled noticeably at the first sentence of Angela's instructions, and continued bristling. By the time she finished speaking he looked like a porcupine. He obviously was accustomed to giving orders and not taking them, except from Turkmenbashi himself. Especially from a woman. No doubt due to an extremely well-developed habit of self-preservation, he thought as long as he needed to before he spoke.

Then he said, "Such was my plan exactly, Miss Chase." (That is *the* best joke I've heard this year, I thought—delivered with wonderfully unctuous sincerity.) "It will all be done precisely as you say. But please let me assure you that we have no suicide bombers in Turkmenistan. There are no terrorists in Turkmenistan."

"I'm glad to hear that, General," Angela said.

"If I may, I'd like to tell you some features of our happy country which will make your all too brief visit more pleasant . . ." And Trymyev did just that for the remaining thirty minutes or so left in our journey, during which I could feel Angela go into the open-eyed sleep mode she went into when we first boarded Sheed's plane in Santa Monica and sat down to dinner. I recalled that she had not slept as I had for twelve hours from Washington through refueling in Abu Dhabi, not to mention her copiloting the flight and expending considerable energy with me in the bedroom suite and not napping afterward. I wondered again how she could do what she does. It was certainly beyond my capacity. But maybe I could do things she couldn't, maybe we could make a great team. And there I went again. Even in this dangerous situation, I start musing about our "relationship." Girlyman, I said to myself silently, but apparently formed the word with my lips.

"Gurbansoltanenedzhe?" Trymyev asked. "Yes, it's true Turkmenbashi changed the word for bread to the name of his mother, much to the amusement of the American media."

I looked over at Angela. Her eyes were now closed and she wasn't even pretending to pay attention. Trymyev realized he had me alone.

"Allow me to ask you a question, Mr. Wilder. Man to man. Do you love your mother?"

"I was an orphan," I said.

"That's wonderful!"

"It is?" I asked.

"What a happy coincidence. Turkmenbashi was also an orphan. He changed the word for bread to his mother's name not at all for personal glorification, but to emphasize the importance of native Turkmenistan culture to national solidarity and order."

I smiled and wished mightily that I had Angela's talent for sleeping.

"Do you realize what a remarkable event we are embarking upon even as I speak?" Trymyev asked. "Turkmenbashi arranged for you and Miss Chase to do President Clinton's business on our native soil. He has never done this for any other nation. Can you comprehend what an exception to Turkmenistan foreign relations he has made to grant the United States this favor?"

"Which is why we're disguised as Saudis," I said.

"A modest request, and you couldn't even paste your mustache on straight," he chuckled. "I hope you'll tell your superiors what Turkmenbashi has done to cultivate American goodwill."

My superiors? I thought. That must be Robin Williams and Billy Crystal. If Trymyev knew he was talking not to an elite foreign-service operative but a soon-to-be unemployed stand-up comic he would probably defenestrate me like in the old days of the KGB.

The convoy pulled off the road and was zipping around sand dunes, astonishing forty-foot wind sculptures, toward what appeared to be a small oasis with a large yurt. The trucks stopped abruptly, as Angela had dictated, one hundred meters from the yurt, and our car drove up to its doorway. Angela was fully awake now. The driver popped the hatchback behind my seat, then appeared carrying a big canvas Santa Claus bag over each shoulder, and entered the yurt. He did this four more times as we watched: ten big duffel bags of money. When he got into the car and fastened his seat belt, Angela said, "Thank you, General. Please pick us up in exactly thirty minutes."

Pretty terse, I thought. Angela Chase, man of few words. She made Clint Eastwood's cowboys seem like gabby Dallas socialites. Just right for here in the Wild West. Except for the yurt, we could have been in the Mojave. The yurt was a big one, thirty feet high at its peak and thirty feet in diameter, covered with a dull dun fabric the color of old goats. Angela strode ahead of me fearlessly, and pulled aside the heavy rug hanging over the doorway. Inside it was so dark after the bright sunlight that she seemed to disappear. I stood there alone in the dark in a yurt in Turkmenistan. Lordy me, how strange life is. I couldn't see Angela in her black hijab or anything else, until a man seated at the far periphery turned up a kerosene lantern.

"Angela?" he said.

"Ahmad," she answered.

It was an odd moment. There was more emotion contained in those single words than in the *Norton Anthology of World Literature*. I felt like I was intruding on their privacy.

Jalalzada stood up and now I could see him clearly. Funny I hadn't thought much about his personal relationship to Angela and not at all about what he might look like. I guess

I expected a ratty little guy in a scraggly beard and turban, the stereotype of the Afghan mujahideen. But he looked like a major league outfielder, big and graceful, rising to his feet in one effortless motion, tall, dark, and handsome. And dressed in khakis and a polo shirt. His shoulder muscles rippled when he moved his arms. Even with a round Pashtun hat and camouflage jacket, he could have stepped out of a J. Crew catalogue.

"Thank you so much for coming, Mr. Wilder," he said, addressing me (to my surprise), courtesy apparently trumping passion in his moral universe. "I appreciate your supporting our cause."

"I'm just along for the ride," I said.

"Long ride," he said. "And Angela, how are you?"

"As ever, Ahmad. Good to see you."

"And you, Angela," Jalalzada replied. Then they both paused, and we all stood there for what seemed like five minutes but was probably five seconds. All their history, whatever it was, was in that silence. Bogart and Bergman in *Casablanca*. I could have been Bergman's hapless husband, the noble freedom fighter, except Jalalzada was not only Bogart but the noble freedom fighter too. I didn't even own an upright piano, much less a nightclub. Would they rush into each other's arms? Not these two. Whatever understanding they had come to, it was etched in steel. Neither of them were people who ever wavered from their resolve, unlike us ordinary mortals.

"May we sit down together?" Jalalzada said, and again in one balletic motion he was cross-legged on a hand-woven Turkmen rug. As shabby as the yurt's outside covering was, the inside was lavish and lush—silk pillows and thick rugs layered on the floor and more rugs draped over the walls. It was also refreshingly cool and comfortable.

Angela had not removed her head scarf, nor did she do so now, but she did remove her veil.

"Same terms, Ahmad," she said, ostensibly referring to the money. "No strings attached."

"Very generous," Jalalzada said. "I will do my best with it. Please thank the president for his trust."

"We both know it won't go very far, don't we?" Angela said.

"Of course. Taliban recruits are pouring in from Pakistan. Twenty-five thousand this year. And they all worship bin Laden. They don't care about Afghanistan, only worldwide jihad."

"What are you going to do?"

"Nothing different. The Afghan people support us. But we can't support them. They need the means to live—food, hospitals, schools—and we can't provide it. The Taliban can—with Pakistani and Saudi money. Without similar support, we'll simply have to restrict our horizon to a small section of the country. The Taliban will not defeat us easily but we also will not defeat them. Eventually they must come to a political solution."

Wake me up when it's over, I said to myself. But Jalalzada had authority. And charisma. And sexual magnetism. No wonder Angela liked him or loved him during their years in Paris and maybe even now. Plus he was unassailably courteous and focused, and when he addressed you he made you feel like the only person in the universe—instead of what I actually was: thoroughly superfluous and dressed like a clown.

He and Angela talked for another twenty minutes: yada yada blah blah blah.

I'd had enough of Middle East affairs (in both senses). I didn't want to admire Jalalzada's apparently selfless devotion and integrity, but I did. He's a better man than I am, I thought. Maybe he was also funnier than I am and could fuck like Jesus Christ after the resurrection. All I wanted was to go home.

Since time fortunately does pass even when it seems like it won't, the last twenty minutes did. They were oddly the most painful of all the minutes of my life since I had first seen Angela in the bank in Santa Monica. I don't know what she or Jalalzada got out of this meeting (except for his getting $10 million), but I was leaving convinced that Angela would never want me the way she wanted him.

Angela stood up and reattached her veil and Jalalzada stood up with her, precisely coordinated. Maybe they would dance away in the moonlight together.

"Allah be with you, Angela," Jalalzada said. He didn't move toward her or attempt to touch her. "And you also, Mr. Wilder."

I said thank you, and shook his hand. Angela had already turned and left without a word and I could see Trymyev's car waiting when she pulled the rug aside from the doorway. I wanted to say something to Jalalzada that would tell him exactly what I thought about him—about how much I admired, envied, and hated him for how Angela felt about him, that I thought he was a truly wonderful and remarkable person and he should go fuck himself with a fossilized camel dick. What I said was, "Good luck, sir."

When I got outside, Angela was in the car with Trymyev. Fortunately we wouldn't be able to say anything to each other for at least the forty-minute car ride back to the plane.

19.

The plane took off two minutes after we got on. Trymyev, God bless him, stood by his 4x4 and waved. Behind him, the honor guard in their tall black Afro hats raised their swords to us in homage and a golden statue of Turkmenbashi glinted in the sun. I thought how apt that I had spent my entire time in Toonloonistan wearing my *thobe* and Prince Abdullah, which I was still wearing. The right outfit for the right occasion. The moment we were airborne, Angela got up and threw off her hijab and stuffed it in the big brown box along with her Kevlar vest and machine pistol.

"Good-bye forever," she said. "Turkmenfuckingbashi be praised."

I just watched and said nothing.

"You looking at me?" she said, mimicking De Niro in *Taxi Driver*.

"'Would you like to talk about something?'" I asked, quoting her in the same tone she had said it to me.

"I would like to go to sleep," she replied, and started for the bedroom suite.

"One question," I said.

"One," she said, holding up an index finger like she was losing patience with her four-year-old.

"Is Jalalzada funnier than me?"

"You are so Robert, Robert," she said, and kissed me on my mouche. "Wake me when we get to Paris."

"Paris?" I asked. She didn't answer, but only gave me a parody of a big sexy wink as she stepped into the bedroom suite and closed the door.

Paris. Did I want to go to Paris with Angela? Does the Pope wear a funny hat? With all my heart, soul, and unreliable mind, not to mention my body from toenails to cowlick, I wanted to burst into the bedroom suite and hump her to paradise. But Angela needed to sleep. I knew her well enough to know she meant what she said. On this occasion. Probably.

This brought me kaclunk right down to earth, where I had been riding this tilt-a-whirl of a woman up down spun around. Every time I'm about to step off I get on again for another fun ride, and why? Do I love Angela? Obviously, except for the minor detail that I have no idea who she is. Do I want Angela? Absolutely and I don't care who she is. She thinks I'm funny and loves to screw me. Stand-up comic paradise. Forget the seventy-two Islamic virgins and delicious fruits without thorns. Forget also that at various moments I had concluded she was: a liar, a con artist, a murderer, a psychopath—and she never would want me the way she wanted Jalalzada. The latter conclusion perhaps an hour ago at most. She laughs, gives me a wink, and bang, I'd follow her anywhere, including Toonloonistan and certainly Paris.

Fact is, I was following what I've always followed: my dick. And there her credentials were impeccable. But was that so bad? Why did I think I could think better with my brain than with my dick? She was overwhelming to me. She was also obviously brilliant, strong, focused, and hilarious herself (Jalalzada, eat your heart out), and all of this entered our sex together. There might be plenty of craziness, but somehow I felt I knew her. And, God help me, loved her. Her words to me in the Malibu kitchen after our first time together had burned their own exclusive neural pathway through my synapses: "You do something to me that goes deep down." Then she dropped her robe and paraded like a stripper in her red Brazilian bikini with the butt-floss bottom. Thank you, Allah, Jesus, Yahweh, Zeus, and whoever else swims in the sky.

This put me into a happy and horny mood for the nine-hour flight to Paris. I was still sitting there in my *thobe* and Prince Abdullah, and despite its obviously facilitating my profound meditation on sexuality and identity, I decided to bury the *thobe* ceremoniously with its female counterpart (Angela's hijab) in the big brown box, Turkmenfuckingbashi be praised. Trouble was that would leave me either in my Arab underpants or exhuming from my suitcase on rollers the pair of underwear I had worn in Irvine, which probably had grown to five times its original size and developed a brain stem and big sharp teeth. Nonetheless I stripped off the *thobe* and Kevlar dominatrix vest and extracted myself gingerly from the Arab underwear and opened the big brown box. Inside on top was the men's silk robe from Malibu and a small piece of notepaper with a heart drawn on it and "xoxxox, Angela." There was even a pair of Calvin Klein briefs and Banana Republic khakis and polo shirt just my size. I was already hooked, but please: could she be this sweet too?

I slipped into the silk robe (happy memories of Malibu). This left the Prince Abdullah to deal with. I didn't want to rip my face off just yet. I might need it in Paris to look fetchingly at Angela. I went into the little airplane bathroom behind the pilot's cabin. There was barely room to stand up straight. Never would I be able to use an airplane bathroom again without thinking of Angela trying to pee in her hijab. I slid the bolt-lock shut since it was the only way to turn on the light and use the mirror. I hadn't seen my Prince Abdullah without the head scarf. The mustache was at least an inch off center and the goatee pointed toward my left nipple. If I had thought I looked ridiculous tooling about Turkmenistan for secret meetings with Central Asia's military commanders, I had never been more right about anything in my life. The mouche stuck out from under my lip like a shoe-polish brush. Nothing remotely like it could possibly sprout from a human face. But the mustache, goatee, and even the mouche came off easily, as if they wanted to leave me as much as I wanted to leave them. There I was again in the mirror: Robert Wilder. I smiled at him rakishly and asked in my best Turkmen accent, "Want to party, Big Boy?"

Two spanking new copies of *Ruhnama* topped a gift basket of Turkmenistan delights waiting for me in the galley kitchen. They must have been loaded on board while we met Jalalzada. Apparently Turkmenbashi eats a lot of meat, because the gift basket was nothing but meat: dried meat, smoked meat, salted meat, canned meat, meat sausages, and especially meat pies. There were six meat pies, each as big as a catcher's mitt, wrapped in cellophane with descriptions of its contents written in Turkmen. I selected a meat pie with ornate red lettering (being in a spicy mood). It was delicious—smoky barbecued lamb in a flaky crust. Georges himself couldn't have done better.

The other almost-nine hours to Paris before I could excusably wake Angela I spent reading Turkmenbashi's *Ruhnama*. Or almost nine minutes anyway. It was worth its weight in Nembutal. A half a page took me right to dreamland.

When I woke up, I couldn't wait any longer to wake Angela. I removed my mouche from the ziplock baggie in which I had planned to store my Prince Abdullah until I could paste it in my Turkmenistan souvenir album, and pushed open the door to the bedroom. Angela, who had apparently trained herself to hear doors open while sleeping, woke the moment I turned the doorknob.

"I brought you a cup of coffee," I said. I was completely naked. So was she. She sat up in bed just as I had, the covers slipping to her waist.

"I don't see any coffee. But I do see something else," she said.

"Private Wanky reporting for duty, sir."

"What's he wearing on his head?" she asked.

"His Turkmen hat," I said.

"That would actually be your mouche," Angela said. "And I hope to God you got the glue off the back or we'll be airlifting Private Wanky to the hospital."

"The good comedian always controls his props," I said, showing Angela the bottom of the mouche, which I had covered with a Post-it.

"Bring Private Wanky a little closer," she said. "I want to give him big Turkmenbashi kisses on both cheeks."

"THAT WAS a very nice experience for me," I said in a dorky falsetto after the requisite pause to consider Postcoital Sacred Awe. I was lying next to Angela in bed with my arm around her while she played with the chest hair at my nipple.

"I'm glad it was, because you're going to have a lot more of them. You touch me like you have little brains in your fingertips."

"I doooo," I said in my best Bela Lugosi, wiggling my fingers in her face. "I dooo have leetle brains in my fingertips."

"I'm serious," she said, sitting up and turning to face me. "I have a confession to make."

"My least favorite sentence in English," I said, still thinking she was kidding.

"There are no Republican ninjas."

This was not what I expected to hear in our airborne paradisiacal pheromone-saturated *chambre a coucher*.

"Right," I said, after a long speechless pause. "Of course. You were just playing Let's Trick The Bonehead. No Republican ninjas pursuing me for what I know about you so they can bring down Clinton."

"No."

"That wild ride to the airport followed by Sheed's explanation on the plane: all planned."

"Yes."

"You're good," I said. "Very convincing. And Sheed too. You people just lie, pretty much all the time, right?"

"Yes. We people."

"So why the truth now?"

"We're going to Paris. I didn't want you worrying a Republican ninja would pop out of your next croissant."

"Very tiny ninja."

"They come in all sizes."

"Kind of like dicks," I said and went into the bathroom and closed the door behind me. Angela was still sitting cross-legged on the bed naked and there I was in the mirror, without my Prince Abdullah this time. I looked at Robert Wilder, all dressed up in his birthday suit. "You are an absolute asshole," I said to him quietly.

I could open the bathroom door and ask Angela why she tricked me into this trip with her, but maybe she'd lie about that too. Maybe anything she'd ever tell me might be a lie. Maybe I should walk back to her and say, "That's it. I'm done." Instead I sat there on the toilet lid for a while, made a goofy face at myself in the mirror, and opened the door without having the slightest idea of what I was going to say or do.

"Well?" she said.

"You want a meat pie?" I asked.

"Somehow I didn't expect that to be your entrance line."

"Turkmenbashi sent us a gift basket of meat. The pies are great. And we each got a personal copy of the *Ruhnama*, which I've begun to memorize so I can pass my Turkmenistan driver's test."

"Are we still going to Paris?" Angela asked.

"Does the Pope drive a Cadillac?"

"No, but he does wear a funny hat."

"Then we certainly are," I said.

She looked at me incredulously.

"Is the meat pie drugged?" she asked.

I smiled enigmatically.

"That's my Mona Lisa smile," I said. "*La Gioconda.* On permanent display at *Le Louvre.*"

"You're not planning to murder me in my sleep?"

"Do you know why she's smiling like that? She's got a load in her pants."

"No drama? No screaming? No insults?"

"We'll work it out. You want a meat pie now?"

"Are you sure you want to associate with one of us people?"

"I'm sure I want to associate with you."

"Bingo," she said. "Toaster oven goes to the handsome gentleman in his birthday suit." She stood up and came over and kissed me—reveille call for Private Wanky. "You are way too good to be true," she said.

"I'm lying," I said. "I'm a better liar than you are."

"But Private Wanky isn't," she said, and pushed me back onto the bed.

So THAT's how that got resolved. Sort of. Angela's primary relationship might be to my dick, not to me, but that was okay. We still had a couple of hours to Paris—or days or weeks, it was such a time warp. We figured it would be early Sunday morning when we arrived. I had slept about fifteen hours since Thursday night when I returned from Irvine to find her in my apartment, and she had slept maybe ten. We had both been jet-lagged back and forth so thoroughly our body clocks were spinning their digits like slot machines.

After much coaching and celebrity product endorsement, Angela accepted a meat pie and I opened another one for myself and we ate them together on the bed still naked. This was odd, too, since before this the only time I had been naked with her was when we were having sex, about to have sex, or had just had sex. I wasn't used to sitting around chatting like nudists. Still she was so breathtaking I couldn't believe my luck.

Unfortunately this feeling of longing for her even when my sperm bank was dry as a Saltine made me need to touch another touchy subject.

"Meat pies," I said. "Yes, another great tradition of the world's cuisines."

"Is this a lecture?"

"Certainly is. I have been invited to all the world's finest institutions of learning to discourse on this fascinating topic. The Institut d'Etudes Politiques de Paris, for example, the school of Europe's diplomatic and political elite."

Stony silence from Angela.

"Yes, I met an interesting gentleman there once," I continued. "A student I believe he was. Afghan, like the hound. I remember because his surname rhymed with the most famous of meat pies, the empanada."

"I had a feeling this was coming sooner or later. I take it back. You aren't too good to be true."

"Empanada, Jalalzada, it's all the same to me. 'No matter where in the world it appears, crusty or crispy, spicy or soggy, a meat pie, ladies and gentlemen, is a meat pie': the final line of my lecture, inevitably provoking standing ovations and thunderous applause."

"All right. What do you want to know?"

"I shall be succinct. Did you fuck him?"

"Oh, Robert. I swear you men are all alike."

"We all look the same upside down," I said.

"That's women," Angela said. "Get your misogynist jokes straight."

"So?" I asked. "Did you fuck him?"

"No."

"Is that what I want to hear or what you think I want to hear?"

"He's a devout Muslim, Robert. In Islam, adultery is a capital crime. He would never have sex outside of marriage."

"Why didn't you marry him?"

"I didn't want to marry him. Or anyone. Ever. What would I be, wife number four? Tending the goats while hubby conducts the insurgency?"

"Why not wife number twenty-three? You could have worn Michael Jordan's jersey. And I bet you can handle a Kalishnikov just fine."

"Let me tell you something about me. There's no shoulda coulda in me. It's a stupid self-destructive habit I decided to break a long time ago. You might consider breaking it yourself."

"That is not the subject. The subject is the meat pie."

"All right, I would have fucked him if he would have fucked me. Is that better? Who wouldn't want to fuck him? Maybe you'd like to fuck him. Let's get Trymyev and Turkmenbashi and Clinton and everybody else in there too. We could all fuck Jalalzada together. Which is good. Because he's obviously already fucked. He doesn't have a chance. So that's where devotion gets you: dead."

"I'm sorry," I said, after an uncomfortable silence.

"It's fine," she said. "I do tell the truth about some things."

"It would be nice to be able to guess which things."

"I admire the man. You understand? He is *devoted*. Do you understand what the word means? It means he is focused and unwavering, or if he does waver or lose focus he never shows it. And he will give his life for what he's devoted to. It makes him powerful. He's immune to self-questioning. And he doesn't have an ounce of bullshit male egoism. Plus he's courteous and kind and actually respects people. And that's incredibly sexy."

"Then why would you want to be with me?" I asked.

"Who said I wanted to be with you?"

"Excuse me. Aren't we in bed together? Have I been hallucinating?"

"What do you know about Islam?" she asked.

"What does that have to do with anything?"

"Just tell me. What do you know about Islam?"

"Nothing. What you said in the meeting with Clinton. That's it. Who gives a rat's ass about Islam?"

"I do. Or I don't about Islam, but I do care about devotion. Because I've never had it. I would like to give a rat's ass about something. I think it might make me happy. Or happy enough."

"Okay," I said, after a long minute. "I think I get it."

"Do you? Do you see what people do to each other? I've done worse. People don't mean anything to me. They are all bewildered. It's all, fuck you and give me your wallet. But that's not Jalalzada. He's different."

"Am I different?"

"You're innocent. For such a consummate stickman, you're incredibly naive."

"What do you mean?" I asked, thus proving her assertion.

"Do you want to know why I lied to get you to go with me? I needed you to go with me. I needed *you* to be there when I saw Jalalzada. You have no idea what you mean to me. You have no idea how lovely you are. You pay attention. Your heart isn't even on your sleeve, it's lit up on your nose. And, as granny says, you have the most beautiful cock in the universe."

I felt like crying. She saw it immediately.

"Oh, you gorgeous man," she said and kissed me tenderly on the cheek as if I were a little boy.

Maybe it was the jet lag or sleep deprivation or Turkmenbashi's meat pie, but the effect of Angela kissing me like this was even stronger than her kissing me deeply, and up came Private Wanky proudly into the picture, as if he wanted to be loved too.

"My God, Robert," Angela said. "You are astonishing."

"I can't help it," I said.

"I am so glad. Come here to me again."

And so I did, and we did, praise be to Allah, all the way to Paris.

20.

Anyone who does not want to fall in love with the person sitting next to him should not ride with her through Paris at dawn on a Sunday in late summer. It could have serious consequences. She might actually be a Komodo dragon wearing lipstick, which would require your forever patronizing restaurants that serve live animals, where your beloved may consume four-fifths of her body weight at a single feeding. Not to mention the difficulty of placing the children in a good preschool. Paris is always preposterously Romantic, as everyone knows, but at dawn on a Sunday in late summer it's even worse. The golden light climbing the enchanting buildings makes them even more enchanting and the city is deserted except for the street sweepers swooshing away joyous Saturday night detritus and the café waiters unstacking café chairs and arranging them around café tables and the quaint boxy lorries of deliverymen idling at the boulangerie: no traffic, no honking, no swearing, no hurrying, and all of it seems to have been created for only the two of you—in this case, Angela and me, riding in the backseat of a Town Car from Le Bourget airport (private jets only) to the Plaza Athénée Hotel (five-star property of the

Sultan of Brunei), down the Champs-Élysées, along the river, and through the Eighth Arrondissement to Rue Montaigne.

She even took my hand in hers as we turned onto the Champs-Élysées, which she had never done before, and I did not mention to her that people usually hold hands before they have sex not after nor cite it as further evidence of what Don called Sheed's reverse dating service: introducing you to the person you've already fucked. Angela had certainly been clear that she didn't have "dates." I didn't think she'd enjoy my pointing out that we had consummated our courtship repeatedly before we had a courtship—not because she would mind the reminder of our consummations but because she'd mind the idea that we were now having a courtship. And she was right: we weren't. I also knew that she didn't want me to tell her I loved her, nor even mention the L-word, much less a word like "courtship" that could imply our courtship might lead to: (horror of horrors): marriage.

So what were my options? As far as I could see, I had exactly one: chill out. Press mute on Mr. Brain and put a sock in my mouth. Take a close look at the reality here. How bad was it? Better than a red hot poker in a Middle Eastern desert prison. Plus, the hotel and everything we ate (conceived and concocted by celebrity chef Alain Ducasse) was free. That's right, folks. Free! Compliments of the Sultan of Brunei, for whom Angela had once done "some work." It must have been "some work" indeed since it entitled her to a lifetime of free stays at any of the Sultan of Brunei's fifteen ultra-luxury hotels worldwide, including the Beverly Hills Hotel, which was, as she put it when I pressed her, her "home base." The only question I had when she informed me of all this is the one I did not ask: what in the hell was she doing with me? I should be dumpster diving in Santa Monica not arriving at the Plaza Athénée swarmed by valets, porters, and concierges dressed impeccably in suits I couldn't afford greeting us with an orchestrated chorus of *"Bonne journée,* Mademoiselle Chase," "So good to see you again, Miss Chase," "Welcome back, Miss Chase," before the manager himself appeared to kiss her on both cheeks and warmly shake my hand. A bell-man loaded Angela's four big bags on a luggage trolley but tucked my suitcase on wheels under one arm. I hoped my underwear would not burst through the zipper and bite him. He turned a key in the elevator to take us to a "restricted" floor—"to the Eiffel Suite, Miss Chase."

And that's where we stayed, without leaving, for the next four days, Sunday at dawn to Wednesday at dusk, fucking and eating, fucking and sleeping, fucking and talking and laughing: out of touch with this world and all its troubles and cares. Forget the Sufi whirling and the Lakota sweat lodge. For my transcendent state, I'll take room service and champagne, caviar, silk robes, 2,000-thread-count sheets, and Mademoiselle Angela Chase to make the *Kama Sutra* look like *Plumbing for Dummies.*

But all good things must come to an end, right? And great things even sooner. On Wednesday evening Angela decided we needed some fresh air. It was time for a picturesque walk along the Seine to have a drink at Café Les Deux Magots, then dinner at L'Excuse, her favorite bistro from her student days—nothing fancy, no Michelin stars, but real bistro fare, out-of-the-way, small, and quintessentially Parisian.

Should I have been suspicious? Or apprehensive? Well, I was. I didn't want to leave our cocoon. I wanted to grab a table leg and refuse to let go. A walk along the Seine on a late summer evening: not exactly on Amnesty International's list of illegal tortures. But too much real world for me. I liked it just fine in "the Eiffel Suite."

Nonetheless I obeyed my earlier resolutions to mute my brain and mouth. Angela seemed to have excellent reasons for her decisions and an aversion to telling me what her reasons are. Fine, I guess, as long as her decisions kept producing excellent results, by which I meant excellent results for me. My judgment could admittedly be a weeny bit unreliable— why not ride with hers for a while? After all, it had gotten us to Paris together. Anyway, she had obviously been the driver and me the passenger probably since I met her in the bank and certainly since she appeared in my apartment in her hijab.

So I told her that some fresh air sounded great and I couldn't imagine anything I'd rather do than have a drink at Les Deux Magots and dinner at her favorite bistro from her student days and how bored I was eating Alain Ducasse's supernal world-famous cuisine and drinking free vintage Cristal. We needed to get out there in the streets of Paris with authentic Parisians and if we didn't do so right away I'd lose contact with the suffering of real people in real life and my art would become jejune. Jejune jejune jejune. I said it twenty times in a row (an old Woody Allen bit), fast and slow, with varied intonations until Angela said, "Enough. Or I'll stuff your mouth with one of my body parts."

I suppose I should have seen that the fates were feeling impish when I pressed the down button and the elevator doors opened and there inside, alone, facing me as if in a mirror, was Prince Abdullah himself. The real one. In *thobe* and head scarf. With a perfectly centered beard, mustache, and mouche. He thoughtfully pressed the hold button while we stepped on. We rode down with him all the way to the lobby. Angela, fast thinker that she is, did not speak to him in Arabic, which might have made him curious, but muttered some French pleasantry, and he responded in English, being not so slow himself and pegging us immediately as Americans.

"My wives insist on coming to Paris to shop while my sons gamble on the Côte d'Azur," he said, with mock gravity. "I don't know which of them spends my money faster." Angela and I chuckled ruefully, in equally mock commiseration.

And that was the extent of our interaction with Prince Abdullah until the elevator doors opened to six burly bodyguards in the lobby and a dozen more guarding a convoy of armored Range Rovers in the porte cochere. They sped away as Angela and I walked out of the hotel still trying to control ourselves like rowdy middle schoolers in sex education class. When we had achieved a respectable distance from the hotel, down Rue Montaigne, we let out our whoops and exclamations.

It must have been seven or eight P.M.—I didn't care anymore—and the light was luscious and the river silk, its slow currents rippling its surface in patterns of blue shades. This was a place made for people. The world seemed peaceful and everyone seemed happy. I'm sure they weren't all happy, but I was. In fact, I had never been happier. It was the high point of my life, no contest.

We walked up a flight of stairs made of medieval cobblestones then a few blocks to Saint-Germain-des-Prés and Café Les Deux Magots famously located on its famous corner. It's situated like a square at an angle, its entrance through french doors fronted by plate glass with tables both inside and out arranged for maximum people watching, the ghosts of Sartre and Camus, Hemingway and Gide, the surrealists and symbolistes all disdaining to act like gawking tourists and established at their usual places inside. So Angela and I sat inside too. We took a crimson-leather banquette in the corner, next to two Japanese girls wearing berets and across from an old man with Einstein hair ferociously reading Le Monde and muttering "Ces idiots!" and "Mon Dieu!" A waiter in a tux and white apron tied around his waist brought our aperitifs: absinthe, into which iced water is poured over a sugar cube. For the surrealists it produced hallucinations. I was hallucinating just fine already. Angela was dressed in a white T-shirt like Jean Seberg in *Breathless* with a crimson cashmere sweater around her shoulders that brought up the henna highlights of her dark chocolate hair. Her eyes seemed lit from inside, and they were zeroed in on mine as we toasted ourselves.

"Here's looking at you, kid," I said.

"You *are* looking at me," Angela said. "You're staring at me. What's up?"

"Do you really want to know?"

"When you put it like that, I don't think so."

"What does Bogart say then? The farewell scene, the plane about to take off and he's telling her she has to get on it with her noble freedom-fighter husband?"

" 'We'll always have Paris,' " Angela said.

"Right. The toaster oven goes to the pretty lady in the red sweater," I said.

"Thanks, Robert. I'll take Big Dick Jokes for fifty."

"Big Dick Jokes for fifty. My dick is so big . . ."

"There's still snow on top of it in summer."

"Another winner!"

"Thanks, Robert. Big Dick Jokes for one hundred."

"My dick is so big . . ."

"A homeless family lives underneath it."

"Bingo. My dick . . ."

"*Your* dick. Absolutely," she said. "Here's looking at *him*."

"You're hallucinating," I said. "Must be the Chinese horny goat weed I've been slipping under your toenails while you're asleep."

"You are an evil genius," Angela said.

I stroked my absinthe glass slowly up and down without realizing it. I wanted to tell her Everything I Felt. Was now The Time?

"Don't do that," she said, as if she had heard my thought, but referred to my stroking. "We'll never make it to dinner."

"Worse things could happen," I said. "You know, you do pretty good schtick. For a girl."

"Oh yes. For a girl. I love that. Comedians are *the* most sexist males in the stratosphere. They make the CIA look like a feminist collective."

"We all sympathize with the aspirations of your people."

"You thought I learned to juggle on the high wire in my spare time. I actually did a few open mics in college."

"Really, where?"

"Comedy Store, Improv, the usual places. After midnight, of course."

"Funny I didn't run into you."

"You had moved on by then."

"Why did you quit?"

"I was actually doing it because of a guy I had a crush on. I gave it up when he got engaged. Anyway I was taking eighteen credits and working for Folsom and that was enough to do in my spare time."

"Who was the lucky guy? I probably knew him."

"Yeah, you probably did," Angela said. Then she just looked at me and waited with the Folsom Sheed autograph model deadpan expression on her face until the lightbulb went on.

"Oh my God," I said stupidly.

"Yup," Angela said. "It was you, my Proud Lion," she said with her Saudi accent. "You think I fuck every customer who walks into a bank?"

"I can't believe it. I swear I had never seen you before that. How did you know me? Where had you even seen me?"

"UCLA, where else? I was one of 800 fresh little freshmen in Professor Bedient's modern poetry course. You were one of his small army of TAs. All the girls hoped he would have you write on the blackboard so they could ogle your butt."

"I just can't believe it," I repeated.

"Why not? You have a great butt."

"You couldn't have been in my discussion section."

"I wasn't in your section. And I came to lectures late and left early and sat in the back row. Then I heard about your secret life as a stand-up comic, so I started tracking your gigs and sitting as far back in the dark as I could with my obligatory two watery drinks. In other words, I stalked you. For months. I can't tell you how many times I heard that midget at the urinal joke. Want to hear it in Arabic?"

"Why didn't you just hit on me?"

"Send my panties to your table? You men have the subtlety of a bull moose. I took the classic girl route: bump into the guy 'accidentally.' But since you were so oblivious, I literally did bump into you once and knocked your drink onto your shirt. 'Fucking drunk bitch,' you said. The only words you ever spoke to me. I've treasured them ever since."

"I don't remember. I must not have seen you."

"It was just a schoolgirl crush. No big deal. I switched majors from English to politics and threw myself into my so-called internship with Folsom. I held onto this desperate crush on you for only about ten years—until approximately now. In fact, I'm apparently not over it yet."

"I could have saved myself ten years of Relationship Building and Communication Skills."

"Timing was bad for me anyway. I was a little shaky my freshman year. Vulnerable, I believe is the word. I couldn't have handled it if you shot me down. "

"Your parents had just died," I said.

"Yeah. They had," Angela said.

"Do you want to talk about it?"

"No."

"No?"

"No."

"Don't you think it might have something to do with what you've chosen to do for the last ten years? What you're doing now?"

"Who cares? You have some secret little theory about me? My trauma yadda yadda blah blah bullshit? Maybe I like what I'm doing."

"You're the one who said you can't be happy."

"Okay, Bucko. You want to do something about it?" The bar-fight challenge again.

"Damn straight I do. I want to fucking marry you."

That stopped her. She started to cry without crying. No tears came out of her eyes but every other facial movement was the same. She didn't make a sound. Instead she stood up.

"I'll be right back," she said. "I'm going to the Femmes, then to call us a cab."

She walked away, just like that, without the slightest indication what she was feeling. She did walk toward the ladies room and the telephones at the back of the café, not out the door to the street, so unless she was planning to escape through the kitchen she had to at least walk past me on the way to never speaking to me again. How badly did I fuck up? 1) Royally 2) Disastrously 3) Catastrophically 4) Apocalyptically 5) All of the above. Well, if I did, I did. I had to tell her sooner or later anyway. Admittedly I kind of bulldozed right past all the pleasant preliminaries. It might have been nice to tell her I loved her first. And I suppose I could have proposed in a more tender manner than "I want to fucking marry you."

And perhaps chosen a more tender and propitious moment. But oh well, too late now.

She was gone a long time, long enough for me to start thinking she did slip out through the kitchen—especially since I noticed there was a whole line of cabs parked outside and she must have known she didn't need to call one. The waiter came by to see if I wanted some food and I ordered another round of absinthes with no intention of drinking them, just to pay table rent. As the Japanese girls were leaving the café, they stopped at my table and one of them said to me in English, "Excuse me, are you Patrick Swayze?" I said, "No, but thank you," and they went off giggling on their Paris adventure. Probably one dared the other to say it. Maybe if Angela didn't come back, I could start robbing banks and the police would arrest Patrick Swayze instead of me.

Then she did come back, acting as if she had never left and I hadn't just asked her to marry me, although I could see there was something else going on under her acting.

"More drinks?" she said.

"No, but thank you," I said.

"Were those Japanese girls hitting on you?"

"Unbelievable. I'm going to report it to the CIA feminist collective. Then organize a multicultural gender studies conference about it."

"I remember all too well," Angela said. "Go Bruins."

"Hook 'em Horns," I replied.

"Shall we go to dinner?" Angela asked.

"Are we getting married?" I said.

"I'll tell you at dinner," she said.

21.

Angela didn't call a cab, she called a car—a Plaza Athénée car, "at the disposal of hotel guests during their stay in Paris." L'Excuse was nestled on a narrow twisty cobblestone cul de sac in the Marais district. She said it might be hard to get a cab back to the hotel but the hotel car would wait for us while we dined. The car was a Town Car like the one that drove us from the airport through Paris at dawn on Sunday, but this ride wasn't much like that one. Angela stared out her window the whole way as the streets darkened. If she sat any farther away from me, she'd have been riding outside. She did not hold my hand, and hardly seemed to be with me at all, much less with the person she wanted to marry. Paris looked about as enchanting as a clogged urinal. If I had any doubt about how badly I had fucked up by telling her I wanted to fucking marry her (Royally Disastrously Catastrophically Apocalyptically), I got my answer: 5) All of the above. Then as we pulled up to the restaurant, she pulled me to her and kissed me on the mouth. Good-bye? Hello? Confusing? Bewildering?

I was about to find out, despite L'Excuse being an unlikely venue for the experience. The owners, Fabrice and Maurice, twin brothers in pompadours and beltless slacks who together weighed less than one Bill Clinton, met us at the door and outdid even the Plaza Athénée staff in gushing over Angela. Whoever she is they seem to like her, I thought. They treated her like the Queen of Cuisine. They showed us to one of ten tables in a tiny room decorated in plywood paneling, hanging plants, and ancient velvet drapes sporting a film of congealed cooking vapor. All the tables were filled at ten on a Wednesday night and the clientele wasn't there for the decor. The brothers put their resources entirely into the food, to spectacular effect. It was straight-ahead bistro cooking as delicious as the Plaza Athénée at one-tenth the price, so Angela was right (as usual)—although I didn't actually taste anything after the amuse-bouche; a soft-boiled egg sweetened with cream that sounds horrific but was sublime.

"So you like to talk endlessly about everything and I don't," Angela said for openers after we were seated.

"We make a great team," I said. "I'm all talk and no action and you're all action and no talk. You don't say anything and I don't do anything."

"What about my tics?" she asked.

"Your ticks? You collect insects?"

"T-I-C-S."

"Tourette's? I didn't notice."

"I'm talking about my habits you can't stand."

"I love your habits," I said. "Especially the way you recite Dr. Seuss during sex."

"You have no idea what they are. What about money?"

"Easy. I don't have any."

"What if you hate wasting money and I waste it?"

"I waste it too."

"Well, I don't. I hate wasting anything. I hate wasting food."

"You only ate half your fish on the plane. Nor did you finish your meat pie. I bet you never ate a leftover in your life."

"So I just lied. I've *studied* how to lie. I lie all the time. You said so yourself. I hardly know what truth is."

"Neither do I."

"I don't care what truth is."

"Me neither."

"What do you care about?"

"Sex," I said.

"Seriously," she said.

"I am serious," I said. "With you, it all goes into sex and radiates out from it. *That's* the truth. It's never happened to me before."

"What happens when I weigh 400 pounds?"

"You'd have to eat a very big dinner, even for Paris."

"So you want to get married, do you? Never have fun together? Have shitty sex, then none? Bitch and nag, little zingers, pointed 'jokes'? Lots of monitoring, opinions, 'helpful criticism'? Sure, let's get married. When's the date?"

"As soon as you want it," I said.

"Come on, Robert. You know the drill as well as I do. Couples drive each other nuts, it's not even their fault, horrible things happen, kids get into the mix, somebody gets sick or fired or depressed or injured, meanwhile frustration and resentment and fantasy eat them alive, not to mention that everyone's so screwed up to begin with. Look what happened to you and Doris."

"I didn't love Doris," I said. "I love you. I think I forgot to mention that."

She started to respond, but the waiter appeared and showed me the wine.

"Please, just pour it," I said, and he did, after taking about seven weeks to open the bottle, sniff the cork, and taste it himself from his shiny silver sommelier's tasting cup, Angela all the while smiling at my impatience at this French national ritual.

"So?" I asked, after he finally left us to ourselves.

"Okay," she said.

I couldn't believe my ears.

"Okay?" I asked. "As in, okay let's get married?"

"Believe me, I never expected this. This is not what I've been waiting for, because I haven't been waiting for anything. I don't understand how you make me feel the way you do. A crush, yes, but I'm afraid this is the real deal. You do it for me, Robert. You're the one. Not Jalalzada. Not anybody else. You. I want to be with you forever."

The waiter had delivered the first course and I hadn't even noticed. We were required upon pain of excommunication to eat it with the first growth Chablis the sommelier had selected for us and poured so religiously.

"Your scallops are getting cold," she said.

"What do you want me to do now?" I asked. "I'll do anything."

"Good," Angela said. "We're almost there. What do you know about Islam?"

"Oh God, that again," I said. "What is this Islam thing? Haven't we been through this already?"

"Do you see how sexy Islam is?"

"Yeah, my *thobe* made me feel like a real stud muffin. And that Prince Abdullah, my God, the man just exudes pheromones. I could hardly breathe in the elevator."

"Do you know where I bought the underwear I'm wearing?"

"Toys Я Us."

"Riyadh. And the red Brazilian bikini you seem to favor? Not actually Brazilian."

"And the point is?"

"Our sex together will be completely private. Just like the last four days only more. No one else knows or ever will know. Only you and me. Total devotion," Angela said. "To each other."

"I'm in," I said.

"*Total* devotion. Restrict your sexual energy to me. You don't get four wives and I get a quarter of a husband. It's got to work both ways. I get all of you. You get all of me. Then it gets better. It gets more intense. Within our marriage, no limits. But we don't go outside it. No past girlfriends, no 'friendships,' no flirtations, no deceptions, no horseshit. Zero Nada Never. You understand? I will love you until my ears fall off. I will devote myself to you and you will devote yourself to me. Could you do that? There aren't many men who could do that."

"With you I could," I said. "I will."

"All right," she said. "You just said your marriage vows. And so did I. You've got me. Forever. If you ever die, I'll fucking kill you."

With that she stood up abruptly, just as she had at Café Les Deux Magots, just as the entrees arrived.

"Eat your dinner, Robert. I've got to make a phone call."

"But the car's outside waiting for us," I said. Now that she said what she said I didn't want to let her out of my sight. She might bump into somebody who would talk sense into her: *you could have any man in the world, why do you want this bumblepuppet?* I realized she had thought the whole thing through before we got to the restaurant—the whole conversation. That's what she was doing in the car. I guess the kiss in front of the restaurant was a hello kiss after all.

Again she was gone a long time. I didn't touch my entrée—roast partridge on a bed of cabbage and bacon with a *vol au vent* filled with avocado mousse. The *vol au vent* was a cup of puff pastry with tiny pastry sculptures of reclining nudes around its rim. It deflated and collapsed as the avocado mousse began to turn brown. After ten minutes, Fabrice and Maurice came to the table with identical pained expressions on their faces.

"There is a problem with the food?" one of them asked.

"Not at all. It's absolutely wonderful, better than Alain Ducasse."

"But you do not eat it," the other said.

"I'm waiting for Angela," I said. "She's in the ladies room having an emergency." As soon as I said this, I realized it implied she was incontinent or something. But Fabrice and Maurice were thinking only of the food.

"We will make you another!" one declared emphatically and the other nodded emphatically and swept my plate away.

When Angela finally returned, her face was white, as if she really had been sick in the pissoir. I knew it had all been too good to be true. Our marriage had lasted fifteen minutes, fourteen of which she had spent in the women's bathroom.

"It's off," I said. "Correct?"

"Postponed," she said.

"The shortest marriage in history."

"Please, don't be angry," she said sadly. "I couldn't take it."

"Well," I said, "I know you don't like to talk about your decisions before you announce them to me, as if I might actually influence them in some minor way. But don't you think I might be informed about this little matter that merely determines the entire rest of my life?"

"See, we're bitching at each other already."

"Pardon *moi*? You just called off our marriage."

"Jalalzada's dead," she said.

I wasn't expecting that.

"I'm sorry," I said.

"He's dead. And I killed him."

"Oh, Angela, that's preposterous," I said.

"Preposterous? What do you know about it? Nothing. The closer anyone is to me the more I hurt them."

"I love you, Angela," I said quietly.

"Don't say that!" she screamed. "Don't ever say that to me again!" She stood up and bolted out of the restaurant. Yet again. But this time she was gone.

I was so stunned, I didn't move. It certainly got everyone's attention. As I said, this was a tiny room—maybe twenty people dining, most of them couples. Fabrice and Maurice and the sous-chefs came out of the kitchen to see what was happening. Everyone stared at me. I didn't know what to say. I couldn't have said it in French anyway.

Then a beautiful elegant old woman seated with her husband across the room said to me in English, "Go after her."

To my astonishment she was smiling at me, and so was her husband.

"Yes, yes, go after her," the woman repeated. "She loves you."

"Thank you," I said.

I threw a wad of francs onto the table and started for the door. The woman's husband raised his wine glass.

"L'amour," he said, toasting, and everyone else nodded and smiled and I heard their wine glasses clinking as I opened the door to the street.

The Town Car was gone and the street was deserted—the narrow cobblestone street of three-story buildings hardly wide enough for the Town Car. I sprinted down to the corner and looked in every direction: nothing anywhere. Desolate.

"Postponed," Angela said. But why? Once again she just did what she did and left me completely out of it. This time I didn't seem to even figure in the equation. If she loved me, how could she do this to me?

I had to find her and talk to her. Things were not going to go well for me if I didn't. But what if she wasn't at the hotel when I got there? She was right about the cabs, though: there were none. I began running—I didn't know which way or to where. All my life I've had a nightmare about being lost in a foreign city and desperately needing to get to some place and waking up with my heart pounding. This was the nightmare. I was in it.

Eventually I stumbled onto Rue de Rivoli and flagged a cab that drove me to the hotel, but by then more than an hour had passed since I left the restaurant. I don't usually pray, but on the elevator up to the room I kept saying aloud, "Angela be here Angela be here Angela be here." Of course she wasn't. Nor was her luggage. Baja all over again, only five bazillion times worse. There was the fucking Eiffel Tower again in the silver-framed window and a fresh vintage Cristal in the silver ice bucket and no Angela. In the middle of the table at the window was an envelope. A note from Angela? No, again. A plane ticket to LA, on the Concorde, leaving tomorrow. First class. But of course.

What could I do? I could throw the silver ice bucket through the window and take a swan dive after it onto the Rue Montaigne. I could do my famous Sex-Pistols-in-the-ultra-luxury-hotel imitation and yell obscenities into the phone at the desk clerk and break priceless antiques and set the mattress on fire. I could wander randomly around the city screaming Angela's name at the top of my lungs like Marlon Brando in *Streetcar*. Or I could call Sheed. Angela must have called Sheed from the women's bathroom at L'Excuse. How else could she have learned about Jalalzada? What time was it now? One A.M.—Thursday. That made it four P.M. in LA—Wednesday. Sheed would still be at the office, no doubt arranging his next covert world-shaking multimillion dollar deal.

I dialed Sheed's number and Tori answered and my life in LA instantly rushed back to me: the gym, the Z, my apartment in Santa Monica, my pathetic career. Maybe I would take the swan dive onto the Rue Montaigne after all.

"Tori, this is Robert Wilder," I said.

"Robb-bert," she breathed. "Where are you? You sound fuzzy."

"I am fuzzy," I said. "Is Sheed there?"

"Are you in Paris? He told me to put through any call from Paris."

"That's me," I said, although I knew Sheed meant Angela.

"Paris. How romantic," Tori said.

"So thick you can cut it with your nose."

"Whatever that means," she said. "Bye, Robert. I'll put you through."

Click. "Folsom Sheed," Sheed said.

"Robert Wilder," I said.

"Mr. Wilder, this is a surprise. It must be one A.M. there."

"Do you know where Angela is? And don't say that if you knew you couldn't tell me."

"Isn't she with you? If I knew I could tell you. Because she doesn't work for me anymore."

"What?"

"She quit, Mr. Wilder. About two hours ago. She said she was getting married to you."

"Two hours ago she was. Now she's not. Did you tell her Jalalzada was dead?"

"I did. He is."

"It upset her very much."

"I expect it did."

Silence. I could see this wasn't getting me anywhere.

"Can you tell me anything that would help me find her?" I asked feebly.

"I'm sorry, Mr. Wilder. I can't imagine what that would be. If Angela doesn't want you to find her, I assure you that you won't find her. She is very resourceful, as you know."

"Yes, I know," I said.

"Do you have a plane ticket home?"

"On the Concorde. First class. Tomorrow."

"I suggest you use it," Sheed said. "The arrangement was for you both to come home on that flight."

"Arrangement? When was it arranged?"

"Before we landed in Washington to meet with the president," Sheed said.

"Really? Angela had all this planned that far in advance?"

"*Very* resourceful, Mr. Wilder. I can't possibly replace her."

"Neither can I," I said.

22.

I pulled into my driveway at midnight, one week to the minute after I pulled into my driveway from the Irvine Improv sailing on adrenaline. Could that have been only a week ago? O Angela. I had been ready to give up women and work day and night like a termite. My life was going to be entirely different. It was watch out world, here comes Robert Wilder! Now it was watch out Robert Wilder, here comes the world. My life was going to be entirely different all right. I was fucking devastated. My heart wasn't just broken. It was crushed, vaporized, annihilated. Again I popped the hatchback, grabbed my suitcase, and rolled it behind me up to my door. Again the door was open, about three inches, but this time I didn't think Krista. I thought Angela. Again the lights were out and the apartment was dark and I pushed the door open and stepped inside and flipped on the lights.

And there she wasn't. The desk chair was exactly as she left it when she swung around like Mrs. Bates's skeleton in full Islamic regalia and told me that if I didn't go with her I'd be dead before morning. Republican ninjas. How stupid did I have to get before I got smart? I should just leave the chair at the precise angle she left it to remind me. If I needed a further reminder, I still had my Prince Abdullah in a zip-lock bag. I should wear it all the time, including the mouche on my dick, attached with superglue, in the unlikely event I ever felt inclined to use it again. "My dick" not "Private Wanky." Court martial: Private Wanky. Henceforth, may his name never be uttered among civilized peoples.

My apartment consisted of three rooms: the living room/study, furnished with one lamp, one Swedish recliner, one desk, and the Angela Chase Memorial swiveling desk chair; the bedroom, with the bathroom on one side and the door to the deck overlooking Renate's garden on the other side; and the kitchen, with the small dining table where I served eggs to Renate and Krista and ate my permafrost burritos. Krista apparently had not been here while I was gone. There were no empty cans of Diet Coke on the floor, no empty bags of Ripples, no empty boxes of Weight Watchers lemon chicken dinner, no heavy metal CDs by Death, Fear Factory, and Weird Looks, and no used dishes in the kitchen sink. Just Sparky's dog bowl and his squeaky pig chew toy at their usual places next to the refrigerator.

Sparky. I had forgotten completely about Sparky. I hadn't thought about him at all during the past week. Poor Sparky had been in the kennel for ten straight days. I consoled myself with the self-berating thought that Madge loved him better than I did. No doubt he was perfectly happy. I'd go pick him up in the morning.

Time for bed. It had been a long day, a long flight next to Angela's blatantly unoccupied seat on the Concorde. Until the cabin door was closed and locked, I hoped she would run onto the plane at the last minute and jump into my lap like the happy ending of a chick flick. She wasn't waiting for me

in my bed either, but my computer was, with a note taped to
the monitor:

Happy Anniversary. Where the fuck are you?
                         Yr former friend,
                         Don

I carried the computer piece by piece to my desk—processor,
monitor, keyboard, and mouse—and dumped it onto the pile
of papers with my unsigned license to marry Doris on top.
That left only my clothes to strip off—the Banana Republic khakis and polo shirt and Calvin Klein briefs Angela had
bought for me in Abu Dhabi. Maybe I would burn them.
Angela took both white silk robes, hers and mine. I thought
this was mean of her, almost vindictive. As if to tell me the
white silk robe wasn't really mine. I was only renting it.

And so it went: my high-speed blender brain. Stuck on
autopilot chop liquefy and puree. Of course I couldn't sleep.
I was beyond exhaustion, having fretted my way home on the
Concorde refusing yet more fabulous complimentary French
food and complimentary French wine and rehashing over and
over the previous evening with Angela. How could she leave
me like that? Right after we had vowed our eternal love? But
what could I do now? I had to find a way to live with what
had happened. Or not.

Then it flashed on me that this is exactly what she had to
do when she was eighteen and her parents killed themselves:
find a way to live with what had happened. Couldn't she have
designed the week to make me feel how she felt when she lost
her parents? The fact is she could. As elaborate and intricate
as it was, she was more than capable of planning it. (*Very*
resourceful, Sheed said.) And she left me because she needed

to make me experience how she felt so I truly understood her and we could be married forever.

Fortunately this story was so implausible it put me to sleep. The next morning I woke to pounding on the front door that sounded like a SWAT team battering ram but turned out to be a messenger in a uniform hand delivering a large brown envelope from Sheed. I made a pot of coffee in the kitchen and opened the envelope: my HBO contract ready to sign and send to Odom Bucket and a letter-sized envelope containing a check for $20,000 with this note, "I hope this lifts your spirits. Best wishes, Folsom Sheed."

It didn't, of course, but aside from being devastated I guessed I wasn't worse off than when I returned from Irvine a week ago—and I was $20,000 richer. I obviously wouldn't have to pay for Sheed's legal services and I could almost pay for the Unwedding Dinner. There was another knock on the door, this one much quieter. I could see it was Renate and I called to her to come in.

"Would you like some coffee?" I asked her when she walked into the kitchen. She was carrying her big straw gardening hat and green metal watering can.

"No thank you," she said. "I saw your car in the driveway."

"Yes, well, I'm home," I said.

"You always tell me when to expect your return and I must have misunderstood. I thought it was one week ago."

"I left again rather quickly," I said.

"Your friend Don came over and he had no idea where you were either, but Krista said you were fine and you were in 'a far-off land.' That's how she put it, 'a far-off land.'"

"How is Krista doing?" I asked.

"She's doing well, remarkably well. She also said you have a broken heart now too. Just like her. I suppose she must be referring to your marriage."

"Yes," I said, knowing Renate meant my first nonmarriage, not my second. Two in a week—must be some kind of record.

Renate continued, "Although Krista also said that she wasn't in love with you anymore, because now you're in love with someone else. She said she was allowed to love you before because she knew you didn't really love the woman you were going to marry—what was her name? I don't want to call her what Krista calls her."

"Witchbitch," I said. "Her name is Doris."

"Doris, yes. What Krista said about you makes no sense of course, but she is much happier and even wants to go out. She has a date with a boy she met in the hospital. He is coming over and they will sit in the garden. Of course I'm not letting her go anywhere with him alone."

"That's great, Renate. I'm glad she's doing better."

"And how are you, Robert? Did you have a good trip?"

"Very interesting trip," I said.

"And your friend Don said you have an HBO special. That's wonderful. And here I am taking up your time. We will all watch your HBO special together," she declared enthusiastically as she went out the door.

I sat at the table finishing my coffee. What Krista told Renate about me was uncanny as usual, but no more incomprehensible than many of the other recent events involving females. Maybe I would join a monastery and apprentice myself to Mr. Hanh and learn how to speak in a falsetto and giggle. Or I could start a paranormal act with Krista. I could call on people in the audience and she could tell them how they feel.

What to do today? There was Sparky to pick up, but that wasn't going to help me find Angela. There was Don to call. And there was Sheed to pester. At least he could tell me the real story about Jalalzada. The newspapers said Jalalzada had been killed when he fell under his Jeep. "*Fier Lion Est Mort*" read the headline in *Le Monde*. "Proud Lion": Angela's I-thought-affectionate ironic nickname for me seemed a lot more ironic than affectionate when I read that it was Jalalzada's not-at-all-ironic nickname in Afghanistan.

I got dressed and was almost at Sheed's office when I realized I could drive to the Beverly Hills Hotel and personally deliver the HBO contract to Odom Bucket at his table in the Polo Lounge where he always ate breakfast. And I could use that as an excuse to snoop around the hotel and talk to waiters or valets or bellboys to ask if they had seen Angela.

But Bucket wasn't there and the staff I talked to either didn't know Angela or said they'd be fired if they gave out information about hotel guests—despite my ridiculously making sure they saw the denomination of the bill I was holding in my hand. They were all very polite, except the maitre d' at the Polo Lounge, an impeccably suave leading-man type who sneered at my hundred-dollar bill and said he considered Miss Chase a personal friend and would never disclose information about a patron no matter the price and he would thank me to leave the premises before he called security.

This left Sheed again. When I pulled up at his office building, the valet parking attendant just smiled. Between Washington, Turkmenistan, Paris, and my various costume changes, I had lost the ticket he gave me at the Santa Monica Airport. But he knew my Z and had let me have it anyway. When he handed me the ticket this time, I said, "No way is this coming back without a stamp." He said, "You will excuse me, señor, if I believe it when I see it."

"Welcome home, Robert," Tori said as I approached her desk. In-your-face black lace was today's theme, peek-a-boo under a blazer. Welcome home indeed.

"How are you, Tori?"

"I thought you weren't going to call me, so I started dating somebody," she answered, as if this were how she was. "He's from the gym too."

"I'll catch you the next time around," I said.

She laughed. "Three months max. The guy's a broker. I've gone out with about twenty of them. They never last longer than three months. They're all so nervous. And they have to be at work before six A.M. when the Stock Exchange opens in New York. They can't go five minutes without checking their pork belly futures. Then they're so tired all they want to do is sleep all weekend. He's buff but who needs it?"

I commiserated with her about that for a while, before I asked if I could see Sheed.

"I told him you were here when the security desk called me. You must be his top priority VIP client. He said you could go right in."

I took three steps toward his office before I recalled the parking ticket in my sweaty little palm. I hadn't put it in my pocket this time so I wouldn't forget. I spun around and asked Tori to stamp it. This surprised her too—that despite my urgent meeting with the high-powered lawyer I would be thinking about my parking ticket.

"It will be waiting for you when you come out, along with a confidential document that needs your signature," she said.

I couldn't imagine what that might be. But I was not, under any circumstances, going to pay for parking again.

Sheed shook my hand, and said he was glad to see me. Before I could open my mouth, he told me Angela had been spotted in Islamabad.

"I'm sure that's why you're here, Mr. Wilder," he said. "And that is all I know. Richard Clarke called me this morning and wanted to know what was going on."

"Do you know what's going on?" I asked.

"I can tell you what I told him. Angela is not on a mission for the president. I did not tell him she doesn't work for me or the president anymore, since they'd kill her if they knew that."

"Who would kill her? Why?"

"They take out rogue agents. They don't allow freelancers in Islamabad, I assure you. Intelligence activity is all about control. They don't play with wild cards."

Despite myself, that made me worry about Angela. It must have shown on my face.

"There's no sense worrying, Mr. Wilder. Angela knows what she's doing, whatever it is."

"What *is* she doing?" I asked, a question I seem to have asked Sheed before.

"Short answer is I don't know. She's not communicating with me."

"Long answer?"

"Long answer is she's probably going to Mazar-i-Sharif for Jalalzada's funeral. She feels she's responsible for his death."

"Is she?" I asked.

"That's a silly question, Mr. Wilder. Everyone in the intelligence community knows the terms of engagement. Moral responsibility is a complex question and ultimately irrelevant. Responsibility for success is what matters. And no one is more successful than Angela Chase."

"What happened to Jalalzada?"

"Betrayed by his own men. His closest cohort was infiltrated by al-Qaeda. He was staging an attack on bin Laden, and that's all they were waiting for. The situation in Afghanistan is more dangerous than ever, which is why I hope Angela isn't there herself. But I'm afraid she is. You know she was in love with him."

"That's not what she said," I said.

Sheed smiled, almost imperceptibly. Either genuinely, or a great piece of acting. "I'm sorry, Mr. Wilder. I wish I could help you."

"Would you contact me if you hear from her?"

"Of course I will. But I don't expect to hear from her."

He then reached up with his tiny hand and actually patted my shoulder in consolation before he showed me out. It felt like a hummingbird resting on me before flying off to the next blossom.

I walked out of his office and past Tori's desk again like a zombie. She must have stepped into the ladies room to adjust her lip implants, and I arrived at the valet parking stand not only without a stamp on my ticket but also without a ticket. The attendant loved it.

"Fifty dollars for a lost ticket, señor. But for you this one is on the house."

He was about to go for my car, when Tori came flying out of the front door with the stamped ticket and the envelope with CONFIDENTIAL printed in red ink all over it. She ran up to me and gave me a big hug, which made me wince, and ran back through the door almost before it had swung all the way shut. She did so much aerobics she wasn't even breathing hard.

The attendant said to me, "I would chop off my arm at the elbow for an embrace from this mamacita, and you make a face like you were at the dentist."

"She's stronger than she looks," I said.

He sighed heavily. "I will never understand Anglos," he said. "I think you are all crazy."

"You understand us perfectly. We *are* all crazy."

He laughed, and got my car. For the absurdity of it, I gave him the hundred-dollar bill the Polo Lounge maitre d' sneered at. He said he'd use it the next time he had to go to the dentist.

I swung by Don's before I stopped at Madge's to pick up Sparky. The kids were at school, Francine was probably off by this time on another lecture tour, and Don was in his attic study consorting with the muse.

"The man from Porlock," he said when he came downstairs. "And I was just getting to the part where Kubla Khan realizes he's delusional and needs therapy. Where have you been for the past week?"

"No way you'll believe this one," I said. I told him everything, as usual. What else are best friends for? It took awhile and, as usual, he listened to the whole story without blinking.

Then he said: "Of all the lawyers in LA, I refer you to the one the sexy bank robber works for. What are the odds of that? Not to mention the rest of it."

"It's great," I said. "I can blame you for everything."

"Say again why Sheed thinks Angela's in Afghanistan."

"He said she was spotted in Islamabad."

"Okay. That's possible. There's also life on Mars. The little green men are just too little for us to see."

"What do you mean?"

"She was *spotted*? In a hijab? With a million other women in Islamabad wearing the same black veils? Angela must have distinctive eyes."

"She sure does. There are no others like them," I said.

"Uh huh," Don said, and rolled *his* eyes. "How many times has Sheed lied to you before today?"

"Twice. Angela's brother and the Republican ninjas."

"Three's the charm. And what's that confidential document you're supposed to sign?"

"I forgot I had it," I said. I was holding the envelope in my hand and tore it open. " 'Nondisclosure Agreement.' The meeting with Clinton."

"Why didn't Sheed ask you to sign it in his office?"

"No idea."

"Maybe it would make his sharing all this classified information about Angela seem less generous? More like an exchange?"

"Never occurred to me."

"Of course not. You said Angela told you she *studied* how to lie. Who do you think was her teacher? So why is Sheed lying to you again? Why would he tell you Angela was in love with Jalalzada? What does he want?"

"I guess for Angela to keep working for him."

"Bingo. If I'm reading him right, he just plays his best card then watches what happens. Like a good politician. I don't think he's invested in anything, which is the reason he's so good. If he loses Angela to you, he's not going to blow his brains out. Wherever she is, I think she'll be back."

"Are you just telling me this so I don't blow *my* brains out?"

"Why would I? I'd inherit your computer and it's a lot better than mine. I installed a surprise on it for you. Did you plug it in yet?"

"I left as soon as I got up this morning. How did you wangle it away from Doris?"

"Doris is a very compassionate woman. I'm telling you, you passed up a gem. Anyway she doesn't love you anymore. She's got a new boyfriend."

"You're kidding me," I said.

"Nope, it's true. She had a religious experience in Maui at the Grand Wailea spa. At those prices you should have a religious experience."

"Tell me. Who's the guy?"

"Who said it was a guy? It is a guy. But I'm committed to secrecy. You will not hear his name pass my lips. You wouldn't believe it anyway. I think the reason Francine and I have crazy friends is so we can believe we are sane. Because by comparison we *are* sane. Look at you. I rest my case."

"Come on," I said. "Who is it?"

"Not telling. It's part of the computer deal. You'll be hearing soon enough anyway. You're going to get a visit from Doris, for the sake of 'closure,' as she calls it."

"Fine," I said. "As long as she leaves *her* gun at the door."

"She's a nice woman, Robert. Much better than you deserve."

"Maybe that was the problem. I only love women who aren't who they pretend to be."

"Fairly large sociological subgroup," Don said.

I stayed a little longer to hear about Francine's return from Maui and immediate departure for another three-week Midwest lecture tour that made the armpit circuit of Rust Belt comedy clubs sound like a cruise to the Bahamas. Don said she was so happy and relaxed after Maui that she wanted him to fly there with her as soon as they could. He thought it might save their marriage if they went every other day or so. But he had learned something that might save their marriage anyway, so he thanked me for standing up Doris at the church after all.

"And what did you learn?" I asked.

"To keep my mouth shut," he said. "Just let her talk and not say a word, but nod sympathetically every once in a while to show I'm not asleep. If I do that, she talks all the crap out of her head so it doesn't back up and choke her. Plus if she thinks I'm listening to her, it makes her horny."

"Okay," I said. "I'll try it on Sparky first. But I hope it doesn't make him horny."

I thanked Don for listening to me. Then I picked up Sparky at Madge's and drove home.

23.

I had never tried to find anyone, much less a "rogue agent" (as Sheed put it) who was now "under the radar" (as Angela put it) and was using all her expertise not to be tracked by the most sophisticated intelligence networks in the world. But I, Robert Wilder, erstwhile stand-up comic, distinguished imitator of screechy violins, *will* find her. With his faithful dog, Sparky, on her trail, I'd climb every mountain and swim every sea etcetera and will not rest until etcetera.

Instead I climbed under the covers. I was exhausted and jet-lagged, so I thought I was just run down and of course clinically depressed. But then I started coughing up a colorful effluvia that seemed to issue from previously untapped regions of my body and I noticed in addition that I could probably fry an egg on my forehead. My mind began cataloguing the untreatable exotic viruses I may have acquired from Turkmenbashi's meat pies or Bill Clinton's secret elevator and their various biospheres. Or I could have been merely(?) somatizing my emotional state, which, in any case, I felt as a whopping physical illness.

So home I stayed, lovesick, in bed. Sparky padded over to the bed once in a while to sniff my face to check if I was still breathing. The time came and went for his walk on the beach, and, saintly doggy that he is, he didn't whine or scratch at the door but waited with his chin resting on his paws in my direct line of vision so I'd see him when I woke up and opened my eyes. I probably would have starved to death eventually if Renate had not appeared at my bedside because—what else?—Krista told her I was very ill and needed help. Krista herself followed the next day, with cool washcloths and warm broth, and, despite my weak protests, kept me alive. She also fed Sparky and took him for his walks and for hours sat in my Swedish recliner listening to her heavy metal CDs on her Discman. When Renate made a meal for Krista she'd bring over an extra portion for me, and as I got stronger we'd all sit on my bed and eat. Renate had called Don the night she found me sick and if he was there when the meal appeared he would join us, although he had to pull up the desk chair because he was so big he would have taken up the whole bed by himself. I was wasted and feverish and winced every time I breathed and almost fainted every time I laughed, but it became one of the better weeks I ever had (pre-Angela). I felt undeserving of these people's kindness, which oddly made receiving it better. I would never deserve it, but that didn't stop them from giving it to me.

At the end of the week, one week after returning from Paris, my little recuperation-idyll ended abruptly. I got three calls back to back that Friday morning: from Bucket, from Tori (calling for Sheed), and from Doris. It was as if they were all waiting poised to snap me back to reality. As it turned out, their calling on the same morning was not a coincidence. Each of them had been contacted by Don, who had convinced them to leave me alone for at least a week while I recovered. Bucket wanted his HBO contract, Sheed wanted his nondisclosure agreement, and Doris wanted her "closure." Her call lasted less than five seconds.

"Robert," she said.

"Doris," I said. "How are you?"

"I'm in your driveway and very anxious about seeing you. Can we get this over with please?"

I said sure, and braced myself for the earthquake.

"I've been sitting in your driveway calling you for the last fifteen minutes," Doris said as she snatched my desk chair and set it facing me propped up on the bed. She had walked right past Krista listening to her Discman in the recliner as if she were invisible. I could see Krista through the doorway to the living room with her hand over her mouth trying to suppress her giggles.

I said, "Just a minute, Doris," and made my way over to Krista.

"Witchbitch," she mouthed silently, her eyeballs nearly popping out of their sockets.

I pulled one of her headphones away from her head. Even at that scratchy low volume the heavy metal music sounded like a houseful of babies being slaughtered with cast iron frying pans.

"I'm going to need a few moments of privacy," I said.

Krista smiled broadly. Doris's discomfort gave her almost infinite pleasure.

"You're feeling much better now, Robert," Krista said.

"Thanks to you," I said.

"I'll be back after she goes away," she said.

I expected a comment about it from Doris, but, obviously from indifference, she didn't say a word. She was dressed in an elegant tailored beige suit and was still tanned from Maui. She took the utmost care with her appearance, no detail missed, no expense spared, everything purposeful but

unobtrusive, an expression of self-respect. She watched me as
I rearranged myself onto the bed. I was wearing pajamas with
little bears holding blue balloons which I suddenly realized
Doris had given me. They had cost about $5,000. (Five hun-
dred, anyway.)

"You look cute in those pajamas," she said.

"You always had great taste in my clothes."

"You're so good looking I could smack you. It just isn't
fair. How can you look great after you've been *sick*, for God's
sake?"

"Because I didn't have leprosy or elephantiasis," I said.

"I'm glad. It would have been a waste."

"How are you, Doris?"

"I'm not in love with you anymore. I'm thankful for that."
She shifted on the chair and crossed her legs. She made a fine
impression, no question about it.

"Don says you're in love with someone else," I said. "He
wouldn't tell me who."

"I know he wouldn't. I hear the same about you."

"I'll have to talk to Don about what he tells Francine."

"Francine didn't tell me. Don did. So I'd go easier on you.
The person I fell in love with didn't respond by abandoning
me like yours did to you. And you did to me."

"So are you going to tell me who it is?"

"Odom Bucket," she answered, without any further ado.

"Ha. Ha. That's a joke, right?" I asked.

"I knew that would be your response but I don't care."

"Doris! He's a monster."

"You don't know him at all. Anyway so are you."

"I guess you have a point," I said sheepishly.

"I don't picture you delivering any sermons on the mount.
Your idea of moral high ground is a privy ditch."

"Okay. Okay," I said.

"No more pretty boys for me. I'm sick of fluff. Odom and I have a great deal in common. Anyway I didn't come here to get your advice on my love life. Nor did I come to accuse you of anything, though God knows I could spend a lifetime doing that. I came here for healing and closure."

"Healing and closure," I repeated.

"You're fucking right," she said.

"Okay. What would you like me to do?"

"Nothing. It's not for you. It's for me. I don't want to be bitter, Robert. It's not good for me. I don't look back. It's the secret of my success. I don't want to be stuck in some stupid useless pain about you."

"How can I help you with that?"

"Just talk to me a minute."

"What would you like me to say?"

"Tell me how you've been. I need to experience you as a normal human being."

"That's going to be a good trick. The past three weeks have been anything but normal."

"How's the HBO special going?"

"Um, it's been a busy week with my bodily fluids. I haven't done a whole lot of run-throughs."

"Odom's agreed to take you on again."

"Really?" I asked. "That's generous of you."

"I've got to be generous. What I want to do is jam my fingers down your throat and rip your heart out and dance with glee while you die horribly. So I'm taking a contrary action."

"Whew. Good thing for me."

"Why did you have to stand me up at the *church*, for God's sake?" she said, starting to cry, then just as quickly stopping before the first tear leaked out.

"Now, Doris," I said. "I'm sorry. I really am."

"God, I'm not going to do this," she said to herself. "You said, 'I'm sorry.' I'm going to accept your apology."

"I am sorry," I said. "It was rotten. I wasn't thinking of you at all."

"Look, you did me a favor. If that was in you to the degree that you even wanted to do that to me, much less actually to do it, our marriage would have been miserable. Who knows how long we would have beaten the dead horse? With my determination and your self-loathing, maybe the rest of our lives."

"You're right," I said.

"I knew it anyway, see? I had been forcing it too. I knew it wasn't going to work. That's why I'm finished with pretty boys. Even now I look at you in those pajamas and I melt. How ridiculous is that? I knew the truth about us, I just couldn't admit it."

"At least you know it now."

"Yeah, I had the crash course. So who's the bimbo? Spun your buns around, didn't she? She's probably the one who gave you the virus. Good woman."

"I can't blame you for being angry. I think I finally know how I made you feel."

"I'm just kidding. I'm really sorry you were so sick. I'm glad it wasn't worse."

"Thanks," I said.

"It doesn't matter to me why you did not show up for our wedding. What difference does it make if you were porking some slut or finding the cure for cancer? You realized you didn't want to marry me, which made me eventually realize I didn't want to marry you."

"Good," I said.

"It is good. We had ten years together. We had some great moments. Our sex was amazing. For me, I mean. You were probably faking your orgasms."

"Men do that a lot," I said.

"See, the point is, it doesn't matter what it was for you. I had a good experience with you, Robert. I loved you, in fact—I mean the person I had convinced myself you were. And that was selfish of me, because I wanted that person so much. I was in love with my own fantasy."

Where had I heard that before? Was this the Psychoflavor of the Month? I think my mouth dropped open.

"You look surprised," Doris said.

"No," I said. "I think you're probably right."

"I know I'm right. You may have done your own shit, you may have been irresponsible and inconsiderate. Despicable even. That's for you to come to terms with. I just need to let it all go."

We talked another ten minutes or so, like friends of mutual friends who happened to have been us. As she got up to leave, she suddenly said, "I don't know you at all, Robert."

"Sometimes I don't know me either."

"Yes, well, it may be time to grow up and find out."

"Something's happened to me," I said. It was another one of those sentences that came out of my mouth before it was in my brain. I had had no intention of talking about this with Doris. She had gotten up and started for the door with her "grow up" comment, but she stopped and turned around.

"What happened to you?" she asked.

"Something has changed. I can't tell what it is. People seem, what, more real? Precious."

"That's a word I never thought I'd hear you use."

"Yeah, weird. It's all probably biochemical."

"Well, keep getting sick then. Maybe you can arrange it, say, every day. You might end up being lovely." She leaned over and kissed me on the cheek.

"Thanks, Doris."

"It was for myself," she said. Then she was gone.

The windows of my bedroom open out into the canyon toward the ocean, and the gauze curtains on them billowed in the breeze. How ludicrous it was to worry about anything, since nothing ever turned out how I imagined anyway. This fact could be either terrifying or amusing. Why should it not be amusing? After sweating concrete blocks about what Doris was going to do to me, what does she do? The loving thing. Plus she takes up with my agent and makes him rehire me. She may think she didn't know me at all, but I obviously knew her even less. I guess she thinks I'm worse than she thought. She's better than I thought.

Krista appeared at my bed.

"Time to take your medicine," she said. "I'm glad you didn't marry Witchbitch."

"She's not so bad, Krista," I said.

"Too bossy."

"Maybe," I answered. "Would you tell me something?"

"What?"

"If I had gotten married to Doris, were you going to take those pills I found in my bed?"

"I don't know."

"You really don't know?"

"That was too long ago. I don't remember. You didn't get married. You got sick. I'm taking care of you. Until Angela comes back and you marry her."

"How do you know her name?"

"I heard it in my head. Don't feel bad anymore. She'll be back soon."

This really *was* uncanny. Maybe we should start that paranormal act.

"How about you, Krista?" I asked. "Do you still feel bad?"

"Not bad. Sad."

"I'm sorry," I said.

"It's okay," she said. "You didn't do anything."

"Let me know if I *can* do anything."

"I'm going back home now. You're okay now, Robert," she said, and picked up her Discman and CDs and walked out the door.

I sat there for a moment, another moment of light and silence with the gauzy curtains and the billowing breeze. It seemed I had a decision to make right then: either live or die. Doris was going on with her life, and so, remarkably, was Krista—at least I hoped for that for Krista. If they could do it, so could I. I might fall apart eighty times a day, every time something reminded me of Angela. I had no delusions about ever "getting over" her. But I got out of bed, cleared the papers off my desk, tossed my unsigned marriage license to Doris into the wastebasket, and turned on the computer.

What appeared on the screen was something I had never seen before on my computer:

Welcome to HoTMaiL

The World's

FREE

Web-based E-mail

I apparently had an e-mail account:

user name: funnyman

password: dickthink.

Don had set it up for me during one of his visits to my apartment during my fabulous all-expenses-paid vacation to Paris. The first e-mail was from him:

> Now we never have to talk again. I can just write
> you insulting messages.
> > Love,
> > Don

There was one more message in the in-box. Its subject line was Silk Robe and it was from Angela:

> The broken heart tattoo I got when you got engaged.
> No one has ever worn the men's white silk robe but
> you. I've packed it and taken it all over the world
> in case by some miracle we'd ever be together. That
> miracle happened. It was better than my wildest
> dreams. You are better than my wildest dreams.
> Nobody should love another human being the way
> I love you. It's not right. It's not fair to you. I *am*
> responsible for Jalalzada's death. But nothing makes
> me feel worse than hurting you. I am so sorry.
> Please forgive me if you can.

The sender's e-mail address was RESTRICTED. That was it. There wasn't a return e-mail address. I clicked the Reply icon but nothing came up. Since I had never used e-mail before, I couldn't tell if I was doing something wrong. To call Don I had to use the phone, but the phone line was being used by the computer to dial into the Internet. If I got off the Internet, would I lose Angela's message? Would it make it impossible for her to write to me again? I wanted to scream and throw the computer through the window. Instead I copied

Angela's message onto a piece of paper and disconnected the Internet and called Don. He said he'd try to find out what the deal was and get back to me. I immediately dialed up the Internet again and logged into HoTMaiL. The two messages, Don's and Angela's, were still in the in-box. I clicked Reply for Don's and wrote:

I'm going crazy.

And sent it. It worked fine. But not Angela's. I couldn't reply to it.

I tried to breathe and calm down a la Mr. Hanh. Where was I now? Same place as before? Angela was somewhere in the world but I didn't know where. At least she was still alive—as of yesterday, Thursday, the day she sent her e-mail. And she still loved me. But again I couldn't tell if she was saying hello or good-bye, or if I'd ever hear from her again.

What could I do? Same answer as before: call Sheed, so he can blow more smoke up my ass. But at least it was smoke and not nothing, and that was my only other option: nothing.

I dialed his number and to my surprise he answered himself.

"Good morning, Mr. Wilder."

"I got an e-mail from Angela," I said.

"I know. I read it."

"She sent it to you?" I asked, appalled.

"All her e-mails go through our office. But nobody else can read them."

"That's comforting," I said. "This one was a little personal."

"I wouldn't take it too seriously if I were you. I've seen this before, Mr. Wilder. It's built into the job description. You can't imagine what sort of pressure Angela has been under for a very long time, and, as remarkable as she is, she has clearly snapped, at least temporarily. She needs a vacation and she's probably taking one, compliments of the Sultan of Brunei."

"She's not in Afghanistan?"

"Not now anyway. She couldn't send an e-mail from Afghanistan."

"So she's safe."

"Let me be honest with you, Mr. Wilder. I know where she is. And when you deliver the nondisclosure agreement I'll tell you."

"You've lied to me at least twice, Mr. Sheed. Why should I believe you?"

"Did you ever hear of tribal ethics, Mr. Wilder? Anyone outside the tribe is not told the truth unless his interests are the same as the tribe's. Our interests—yours and mine—have not always been the same. There's nothing personal in this at all."

"Are they the same now? Why would you tell me where Angela is, if in fact you really know where she is?"

"Because she will tell you she's finished with you."

"You seem to be pretty sure of that."

"I've been working closely with Angela for ten years. I know her better than she knows herself."

"That's quite a claim, Mr. Sheed. It may be the most arrogant thing I've ever heard anyone say."

"I look forward to seeing you in my office, Mr. Wilder," he answered, and hung up.

Now what? Call Don? Check my e-mail again? Check my e-mail again.

Sure enough, another message from Angela (Subject: Your Secret Little Theory):

> The night before I was to leave for boarding
> school my father came into my bedroom. This was
> an Episcopal priest, a man of God. He was groomed

to be a Bishop and ended up as pastor at Our Lady
of Malibu church. Our Lady of Malibu, who's that?
Michelle Pfeiffer? He was completely out of his
mind. He came into my bedroom, and sat down
on the edge of my bed and said he had to tell me a
story. This was the story:

God and The Devil play bones for souls God lets
the Devil win a few so he'll let all the other souls
alone and the Devil's souls are always trying to crawl
over to God's side but the Devil has a thick rubber
rope tied around their ankles and sometimes he lets
them get almost to God's side sometimes less than a
tenth of an inch away before he snaps them back and
no matter what they do or how they try, their souls
belong to the Devil until he gets bored with them, or
the game, or both, and crushes them one by one like
black ants under his thumb.

Then my father said, "I belong to the Devil. So
does your mother. Get away from us, Angela, and
stay away." He got up and left and was nowhere to
be found the next day when I went to the airport.

I was thirteen years old. I loved my parents
totally. They were so good to me until they stopped
loving each other. That was the one thing they
couldn't do for me. Love each other anymore. I'd
hear them fight upstairs, never in my presence, but
I'd sneak up and listen outside their door. I heard
every horrible word they said to each other, brutal
brutal things. They didn't catch me doing it until I
was thirteen, which is when they decided to send
me away to Lucerne. I still didn't want to go. It was
awful. I cried and cried. You know I haven't cried
since? Even when they killed themselves. My life

since then has been one big Fuck It. It looks like
super achiever but it's really Fuck It.

Your secret little theory about me is right on the
money. I'm a psychoanalytic cliché.

I can't do this to you. No one is allowed to
burden anyone else with the way I would love you.
It's not going to happen. I don't care how much I
fucking love you. It's killing me.

I thought, Angela has snapped. Sheed was right. Then I realized he was the one who planted that reaction in my head. Then
I thought he wrote the e-mail himself—if he could read her
e-mails maybe he could write them too. It was only after those
thoughts that I noticed that this e-mail was sent from a different
address: hijabpee@hotmail.com. And I could reply to it.

Dear Angela,

What happened to you should never happen to
a child. Thank you for telling me about it. I'll never
forget it.

Hurting each other is unavoidable. We're human
and inconstant. You are beyond wonderful to me, but
you're still a human being. And so am I. Devotion is
a practice, not a perfect static condition. My vow to
you stands: I will devote myself to you. I will try to
love you in everything I say and do with you. Even if
I fail sometimes, I will try. Please tell me where you
are. I want to marry you and be with you forever.

I love you,
Robert

No jokes. Not one. I hit the Send button and off it went
into the ionosphere to I didn't know where—except probably

Sheed's computer. Or maybe not. It was disturbing to say the least that my most intimate feelings about Angela and hers about me were being monitored and gauged and analyzed for how they could be manipulated. Or even changed entirely. The response she got from me could say, "Fuck you. Don't ever contact me again."

My whole life seemed on the line now, and—more importantly—so did Angela's. It made me surprisingly happy that this was my response: that she was more important to me than me. It was the first time in my life I felt that someone else mattered more than I do.

I got into my car and drove straight to Sheed's.

24.

"*Buenos días, señor*," my favorite valet said as I stepped from the Z and handed him the ignition key. "Mr. Sheed's doing big business for us today. Miss Chase was just here too."

"What? Where?" I asked.

"Right there," he said, pointing to a low steel-blue sedan with quadruple exhaust pipes, just pulling away then roaring off like a cruise missile. "She told me she was signing out, señor. That she wouldn't be seeing me here again."

"Angela!" I screamed at the top of my lungs. My best Marlon Brando/Stanley Kowalski of all time. The people streaming in and out of the office building carrying their Louis Vuitton bags and briefcases all stopped and stared at me. It was as if I hit freeze frame. The whole world stopped. All my agony and desperation was in that scream. But Angela's car kept going.

I grabbed the key and jumped back into the Z and followed her car. I hadn't actually seen Angela herself. Then I did. She had pulled over a block ahead of me and was standing outside her car, dressed in the elegant black suit she wore to the meeting with Clinton. Her power outfit. Her spectacular legs. Even in my distress, her beauty knocked me flat.

I pulled up behind her and climbed out of the Z, but as I did she shouted, "Follow me, Robert," and dove back into her car and roared off again.

I had no idea what she was driving—some foreign turbo V-12 limited edition something—much less where. O for that missed unit of High Speed Evasive Maneuvers in high school driver's ed. Her car made the Z look like an in-home scooter. She turned up Pico heading toward Santa Monica Airport. Off to Toonloonistan again? Or Paris, for another memorable meal at L'Excuse? She turned onto Twenty-Third then shot down an alley and right on Twenty-Fourth then right down the next alley and left onto Twenty-Third again—exactly the little jaunt we had taken to avoid the fictional Republican ninjas in their fictional Black Mercedeses. Then instead of entering the airport gate she performed a nifty u-turn and headed back where we came from.

If she could be crazy, so could I. I started honking. And kept honking. Let's step up the volume. Let's get the police involved and spend the night together in city jail. In response to my honking, she slid back her moon roof and swung a red flag around her finger. Why not? I thought. Next we'll have the crotchless Donald Duck outfit and Cuban cigar. Then I saw the red flag wasn't a red flag. It was the butt-floss bottom of her Saudi bikini.

People once used flag semaphores and smoke signals and all manner of inventions to communicate visually when they couldn't hear each other. Angela's message was loud and clear. By this time she had turned onto Ocean Avenue bordering the long skinny park fronting the Pacific where the homeless people bed down in clumps. She was leading me along the exact route we had driven to Santa Monica Airport from my apartment two weeks ago—only in reverse. She was taking me home. Again we hit all the lights green. I honked my joy and she honked back. She waved to me through the moon roof. She swung into the Santa Monica Canyon and into my driveway. I stopped behind her. My driveway was barely long enough for one car, much less two, so most of my Z was sticking out into the street. I didn't care. We both got out of our cars and she ran into my arms, the mandatory shameless chick flick ending. Fine with me. She kissed me deeply and she kissed me tenderly and Private Wanky miraculously rose from the dead. After a week in the dark and lonely tomb, he stood proudly among us again. Based on this miracle we would found a new religion. It would be called Wankianity.

"What *is* that rocket ship you're driving?" I asked Angela when she allowed me to take a breath. "I've never seen one of those before."

"Remnant of a former life," she said. "I'm getting married."

"This is becoming an interesting day," I said, trying to imitate her lopsided grin.

"Let's make it more interesting," she replied, and took my hand and led me into my apartment.

On May 1, 2011, I called Angela's cell phone from the studio, after I had finished filming yet another edgy pilot in which a stand-up comic plays himself. It had about as much chance of flying as I did if I stood on the cliff behind our house and flapped my arms. Angela was at the gym, on what she called her Sisyphean Stairmaster.

"They got bin Laden," I said, when she picked up.

"Who's he?" she asked.

"Let me guess," I said. "You're not interested."

"Never heard of him."

"Let me guess again: you don't want to talk about it."

"Been there, Robert. Done that. Got the T-shirt."

"You look great in T-shirts. I still think of that one you wore at Les Deux Magots."

"So are you picking up the kids?" she asked.

"Which ones?"

"Ours."

"*All* of them?" I asked.

"Just the cute ones," she answered.

"You're the cute one," I said.

"I knew there was a reason I married you."

"Someday you might tell me what it is."

"I'd rather show you, if you're not doing anything before school lets out."

"You're on."

"Oh yes, I am, my Proud Lion. Thanks to you."

"The pleasure is mine, my dear."

"Ours, Robert, my love," Angela said, and what a music it was. "This pleasure is ours."

ACKNOWLEDGMENTS

Thanks to the Borchard Foundation for a fellowship and residency in Missilac, France, where I wrote the first draft of what turned out many years later to be this book. Thanks also: to Charles Baxter, Tina Bennett, Douglas Brayfield, Stuart Dybek, Ryan Harbage, Martin Shepard, and Chuck Verrill for their sharp, generous responses to earlier drafts; to John Skoyles for introducing me to The Permanent Press; to Judith Shepard and Barbara Anderson for their brilliant, meticulous editing; and to Doreen Gildroy for her insight, love, and patience while listening to more readings of these chapters than anyone should have to endure. *Guy Novel* is her book.